A HACKER MYSTERY

DEATH *in a* GREEN JACKET

JAMES Y. BARTLETT

This Yeoman House softcover edition of ***Death in a Green Jacket*** is an original publication. It is published by arrangement with the author.

Cover Design: Caleb Clarke
Printed in the USA.

ISBN: 978-0-9754676-6-4
Library of Congress Control Number: 2007925004

For Susan

Always

Prologue

GEORGE CARRUTHERS III, a distinguished banker from Atlanta, was the one who first noticed the foul smell. Carruthers, a high-handicap golfer and longtime member of the Augusta National Golf Club, had managed to hit his golf ball into the large, sweeping bunker that sits some 50 yards in front of the 10th green at the National. That in itself was an accomplishment, though of dubious distinction. That big sweeping bunker is almost never in play during the Masters tournament. When the course was first built in 1932, the bunker had been situated next to what was then the first green. But a few years later, after the nines were reversed, part of the never-ending fiddling that goes on at Augusta National, the green was repositioned up the hill and a bit off to the left.

But they left that big, sprawling bunker right where it was. With its big, upsweeping face, the bunker partially hides the fairway that sweeps uphill to the green, and from some parts of the fairway it looks like it's protecting the front edge. But it's all camouflage, which was what the architect of Augusta National, Dr. Alister Mackenzie, had learned about while serving in the British Army during World War I.

Hackers like George Carruthers III do not play the same game as the professionals who visit Augusta every April. He had popped his tee shot high in the air, so it stopped halfway down the great slope of the steep hill that drops away from the clubhouse. Trying to make up his lost distance, despite the unfriendly hanging lie on the side of the hill, Carruthers then tried a fairway wood, which he topped dreadfully, sending it skittering along the fairway until it chased into Dr. Mackenzie's bunker. Had this been the Masters, the TV announcer might have fallen out of his booth in amazement—no one *ever* hit a ball into that bunker. But this wasn't the Masters, there were no announcers, and the members of the hallowed old club are all too familiar with that bunker.

Carruthers cursed, grabbed a nine-iron and sent his caddie on ahead to the green while he climbed down into the bright white sand, littered with bits of pine straw that dropped from the surrounding canyon of loblolly pines. He was thinking that if he could somehow manage to knock his ball up on the green, he had half a chance to make bogey. For golfers like George Carruthers III, bogey is always something to celebrate at Augusta National.

But as he entered the expanse of sand, he immediately noticed the smell. It was the smell of death. Sickly sweet, the odor of decay, it announced that something was dead and decomposing in the warm Georgia sun. Nose wrinkling with distaste, the fastidiously groomed Atlanta banker looked around for the tracks of an animal he was certain had died somewhere in the vicinity of his golf ball. But the bunker was empty, immaculately swept, the sand virtually undisturbed. Around the edges of the bunker, the grass had been neatly trimmed and carefully edged, as if Carruthers' own barber, whose shop he visited in the basement of the Candler Building once every two weeks, had gone around the entire bunker with his clippers, combing and trimming so that every blade of grass was in its prescribed place.

Shrugging, Carruthers stepped up to his ball, swung, and bladed it neatly over the green and down the grassy bank beyond. When he trudged up to the green, his playing partners chided him humorously. He could only shake his head.

"Phew," he said. "Something is dead down there. How can I play a tough shot with that smell?"

"The only thing that stinks around here," said one of the wags in his foursome, "Is your golf swing."

Carruthers and company played on, and, as they chopped their way around the rest of Augusta National's fabled back nine, the incident was soon forgotten. Several hours later, as Carruthers and his friends sat in the members' lounge, enjoying a cold beer, Augusta's head golf professional, Martin Tynsdale, walked by and asked the gentlemen how their round had fared.

"We stunk the place up," said one, looking at the scorecard in disgust.

"That reminds me, Marty," Carruthers piped up. "I smelled something dead in the front bunker on 10. You might have one of the fellows check it out. Most unpleasant."

"Yes, sir, Mr. Carruthers," Tynsdale said. "We'll get right on that. Was that the bunker to the right of the green?"

The table laughed, all except Carruthers. "No, Marty," he said, his face turning red. "The front one. Down the fairway."

Tynsdale smiled knowingly and gave George Carruthers III a friendly squeeze of the shoulder. "Thanks," he said, "I'll have someone go down and look around."

It was an hour before sunrise the next morning when Bill Beckham, the course superintendent, motioned to Chas Johnson. Johnson was getting ready to drive out onto the course to mow the greens on the back side. He and two other workers had already been up for an hour, mowing the front side greens in the chill darkness with the bright headlamps as their guide.

"Chas," Beckham said. "Marty called yesterday afternoon and said one of the members complained about something dead and smelly down in the front bunker at 10. Check it out, will you? Must be a squirrel or something that a hawk left behind. And check all around the area—smells are funny. They can drift in from anywhere."

"Yessah," Johnson said, getting up into the seat of his triplex mower. It was the newest model and it looked as clean and shiny as they day it had rolled out of the factory. Nothing at Augusta National ever looked worn or used. What Johnson didn't say, but was thinking, was "Goddam members prolly think their own shit smells better than anyone else."

Johnson had to drive a circuitous passage down to the tenth green—machinery was to be kept off the fairways at all times. There were secret pathways and openings through the woods that the grounds crew knew to use, so it took Chas several minutes before he pulled up next to the green. Dismounting, he walked back the 50 yards or so to the Mackenzie bunker, its yawning expanse glimmering the in the dawn light.

He smelled it, too. It was obvious, overpowering. Chas Johnson, who had served with the Marines in Viet Nam, was familiar with the smell of death. Something near this bunker was very, very dead. Pulling his jacket collar around in front of his nose and mouth to filter out the nauseating stench, Johnson walked around the perimeter of the bunker, looking for something out of place. There was a set of animal tracks in the soft white sand, but he could see where the critter had entered, dug a little, and where it had left. Nothing else seemed out of place. He walked back up to the green, and examined the bunker to the right, the place where pros often bailed out on Sunday afternoon to avoid the certain bogey of a pulled shot down the bank to the left. The odor of death lingered here, too, but again, nothing seemed out of place.

Johnson walked back down the hill to the high lip at the upsweep of the bunker. He stared at the sand with the practiced eyes of someone who had worked on this golf course for nearly 30 years.

There! To the right, where a finger of green turf probed into the white sand, providing both a curvilinear design on the bunker's edge and a place for golfers to enter and exit the sand. Just where the green finger ended, Chas Johnson thought that the surface of the sand looked slightly convex, slightly bulged. Not perfect, and therefore not normal.

Looking around, he found a bunker rake and walked around and back down into the sand. To his practiced feet, the sand felt slightly harder than it should. He took the rake and began gently digging into the white silica. The sand, which should have been silky and loose, seemed hard and packed. Something wasn't right. He kept digging and moving sand back with the rake.

Suddenly, one of the tines caught on something. Chas Johnson pulled. The rake was caught. He pulled harder. Slowly, whatever his rake had snagged out began to pull free from the sand. Then it came up out of the sand and into sight.

Chas Johnson stared with wordless horror as he pulled a human arm out of the sand. The rake had caught beneath the band of a wristwatch. The arm, grey and green in the dawn light, was still connected to a torso buried deeper in the sand. But Chas Johnson wanted nothing more to do with his grisly job. He dropped the rake, ran back to the green, jumped into his mower and, ignoring all the rules about keeping off the fairway, blasted back up the hill towards the clubhouse as fast as his mower could go.

The fingers of the hand, which had fallen back onto the sand, next to the rake that Chas dropped, pointed towards the green.

Chapter One

We were in Ponte Vedra Beach, getting ready for the Players Championship, when the story came across the wires about the body found in the bunker at Augusta National. "We," of course, are the traveling band of brothers known as golf writers who follow the Tour around the country for the benefit of our readers back home, the members of Hacker Nation. In my case, that's literally true. "Hacker on Tour" in the ***Boston Journal.*** Catchy, huh? Blame that barely functioning idiot known as my editor.

It was Tuesday morning, and the field of most of the world's best players were out on Pete Dye's golf course trying to figure out how to golf their balls around the course without running afoul of the acres of sandy "waste area" and the oceans of gator-filled water hazards or, perhaps more importantly, how to get their approach shots to find those sections of the greens that are not on the wrong side of the buried elephants Dye installed beneath the gentle green turf of the Stadium course.

The press room at The Players is both large and luxurious—the tournament is the marquee event for the PGA Tour, played at their headquarters, and they really roll out the red carpet for the press during the week. Because this tournament is one of a dwindling few that manages to attract most of the top players in the world to the same place at the same time, the press contingent—both domestic and international—is quite large. Most of the British golf press come over for the Players, then head for the nearest beach to burn themselves lobster red before they make their way up to Augusta. So the PGA Tour built a state-of-the-art press room, with electronic scoreboards, Wifi connections for our laptops, hot buffet lunches every day, a regular procession of players trotted in and out of the interview area to provide those sound bites upon which we all have come to depend, and a large staff of attractive helpers ready to hasten to do our bidding, should we have any needs.

Well, journalistic needs, anyway. But on this Tuesday morning, the cavernous press room was less than half full, as many writers were themselves out sampling some of the Jacksonville area's finest golf courses. Normally, I would have been out there too, getting in eighteen up at Amelia Island, or out at The Ravines, or even along the beach at the old Ponte Vedra Inn. But I actually had a little catch-up work to do. Last weekend, the Tour had been over in Orlando, at Arnold Palmer's Bay Hill, and Mary Jane Cappaletti and her precocious young daughter Victoria had flown down for the weekend to "do the parks." Mary Jane lives in the apartment below mine in Boston's North End, and we had not that long ago embarked upon that journey known as "a relationship." It had actually been nice having them around, taking them out to some of the millions of family and theme restaurants in O-town and listening to their excited jabbering about the rides they had been on and the things they had done while I was at the golf course, watching Ernie Els smooth his way around Arnie's tough course for a win. They had an early-afternoon flight home on Monday, so we slept in, and then had a nice breakfast. I had driven them over to the Orlando airport, hugged and kissed them both goodbye, and headed up the interstate for the Atlantic coast and Jacksonville.

So when the news from Augusta crossed the wires late that morning, there weren't too many of us around to discuss all the ramifications. The facts were pretty sparse anyway. The Augusta police reported that the body of one John H. Judge, aged 26, had been discovered Monday morning buried in a bunker on the tenth hole of the famed Augusta National Golf Club. Judge was a resident of Grovetown, Georgia, located outside Augusta near the U.S. Army base at Fort Gordon, and an accountant for the local office of BellSouth. He was not a member of the club, no one there seemed to know him at all, and no one had any idea who had killed the man or why he had been buried in a bunker. Investigation continues, autopsy scheduled, etc. etc. etc.

John "Quigs" Quigley from the ***Detroit News*** was sitting a few desks from me.

"Body in the bunker?" he said, speaking mostly to himself, his reading glasses pushed up atop his mostly bald head as he scanned the news sheet that had just been handed out to all of us. "Isn't that the name of a novel by Agatha Christie?"

"I think her book is 'The Murder on the Links,'" I said.

"Yeah, it's a little too trite for the Dame," he said. He scratched the side of his nose thoughtfully. "Whaddya think, Hacker?" he asked me. "Why would someone bury someone they just killed in a sand trap at Augusta National three weeks before the Masters? You'd have to be nuts."

"Whereas if you killed someone and just dumped the body in the Savannah River, you'd be sane," I said.

He chuckled. "Point taken."

"But you're probably right," I said. "Whoever did this wanted the body to be found. That's why he stuck it in one of the most public private places in Augusta, if not the entire country."

Quigs looked at me sideways.

"You know Hacker," he said. "You keep getting involved in all these murders and stuff, people are gonna talk. Or at the least, not want to hang out with you."

"I didn't do it!" I protested, laughing. "I just made an observation."

We started talking about the NCAA basketball tournament that was beginning to heat up, and swapped a few baseball tidbits from spring training, and soon forgot all about the body in the bunker at Augusta National.

But there was still a piece of gray matter in the back of my head that was turning things over, poking at them, trying to understand. Who was this John Judge and why did he have an enemy who wanted him dead? Where had he been killed? Why had he been planted in the sand on the tenth hole? And how come none of Augusta's vaunted Pinkerton guards saw anything?

Quigs eventually went back to his laptop and I stared off into space. Finally, I shook my head and decided to get back to work. There were plenty of questions, but none of them were my business. I had a bunch of quotes and notes to put together for the morning paper and it was up to the Augusta police to ask all the questions about John H. Judge, age 26, deceased.

Besides, if I got my stuff done, I might still make an afternoon tee time to get in a quick nine.

Chapter Two

On Sunday night, after Tiger Woods had rolled to another impressive victory at The Players, pretending to let Phil Mickelson and Vijay Singh have a sniff at the lead before going out on that afternoon and throwing a nifty little 65 at them, leaving all of us with no choice but to install him as the prohibitive favorite heading into Augusta National in three weeks' time—hell, he would have been the prohibitive favorite at the Masters if he had shot a 79 and broken his leg along the way—I sat back in the slowly emptying press room and tried to decide what to do with a free week.

The Tour was moving on to Atlanta, but most of the best players were going home for a week to practice, consult with their swing and mental gurus and generally get their game faces on for the first major of the year. The field left for the TPC at Sugarloaf was ho-hum at best. A bunch of the golf writers were heading up the coast to Myrtle Beach, South Carolina and the annual golf writers' golf tournament, a weekend of fun, booze and bad golf. I hadn't signed up for the tournament, because I'm getting too old for the boozing nightlife, my golf game was nonexistent and I pretty much hate Myrtle Beach, which has turned into a 70-mile-long traffic bottleneck filled with franchised restaurants, putt-putt emporiums, red-neck attractions and too many bad golf courses to count. Other than that, I'm sure it's swell.

I was thinking very seriously of going home and spending more time with Mary Jane and Victoria, despite the fact that I would have to make some extra flights to get back to Augusta in a week. Frank Donatello, that idiot boss of mine back in Boston, would throw several conniption fits about my expense report. But then, he does that anyway. I think it's in his job description.

But I hadn't made up my mind on what to do when my cell phone bleeped at me.

"Yo," I said. I believe in brevity.

"Hacker?" said a voice I recognized but couldn't quite place. "Are you on deadline? This is Brett Jacoby at Augusta National."

Brett Jacoby was a former golf writer for the Atlanta newspapers who had been hired about five years ago to be the first in-house public relations executive at the National. It had been a hire long overdue. Before Brett, all matters concerning credentials and such had been handled by a sweet old dear who was always polite but firm in her denials of special requests, and all statements made by the club were issued by the Chairman. After Brett, the club fast-forwarded its press relations into at least the twentieth century, if not the 21st, built a fancy new press facility with satellite uplinks and wireless Internet access, upgraded its historical facts and figures resources, digitized its photo library and otherwise tried to make life a little easier for those who covered the tournament. Of course, most of what Brett did still involved saying "no" to people, but as a former newspaper reporter himself, he knew how to do it without being insulting. That was a first for the club.

"Brett!" I said into the phone. "How's things? Getting ready for the invasion of the world of golf?"

"Oh, are people coming this way?" he said drily. We laughed.

"Hack," he said. "I was wondering if I could talk you into coming up early. Kind of as a personal favor."

"What's up?" I was curious.

"Well, you probably heard about the crime we had this week up here."

"Oh, yeah, the body in the bunker," I said. "I haven't seen much more about it in the news."

"No, it's been pretty quiet," he said.

I paused.

"That your doing?" I asked.

I heard him sigh.

"That's part of what I'd like to talk about with you, if you can come," he said. "There's some things happening on that front, and I'm tied down, as you can imagine, with all the tournament stuff."

"Why me?" I asked.

"You've got some police reporting background," he said. "There's a lot going on I don't know anything about, and I'm afraid we might be getting slammed from certain directions. I really need another pair of eyes and ears up here on the ground."

"You want me to work for Augusta National?" I asked, incredulous.

"Officially? No," he said quickly. "That's the favor part. Listen, I know this is all kind of screwy sounding, and I'll understand if you don't want to do it. Or can't. But there's more to this story than has been released to the public, and I want to try and protect my employers if I can. To do that I need more information, and to get that I need someone like you. And you might stumble onto a pretty good story."

I felt the small hairs at the nape of my neck rising. That's a sure-fire signal that there was something interesting going on. Something I'd probably have to find out about. And I suspect Brett Jacoby knew that.

"Can I get in a round of golf?" I asked, laughing.

He sighed again. "The golf course is closed in preparation for the tournament," he said automatically. Then he chuckled a bit. "I can pull some strings and make sure you get into the Monday press round." Every year, after the Masters tournament, names of the members of the worldwide press covering the tournament are drawn from a hat and 30 lucky stiffs get chosen to play the Augusta National course in its tournament trim on Monday morning. I had never been one of the chosen few.

"Done," I said. "Actually, I've been trying to figure out what to do for the next week. Even though an extra week in Augusta, Georgia is not exactly at the top of my to-do list, it sounds interesting. I'll do it."

"Great, Hacker, thanks!" Brett said. His relief was evident. We talked some logistics. He said the club would arrange accommodations and we made arrangements to meet for breakfast Tuesday morning.

He rang off and I sat there for several minutes revising my list of questions concerning the strange-sounding case of the body in the bunker.

Chapter Three

Monday morning I slept in. It's my off day. I had the entire day to get to Augusta, and figured I could put off doing laundry for another day or two. So I caught a few extra winks, had a large and leisurely breakfast while perusing ***USA Today***'s report on the just-concluded Players Championship. Ricky Donovan, that paper's golf writer, seemed to think Tiger's shot on the island-green 17th, a one-hop-off-the-flagstick-for-kick-in-birdie, was one of the "shots of the century." Whatever. I packed up my stuff and headed out.

I decided to take the cross-country route to Augusta, because there is no Interstate way to get there from Jacksonville without going up through Macon and Atlanta, which made no sense at all. So I jumped on I-95 north for an hour or two until I crossed over the Savannah River and then, at Hardeeville, I took old U.S. 321 which roughly follows the river as it angles northwest up through the Carolina Piedmont. I was on the South Carolina side of the river, and once I left the coast, I found myself deep in Dixie. The Old South. As the highway passed through little towns like Baker Hill, Tillman and on past Groover Landing, I found myself wondering, as I did every time I drove through a rural section of America, just who were the people who lived here and what did they do to make a living?

At first appearance, the answer was not much. Traffic on the highway was limited to the occasional trucker hauling timber or chickens or some unknown something locked tight in a silver rectangle of steel; a few pickups, dusty from the fields, and me. The little townships I slipped through silently each seemed to contain a seed & feed store, a Hardee's hamburger joint, the local bank and maybe a gas station. One side of town would be the "colored" section, where the homes were ramshackle, unpainted, propped on concrete blocks and guarded by mangy dogs. Across Main Street or over the railroad tracks would be the "good" part of town, with neat brick homes and orderly, trimmed lawns encircled by chain link fences, magnolias and azaleas in bloom, and, occasionally, a large Gothic-looking mansion-type place up on a hill.

Did these people like living out here in Nowheresville? I used to think that one had to live in a city to be fulfilled. But now I was beginning to think that the folks who managed to find a quiet little podunk like the ones I was driving through perhaps had the better deal. They knew all their neighbors. They knew practically everyone in town. If they wanted to be left alone, they probably were. They could park anywhere they wanted and probably didn't have to lock the car door. Or the front door. There was quiet. Peace. A connection with the seasons and with the land. What more could one want?

I drove through another little town and out into the empty countryside, which was coming alive in spring. The trees down here in the South had already leafed out, the hedges of forsythia and banks of azaleas were in full bloom, and the long dark fields on both sides of the road were beginning to show green sprouts of something, poking their heads hopefully up into the warm bright sunshine.

I suppose one could want to go see the latest movies. To buy, if in the mood, some Thai fish paste for a marinade. A hefty Sunday newspaper with a maddening Op-ed page and good long sports stories. One might want a neighborhood hardware store where one could get a key made or find a PVC elbow joint to fix that undersink problem. One could want friends to come over for an evening of laughter, debate and good food and wine. One might want any of the millions of things that a big city offers and a country town does not.

Somewhere in the middle, no doubt, lies nirvana.

I turned my thoughts to what lay ahead, waiting for me in Augusta. It sounded like Brett Jacoby had an intriguing problem. I wasn't sure I could help, but I was willing—intrigued even—to find out what he had in mind. I had called Mary Jane the night before, as I did almost every night now, to talk about our day and connect with a kindred soul. I told her of Brett's call and my decision to go up to Augusta a week early and see what he wanted.

"Let me get this straight," she had said. "You are going to go help the Augusta National Golf Club pull whatever chestnuts they've got burning out of the fire?" She had paused and let me think about that. "You? You hate the Masters."

Well, I argued back now, silently in my head, perhaps "hate" is too strong a word. Let's just say I have never fallen under the magic spell of the Masters. It's easy to do, and most of those who go there every April to watch the golf tournament unfold eventually submit to the charms of the place. I mean, you walk out in back of that big white clubhouse and the ground opens up and falls away down the sweeping slopes of the hill that comes to an abrupt stop at Rae's Creek. Those huge old pines tower alongside the fairways, and it can take your breath away. And before you get it back, you catch a whiff of the hundred-year-old wisteria climbing up the side of that antebellum clubhouse, and you see the tables scattered beneath the gnarled limbs of that famous old oak out back, and people you haven't seen for a year come up with smiles on their faces to greet you. The warm Georgia sunshine hits your face and you hear the first bursts of applause sounding like the wind in a mountain ravine wafting up from Amen Corner and it's very easy to get swept away into that magical Masters land.

But I've always resisted drinking the Kool-Aid. It's because of that magic spell that gets cast every spring that the crusty old bastards who run their little boy's club can get away with acting like, well, crusty old bastards. They can snap their cigar-stained fingers and make a venerable national television network dance to their will. They can disinvite anyone they want, for any reason they make up. Hell, they could probably institute a rule saying all competitors must henceforth play in the nude and most of the players would do it, just because of that magic Masters crap.

One reason I've managed to resist the magic is that for me, the Masters is just another work week. The players may all wax Wordsworthian about how they love coming to Augusta, how well they're treated, how wonderful life is...but for me, it's just another stop on the never-ending Tour. It's another week away from home, living out of a suitcase, trying to get one or two of those golf-playing morons to say something halfway interesting. It's also a week in which I, and about three dozen other regular Tour writers, have to wrack our brains to come up with something new and interesting to write about a golf tournament that's been played at the same hilly old golf course since 1930-something. Try doing that about twenty times in a row and see if you can find something magical to write about.

Another reason I've always resisted the magic is because I believe the club long ago came to an important fork in the road and took the wrong one. Augusta National, as we all know, was founded by two men. The first was the great Bob Jones who, at the end of his brief career as the world's best golfer, wanted only one thing--to get away from the rest of us. After his fourteen year career—seven years in the wilderness followed by seven in which he was practically unbeatable—he became a national celebrity in the manner of The Beatles, Elvis, Michael Jordon and Bill Clinton. He could go nowhere without being mobbed by fans desperate for a touch, a smile or a word. That stops being fun very quickly, and that's why Jones, when he decided he wanted to build a golf course where he could go to relax with his friends, wanted someplace very private and way off the beaten track.

History records that he turned to Clifford Roberts, a Wall Street financier, future rainmaker for Dwight Eisenhower's presidential run, and a self-described "designated bastard." Roberts' job was to raise the money to build the club—not an easy thing to do in the depths of the Depression in 1930-31—and Bobby Jones' job was to attract the right kind of member. That would be someone who loved golf in its purest form, and had the means to pay to keep everyone else outside the gates.

Bob Jones was happy to turn over the business details to Roberts. Jones was a genial man, someone who loved a good story and a strong drink, loved to laugh, and who enjoyed life, his wife and family and his privacy. Roberts loved to be a bastard, to say "no" to things, and to keep white-knuckled control on all aspects of Augusta National. The partnership worked well until Jones gradually grew weaker and sicker with the muscle-wasting disease that eventually killed him. As Bobby slowly faded—he somehow managed to hang on until 1971—Clifford Roberts took over more and more control of the club, until he became the sole power. And at some point along the way, Augusta National Golf Club became the personification of Clifford Roberts.

It became—and still is—an unfriendly place. The members there, for whatever reason, decided to adopt the Roberts façade of being grumpy bastards. Maybe they all are grumpy bastards, drawn as they are from the top ranks of business, finance and the professions. Certainly, few of them let the Masters magic dust inject some sunniness into their personalities. But I've always wondered what kind of personality the place would have assumed if Bob Jones hadn't fallen ill, but remained hale and hearty until old age. I'd like to believe that the Masters would have developed into the kind of tournament Jones first envisioned—a joyful gathering of good friends in the warm spring sunshine, to celebrate the return of warm weather, the camaraderie of golfers, and the sheer exuberance of competition. The Masters, as Jones himself often said, is the championship of nothing. For that simple reason alone, it is probably the most cherished title in golf.

But under Roberts' churlish hand, the tournament long ago stopped being fun. Despite all the famous innovations he came up with—from gallery ropes to plus-or-minus scores to par to free parking for the fans to the green-wrapped pimento-and-cheese sandwiches—Clifford Roberts sucked all the joy out of the Masters. He turned it into a place where you have to tiptoe past the graveyard and speak in respectful whispers so you don't get thrown out on your ear.

A rumbling from my empty stomach interrupted my reverie. I was still motoring through the Carolina farmland, but I decided that I would stop in the next crossroads town and find something to eat. In a few minutes, a neat wooden sign announced that I was entering the town of Blythe, South Carolina. That sounded nice. First, I passed about a two-mile section of franchise row, with, in rough order, a MacDonalds, Wal-Mart, Wendy's, Taco Bell, Pep Boys, the Red Dots liquor store, Hardee's, and a couple of car dealerships, which were apparently competing to see who could fly the most obnoxiously large American flag. I think the Ford place had Toyota beat by maybe four square feet.

Just for the heck of it, or perhaps following my inerrant reporter's sense, I turned off the two-lane highway at the sign for downtown, which turned out to be one block of low, one-story buildings ending in a public square of sorts, with a cupola-topped courthouse building shaded by large magnolia trees. And there on the corner, with a slanted, nose-in parking space right in front, was Walt's Diner. "Home Cookin'" the sign in the window promised. Just the kind of place I prefer to one of the franchise burger places, where you're never entirely sure what it is they put between the buns.

I pulled in, locked up, and stood and stretched in the bright afternoon sun. It was a little after one, so the main lunch crowd had come and gone. The bell above the door tinkled as I walked in. A long counter with round swivel stools ran down the left side of the diner, while about six small wooden tables covered with red-checked vinyl sat against the wall on the right. Half the tables were full, and all but one of the stools was empty. I decided to sit at the counter, where I could watch Walt, or whoever it was doing the cooking, working in the kitchen along the back.

There was just one waitress working the lunch shift at Walt's. She was a slightly frumpy middle-aged woman, with brown hair piled haphazardly atop her head, pinned in place with some leathery things and festooned with two yellow pencils. She was wearing a yellow long-sleeved oxford shirt, blue jeans and a white apron that looked the worse for the lunch rush.

I plopped down on my squeaky swivel seat and picked up the menu stuck in the holder of the amenity tray in front of me. The waitress gave me a few seconds before she came up, pulled a worn order pad from her hip pocket and we went through the southern ritual of fine dining.

"Som'thin' to drink, hon?" she asked.

"Ice tea," I said.

"Sweet or unsweet?" she asked.

"Sweet, like me," I said.

I got the usual half smile. It was probably the four hundredth time today she had heard that. She scurried off to get my tea and I went back to reading the menu. The specials for the day included stuffed grape leaves. I needed to know Walt's last name, and how many generations removed from Thessalonica he was before I went for that. Fried chicken, which I could smell bubbling in the hot grease in the back. Baked lasagna, which would never match up with Mary Jane's, whose recipe was borrowed from her Italian mobster in-laws. Or a ham steak smothered in red-eye gravy, with a selection of two sides.

The waitress came back, slapped down the red plastic tumbler filled with tea and ice cubes, laid down a long-handle spoon, the square sugar-packet holder and a napkin which was rolled up with the rest of my silverware. She whipped out her order book again.

"What'll it be?" she asked, pushing a stray strand of hair back on top of her flushed head.

"I'll have the ham steak, mashed and slaw," I said.

She nodded, scribbled her notes, tore off the page, slapped it down on the counter and yelled the order to the cook in the back. She grabbed a pitcher of iced tea and dashed off to refill the glasses of some of the other patrons.

I sipped my sweet tea and looked around. Walt's had obviously been around for a few years. The ceiling in the tall, narrow room was covered with panels of tin pressed into a flowery design. The counter with stools would have dated the place some, but the walls above the row of tables were covered in old black and white photos. There were high school football teams, Little League baseball teams, a framed page from a newspaper—the Blythe Herald—with a huge screaming headline splashed across the front: "Tornado Hits Town." Lace curtains draped on a rod covered the front windows at about waist height, allowing the sunlight from outside to come in, and allowing the patrons of Walt's to look outside and see what was going on in the courthouse square. Which, at the moment, was exactly nothing.

"So what brings y'all to Blythe?" the waitress, who had snuck up on me and was refilling my glass of tea reduced by all of one sip, was asking.

"Passing through on my way up to Augusta," I said.

"You Army?" she asked, looking doubtfully at my longish hair.

"Nope," I said.

"Nuclear?" She was referring to the Savannah River Plant, where they had been making, working with and storing nuclear materials since DuPont built the first reactor in the early 1950s. All I knew about the massive and highly secretive site along the Savannah River was that it was the second-largest employer in the greater Augusta area, after the Army's Fort Gordon.

"Nope," I said. "Going up for the golf tournament next week."

"Ah," she said, and cast her eyes somewhat nervously back towards the kitchen. "You might not want to mention that if Walt comes out."

"He doesn't like golf?" I said, smiling.

"Naw," she said. "His nephew was murdered a few days ago. They found his body on the golf course. He'd been shot."

"I heard about that," I said, noncommittally.

She pushed her hair back and nodded. "Well, nobody in the family has been able to find out anything," she said, shaking her head. "The po-leece has clammed up tighter than a tick. And that damn club ain't sayin' nothing. Walt and his sister—Johnny's mother-- is all tore up. They buried him Sunday."

"And no idea who did it or why?" I asked innocently.

"You a cop?" a rough voice rasped.

The waitress and I both looked up, surprised. A large man with a huge, red, bald head was standing there, holding an immense plate of food in his hand. It looked like a ham steak cut from a five-foot-long pig. This was apparently Walt, with an apron strung across his massive chest, covering a tee shirt. His jowly face seemed to melt necklessly into his torso. I would have bet the farm that he'd played the interior line for Blythe High School, and maybe for Clemson or the USC Gamecocks after that. His arms were also beefy, but compared to that chest, they looked almost puny holding my lunch.

He put the plate down in front of me and fixed me with an unfriendly stare.

"No, sir, I am not," I said carefully, picking up my napkin-wrapped silverware. "I am a reporter, a sports writer, on my way to cover the Masters next week."

He continued to stare at me, his beady little eyes peering out from beneath his massive, sweaty forehead. After the eyebrows, there wasn't another hair in view on the man, if you didn't count a few strays peeking out from his ears.

"Reporter, huh." It was a statement, not a question, and it didn't sound like he was a fan of the Fourth Estate. But then, who is these days?

"Yes sir," I said politely. I was trying as hard as I could to maintain an even, pleasant tone of voice with Walt. He was big, he looked mad and I'll bet he had a sharp cleaver back there somewhere. "This nice young lady was telling me about your nephew," I continued, nodding at the waitress, who was looking at me with what I assumed was a warning not to go where I was heading. "I am sure sorry for your loss. We were just talking about the lack of information forthcoming from the police about the crime."

His thick eyebrows twitched up and down a few times while he digested that.

"They have clammed up on me," he said, finally. "Somebody has put the kibosh on the thing."

"Why?" I asked, genuinely curious.

He leaned against the counter and crossed his arms. "Damned if I know," he said. "Johnny was a good kid. He worked hard, kept his nose clean. He was one of them accountant types... quiet, neat, everything in order. He went to church on Sundays, came home a lot to visit his Mom. Handled my books every year and we never had a problem. Why the Good Lord saw fit for him to have this end ... "

His eyes filled with tears, which he fought back. The waitress put a comforting hand on his arm.

"Maybe the cops are working on an angle and don't want anything to get out in public before they make their move," I suggested. I tucked into my lunch and was shoveling it in as fast as I could while we talked.

Walt shook his head. "Nope," he said. "Someone up top has said to bury it, and it is buried," he said. "The cop I know up there in Augusta made a few calls, talked to some of them in the homicide division. They tole him to forget about it. The lid was officially clamped on."

"By who?" I wondered.

"That, sir, I don't know and would like to find out," Walt said, his jaw quivering in anger. "I gotta figure it's those damn high-falutin' golf types at that golf club. Ever'one knows that when they snap their fingers, everyone in the damn city jumps."

"But I thought Johnny didn't have anything to do with Augusta National," I said.

"Far as anyone knows, he didn't," Walt said. "But that ain't very far."

I finished up my lunch, drank the last of my tea. The waitress poured my glass full again. No one who dines out in the Deep South is ever in danger of dehydration. I figure it must be a state law that every restaurant customer must float out the door filled with about a gallon of tea.

"I tell you what," I said. "I'll ask around some. If I learn anything, I'll let you know."

Walt's eyes filled again and he looked away for a moment. Then he grabbed a spare order pad from the counter and scribbled something on it. He ripped it off the pad and handed it to me. "My numbers, here and home," he said. "Any time, day or night. Name's Walt, Walt Cromwell."

I nodded, pulled out my wallet and tucked the paper away.

"What do I owe ya?" I asked. "It was damn good."

Walt waved his hand. "It's on the house, young feller," he said.

I protested. "I can't guarantee I'll find out anything," I said.

Walt was firm. "You just do the best you can," he said. "That's all the Lord asks of any of us."

I shook his hand, and the waitress', went out through the tinkling door, and got in my car. Quite the coincidence, showing up for lunch here in little Blythe and running into the family of the victim of the incident in Augusta. But like they say on the golf course, if you can't be good, might as well be lucky.

Chapter Four

Augusta, Georgia, is a funny little town. It was laid out originally by the same General James Edward Oglethorpe who gave Savannah its distinctive gridwork of streets and intersections of leafy green parks. Oglethorpe obviously expended every ounce of charm he had on Savannah, because when he got to Augusta, some 200 miles up the Savannah River, he had nothing left.

Perhaps form does follow function and where Savannah was a commercial interchange, where goods came and went from the seaport and the merchants and the lawyers needed elegant, wrought-iron-bedecked, fanciful homes and offices and churches, Augusta was always a workingman's town, two-fisted, no-nonsense, down and dirty. The Savannah River is shallow and shoaled at Augusta, and that fast-moving water was harnessed to run the cotton gins and mills that gave the town its reason for being. Instead of clipper ships from London, Augusta was the destination for cartloads of Georgia cotton, driven by mule team and redneck to the ugly brick mills along the river and canals.

Rather than elegant salons, downtown Augusta was a beer-and-a-shot kind of town, filled with bars, gambling dens and whores. Iniquity City. Rednecks just wanna have fun.

It's also a town that has always had something of a chip on its collective shoulder. While Augusta was busy churning out the raw goods, Atlanta became the South's financial crossroads and Savannah the South's premiere party town. Even in the Civil War, after Sherman finally conquered and burned Atlanta—giving that city victim's bragging rights for eternity—everyone in Augusta expected that they were next on the General's hit list. The town, after all, had converted some of its mills into powder works to make ammunition for the Rebel army. But no. Sherman merely feinted in Augusta's direction and then cut his broad swatch south and east through Georgia, before arriving at the gates of Savannah, which quickly rolled over and surrendered, thus preserving for future generations the on-going cocktail party of life in that elegant town.

And while the rebuilt Atlanta prospered and Savannah stayed pretty much the same—the two sides of the Southern miracle coin—Augusta merely faded into the background. It had a brief Renaissance as a winter destination for the rich and powerful during the Gilded Age, but as the railroads pushed deeper and deeper into Florida, which was warmer and had beaches, Augusta's fame and fortunes waned again. Many suspect the reason why Bob Jones and Clifford Roberts selected Augusta as the site for their golf club was that it was such a quiet backwater podunky kind of place that Jones would be able to visit and play there in relative peace.

But that's not to say there were no pretty places in Augusta. Up on The Hill, a neighborhood also known as Summerville, there are several blocks of mansions, many with nice views across downtown and the river. I made my way through the city and up into this district, where Brett Jacoby had booked a room for me in a quiet bed and breakfast inn. After a few missed turns and consultations with my map, I finally found the Olde Magnolia Inn, a gothic-looking Victorian home with a turreted tower and a long, winding drive shaded by the eponymous tree. I drove around to the back where there was a crushed-stone parking area next to a gently sloping, shady lawn. Groupings of chairs dotted the lawn, and a large porch wrapped around the entire back of the house.

It was a far nicer place than the one I had booked for next week, during the tournament. Like most other members of the press, I was scheduled to stay in either the Comfort Inn or the Motel 6 over on Washington Road, at the intersection of Interstate 20, one of those deliberately ugly interfaces filled with strip shopping malls, gas stations, fast-food joints and motels. Lots and lots of motels which try to hang on to negligible business for 51 weeks a year just so they can jack the rates up four or five hundred percent during Masters week and make their yearly numbers. The rest of the year, they'd be lucky to get $75 a night. The ***Boston Journal*** and other newspapers across America, not to mention the legions of golf fans who invade Augusta every April, paid $295 a night for the same room. Ain't capitalism grand?

I don't know what the Olde Magnolia charged, because Augusta National had picked up my tab, at least until Sunday. A pleasant elderly woman checked me in, bade me welcome and showed me upstairs to the Stonewall Jackson Suite, which featured a four-poster bed, chintz wallpaper, heavy mahogany wardrobe and dresser, and a claw-foot bathtub in the bath. There was a cut-glass beaker of sherry on the dresser for my complimentary nightcap, and she said there'd be fresh-baked cookies left outside in the hall in case anyone got the munchies at midnight. Breakfast from seven to nine and did I require anything special?

I thanked her kindly in my best faux-Southern manner and unpacked a bit before placing a call to Jacoby. He said he'd meet me for breakfast at eight, and did I need some recommendations for dinner? I thanked him very kindly, starting to feel queasy at all this unnatural politeness, but said I knew some folks in town I could call.

I flipped through my book and found the number for Connaught Thackery IV. I had met the Conn Man several Masters ago at, best as I could recall, the Aussie party. Every year, the Australians in town for the Masters get together and throw a little "barbie" at one of the rental homes they take for the week. Invited guests include all the Australian Golf Union bigwigs, assorted friends and magnates, and they fly in a planeload of Fosters lager for the event which always attracts the A-list of visiting celebrities, hot babes and residents of Augusta who haven't rented out their homes and fled town.

Conn was one of those unfortunate Southerners who had been tagged with two last names in what was, I thought, one of the stranger traditions of Dixie. But he had overcome this infliction by embracing the Southern aristocracy, where strange names are both common and accepted. He had coasted through the University of Georgia, managed to get a law degree and come back to Augusta. He didn't have to work too hard—the family trust fund, run by savvy gnomes over in Atlanta, provided a nice independent income—but he took on cases that interested him, which ran the gamut from high-society divorce cases to First Amendment challenges to the ***Augusta Chronicle*** to civil rights cases for the working poor of "The Terry," or The Territory as Augusta's downtown black neighborhood was known. As a result, he knew just about everybody in town, one way or another, and knew their secrets.

We had become friendly over several Fosters, while some Aussie band called the "Dreadful Dingos" thumped in the background, and we had spent most of the evening chatting up two vapid sheilas from Adelaide. We promised them a starring role in the next Rigid Tools catalog, but they didn't know what that meant and eventually disappeared into the night. But we had enjoyed ourselves anyway.

Conn, as always, was happy to hear from me.

"Hacker!" he said when I got him on the phone. "You're in town? Did you get the dates wrong again? The damn tournament doesn't start until next week!"

I laughed and told him I was in town a little early to do some advance work. He asked where I was and whistled when I told him about the Olde Magnolia.

"Damn, son, you're moving up in the world," he said. "That place is one of the National's stash houses. It'll be filled with fancy pants. That's where they put all the international golf officials. My, my. Remember to keep that pinkie in the air."

I asked if he was free for dinner and we agreed to meet at a rib joint downtown by the Riverwalk.

Evening plans made, I took a nap in my fancy chintz bedroom. Whether or not my pinkie was suitably raised, I could not say.

Chapter Five

A soft rain had begun to fall and the air was chilly as I drove down off The Hill and found my way down to the Riverwalk, an area of former cotton warehouses and brick factories that had been gentrified and converted with your tax dollars into art museums, shops, uninspiring views of the murky Savannah River and a bedraggled South Carolina on the far shore. I suppose I should give the city some credit for the effort, but in the cold spring rain, downtown Augusta—Riverwalk or no Riverwalk—was dreary and depressing.

Inside, Beamie's on the River wasn't much better. Open, bricky, with a big bar in the center of the room, Beamie's was pretty dead. I didn't see Conn anywhere, so I took a seat at the bar, ordered a Scotch and ate some stale peanuts while watching the latest news from ESPN. It was all about steroids in baseball and the arrest of some NBA star.

I was halfway through my Scotch when the Conn Man walked in, shaking the rain off his jacket. He was tall, about 50 years old, with salt-and-pepper hair all aflop. But he was obviously in good shape, trim and strong-looking. He was wearing a casual long-sleeved shirt, neatly pressed khakis, and polished loafers. He looked the very part of a Southern aristocrat. I watched him work the room as he made his way up to the bar. He air-kissed the hostess, shook hands with a couple in a front booth, hugged two other waitresses who saw him and came running up, and high-fived the bartender before he finally turned to me.

"You running for mayor?" I asked as we shook hands.

"Got a few too many skeletons in the closet for public service," Conn chortled. The bartender set a drink down in front of him and gave him the thumb-shoot sign. Conn shot him back. "Besides, who wants the responsibility of running this dog-ass old town?"

We spent a jolly half-hour or so catching up with each other. He was aghast to learn I had a serious Significant Other; I was happy to hear that he hadn't changed much. His father had died and left him another small pot of cash, and he had recently concluded, successfully, a big divorce case for a client.

"So you're basically rolling in it," I concluded.

"It's not the money, Hacker," he said, looking at me seriously. "It's the fun the money will buy."

"So you're having tons o' fun?"

He grinned at me. "Tryin' to."

We moved over to a booth with a view of the gray river sliding slowly past and ordered some steaks and a bowl of the restaurant's prized seafood gumbo.

"So what are you doing here?" he asked as we tucked into our dinner.

I explained that Brett Jacoby had asked me to come up a few days early and help him with something that had to do with the murder that had been discovered at Augusta National the previous week. "We're having breakfast in the morning," I told him. "So I don't really know what he wants me to do, specifically."

Conn's face turned dark, and he frowned.

"That's a bad business," he said, shaking his head. "Watch your back."

"What do you know about it?" I wondered. "And how, exactly, is Augusta National involved?"

He fished the last of his gumbo from his bowl before answering.

"Rule Number One in Augusta," he said, raising his forefinger like a schoolteacher, "Is that the National is always involved. Even when they say they're not involved, that means they're involved but they just don't want anyone to know it. There is no separating the golf club from anything that happens in this town. Anything." He wagged that finger for emphasis.

"So you're telling me that Augusta National knowingly had this nice quiet little church-going, mama-loving, accountant bumped off?" I was incredulous. "For what purpose?"

Conn was shaking his head at me. "Oh, Hacker," he said, "Typical media. Jumping to the wrong conclusions with half-baked information. I suppose I should have told you Rule Number Two in Augusta—nothing is ever as it first appears. There are layers, my friend. Layer after layer after layer. Most of which go back decades, if not generations."

"Sounds kinda Gothic," I said.

He nodded. "Oh, yeah," he agreed. "Up to and probably including the crazy aunt in the attic."

"So tell me what's going down," I said as our steaks arrived. We stopped talking long enough to arrange all the condiments, load up the baked potatoes, and each eat several bites of meat before Conn began talking again.

"Okay," he said, chewing rapidly. "Let's look at what we know and examine what we probably don't know. First, poor little Johnny Judge was killed."

"I haven't even heard how," I said.

"Two shots in the chest," Conn told me, eyes dark, shaking his head.

"Could be a Mob hit," I said. "You got one of them down here?"

He chuckled softly. "La Cosa Nostra? Naw. Down here, most of the traditional criminal activities are run by the boys down in The Terry," he said. "Law enforcement chips away at the edges when they need to, but the unspoken arrangement is that The Terry is the place to go when you need a hooker, some cocaine, a quick loan to carry you over, or to lay down a bet. Unless someone gets carried away, they let all that go on."

"Somebody got carried away then," I said, thinking of the body in the bunker.

Conn shook his head. "But the shooting of this Judge boy doesn't fit the usual pattern," he said. "The fellas that run things down in The Terry know one thing very, very well: if they start shooting up white people, the game will be called off damn quick. Especially if they start shooting nice, plump, God-fearing, Mama-loving white boys like that Judge kid."

"So he wasn't shot by the local bad guys," I said. "Then who did it?"

"Ah, well, that's the next interesting question, isn't it?" Conn said. "To me, it's very illuminating to consider where the body was...ah...positioned."

"In a bunker at Augusta National, two weeks before the biggest golf event of the year," I said. "Sounded like a deliberate act to me, too."

"More like a warning, I'd say," Conn said.

"About what?"

He smiled enigmatically and shook his head. "To tell you the truth, Hack, I don't know. Over the last year or so, I have heard some whispers and the usual assortment of rumors have filtered their way through town. People are always gossiping about what happens out there at that club. It's one of the great participatory sports here in Augusta, and it goes on after church on Sunday, at the chamber of commerce, at the garden clubs and down in the dives of The Terry. One learns to pick out the gossip that sounds ridiculous or mean and impossible and discount it. But one also learns to listen for the true notes, and piece together stuff that really happens."

"And your rumor antennae have told you what?"

He shrugged, and cut himself another slice of steak. "There's a new leadership group out there," he said. "Ever since Grosvenor took over a year ago as Chairman, there have been all sorts of rumors of discontent."

He was talking about Charlie Grosvenor, who had been appointed Chairman of the club some 18 months ago. The appointment had been endlessly analyzed in the golfing press because Grosvenor was the first chairman of Augusta National since Clifford Roberts whose home territory was Wall Street and not the Olde South. He spoke in clipped, patrician tones, rather than the folksy, down-home drawl that many had come to associate with official Augusta National since the days of Jackson Stephens and Hootie Johnson. And like your typical Wall Street investment magnate, when Charles Grosvenor spoke, he expected people to jump to do his bidding.

Conn continued to talk as he ate. "Some of the old guard don't like the way the man runs the place. Feel rubbed the wrong way. Is it generational? Natural progress? The way clubs go? Nobody likes change, least of all some of those troglodytes at the National. And every chairman makes his own enemies at that place. It's the main recreation at the National—complaining. Of course, they can't do it openly or else they get bounced, so they whisper. But some of the whispers I've heard have been a bit deeper than the usual fight against change. Nothing I can really put a finger on, but there's something going on that has people deeply upset."

"Upset enough to have someone shot to death and buried on the tenth fairway?" I wondered. "And how does this Judge kid fit into the picture?"

Conn shrugged again. "Sorry, Hacker, I don't know everything. Far as I can tell, John Judge worked out at the regional office of BellSouth, and was in charge of construction oversight. Y'know...they buy telephone wire and poles and switches and things, and someone has to tote up the costs and make sure the invoices get paid and such like that. There's a lot of new home construction going on all around us, so I imagine they kept him hopping. Sounds hopelessly boring to me, but just about perfect for someone like this Johnny Judge, who apparently liked to fish and hunt, go visit his Mama now and then, and live a quiet life. He seemed like one happy to have a job, a regular paycheck and weekends off."

"You said his murder might be a warning," I said, pointing my fork across the table. "A warning about what?"

Conn shrugged again. "Dunno," he said. "But that brings me to Rule Three."

"Which is?"

"Follow the money."

"That's Rule One in most places," I said.

Conn shrugged. "That's Augusta for you," he said. "We like to be different."

Chapter Six

The nice lady at the Olde Magnolia was gobsmacked when I told her I wasn't going to take breakfast at the inn. "Oh, what a shame!" she exclaimed, as though her heart had been broken. "The chef is making his coconut French toast!" I allowed as how it did seem a shame to let all that work go to waste, but that I had a previous breakfast appointment. She let me go, but didn't look happy.

It didn't take long to drive from the inn over to Washington Avenue. Passing by all the concrete and asphalt detritus of modern-day Americana--the strip malls and gas stations and drive-thrus and car washes—I turned in at the entrance to Augusta National, which had only a modest white sign announcing the most famous golf club in the world. A steel gate blocked the way one car-length into the place, and a grey uniformed Pinkerton guard came out of his wooden guard house. He had epaulets on his shoulders, a holster on his hip and a clipboard in his hand and I felt thankful he didn't approach my car with weapon drawn.

I told him I had a breakfast appointment with Brett Jacoby. He looked down at his clipboard, asked me to wait, and went back inside his little hut to make a call. The gate magically opened and he waved me on towards the clubhouse. As I drove through the gateway I resisted the impulse to shout back at the guy "Aha! Al Qaida has once again tricked you, you infidel dogs!"

I had never actually driven down the famous Magnolia Lane—the press parking lot is further down Washington Avenue with its own entrance. The green waxy leaves of the twin row of ancient trees created a dappled sunlight pattern on the ground as I drove towards the clubhouse. The driving range was on my left as I swung around what they call the Founder's Circle, a grassy area outside the front door. Next to the flagpole, twin monuments enshrine the memories of Jones and Roberts. A gardener was busy setting bright yellow pansies into the planters that create the club's logo: a yellow map of the USA into which a flagstick would be set roughly in the location of Augusta. Thousands of people would take a photograph of the scene in the next week.

A white-jacketed attendant came out of the clubhouse entrance, greeted me by name and offered to park my car for me. I graciously allowed him to take the wheel and followed his directions inside. There was a deep mahogany counter inside the door where another Pinkerton guard was watching the four video monitors that seemed to have the place covered. He motioned me up the stairway off to the right, telling me that Mr. Jacoby would be waiting for me in his office, second door to the left.

For a place that was going to host the first major golf tournament of the year in six days, it was amazingly quiet inside the thick concrete walls of the clubhouse. Beyond the counter, a green runner occupied the center of a wide hardwood hallway whose floor was polished to a mirror-like finish. I could see that the old house—it had been built in 1857 by Dennis Redman, an indigo farmer—had the antebellum system of air conditioning seen throughout the South: a roomy central hallway with large door openings on both ends which could be flung open to allow whatever breeze existed to drift through the house. Today, the doors were shut and the air conditioning was turned on.

Upstairs I found a nondescript hall filled with offices. There was a slight humming sound of fluorescent lighting and computers turned on. But there was no one in sight. I guess I expected more chaos the week before the Masters—people running about tossing paper at each other and shouting "You forgot to order the pimento-and-cheese sandwiches???" Instead, it seemed like I'd walked into the deepest recesses of Ernst & Young, where all was calm, cool, controlled and number-crunching.

I peeked inside the second door to the left and saw Brett Jacoby at his desk. His office was small and orderly, with a view out over the now-empty driving range.. The desk held a computer, a full-size calendar blotter, a picture of Mrs. Jacoby and the two kids and nothing else. Brett was talking on his telephone, facing away from the door. Jacoby resembled nothing so much as a college professor. He had lost most of his hair, except for a furry strip around the sides and in back, and his bald pate was shiny and seemed to have been buffed into perfection. He was somewhere in his fifties, a bit paunchy around the middle, not too tall. He was wearing a blue-on-white pinstriped dress shirt, matching necktie and pressed khakis.

He hung up the phone, saw me standing there and rose to greet me. He waved me into a guest chair in front of his desk. We spent a few minutes catching up—something we usually do the week of the tournament. Jacoby had worked at the Atlanta newspapers for almost twenty years before Jackson Stephens had asked him to become the club's public face. It had taken him a year or two to get settled into the job, but he stuck it out. Now, he told me, he loved his work, his family liked the Augusta area and all was well.

"C'mon," he said finally, "I promised you breakfast."

He led me down the hall, down a small back staircase and into the Trophy Room, where a few tables were set for breakfast. The portrait of Eisenhower beamed from one wall and the painting of His Holiness Bob Jones occupied another. I looked around for the massive silver reproduction of the National clubhouse, which is the trophy given to the winner of the Masters, but it wasn't on its usual plinth. Brett saw me looking and said "They send it out every year about this time to get it polished up."

We sat down near a window looking out onto the golf course and a waiter materialized out of nowhere. "Mornin' Mr. Brett," the man said, his deeply black face wreathed in a pleasant smile. "Who is this fine gentleman you've got wid' you this mornin'?"

Brett introduced me to Calvin, and after he shook out our napkins for us, he strolled off in search of the coffee pot.

"When he comes back, just tell him what you'd like to eat," Brett told me. "They don't have menus for breakfast—chef just whips up whatever anyone orders."

"I can see how one could get used to living in the lap of luxury," I chided him.

"Yeah," he said, turning a little red, "It don't suck working here most of the time." Brett went on to explain that because the club is closed down during the summer months—from May until October 1st—it was usually quiet if not boring for that part of the year. But when the members were in town, both the activity and the level of luxury ratcheted up a few notches.

Calvin came back and we ordered. Just for the heck of it, I ordered an egg-white omelet with chorizo sausage and fried green tomatoes. "Yassir," Calvin smiled at me, as if he had an order like that every single morning of his life.

Brett and I discussed the world of golf and sipped our coffee for the next few minutes, until Calvin brought our plates. I'll be damned if the kitchen hadn't filled my order, right down to the grilled chorizo. "Tell the chef he's on his toes," I said. Calvin's face broke out in a wide, wrinkled smile as he refilled our coffee cups. "Yassir," he said, nodding his head. "I'll tell Miss Daisy that yo' is happy. She gon' like that."

"Hell," Brett said, "She didn't even have to break a sweat. I've seen Japanese guys order the Tokyo Special and out it comes just like they like it in Osaka—raw fish, steamed rice and tofu."

"I get the feeling that the one thing this place is not missing is resources," I said.

We ate quietly. The food was delicious. I was hungry.

"So," I said finally, pushing back my plate and downing the last of my coffee. I saw Calvin out of the corner of my eye start forward with the coffee pot again, and I waved him away. "What's going on around here and what can I do to help?"

Brett put down his knife and fork. He poured a little cream into his coffee cup and then picked up his spoon and stirred the coffee thoughtfully. I got the sense that he was stalling, thinking.

"Look," I said. "I know how buttoned down this place can be. If you're having second thoughts about letting some outsider sniff around whatever dirty laundry there is, if there is any, then don't worry about it. I got a good breakfast and a nice inn to stay in and I can waste my time this week playing some golf. No problem. On the other hand, if you think there's something I can do to help you, just ask. If I don't think I can do it, I'll say so."

Brett looked at me gratefully. "There are a lot of people who would like to harm this place," he said. "Especially after that whole Martha Burk circus...hell, even before that. We seem to represent something a lot of people resent. And there are plenty of guys in the press and outside that would love to dig up some dirt and use it to drag our name through the mud."

"Brett," I said, "I've never been a big fan of the way you guys do business. I think you know that. But it's not my club and I don't lose any sleep over it. You guys put on a pretty good golf tournament every year, and that's all I'm interested in. Everybody in the press room has an opinion on how you guys should run this place, and my opinion is the same as everyone else's: not worth pig's snot. It's your club. On the other hand, if Augusta National is doing something illegal or immoral or something, then that's a legitimate news story and, since I'm a legitimate news reporter, or so they say, I'd be interested in that."

Calvin came over unbidden and filled our coffee cups again.

"But I came over here yesterday because you asked me for a favor," I said. "You and I go back a ways. I know you're a straight shooter, and I think you know I am, too. So, again, tell me what you want to, or tell me nothing. No hard feelings either way."

Brett looked relieved.

"Thanks, Hacker, I appreciate that," he said. "Let's go take a walk."

We walked out the central hallway to the back entrance which led out to the grass lawn behind the clubhouse. For the umpteenth time, I took in one of the grandest vistas in golf, and for the umpteenth time, it almost took my breath away. There is a scale to Augusta National that never translates onto the television screen. You have to stand there on the sunny grass behind the clubhouse and let it overtake your senses. There were dozens of workmen in yellow construction hard hats milling about, putting the finishing touches on the grandstands and draping ropes along the fairways and touching up the various wooden parts with green paint. But even with all that activity, the view assaulted one's senses.

First, it's the way the course drops away down the hill towards Rae's Creek. I always think that the golfers should be wearing crampons instead of spikes to maneuver their way up and down those hills. Then, there's the contrast between the wide-open spaces of that hillside, and the tall loblolly pines that define most of the fairways. Then, there's the flowering things in bloom everywhere one looks: the azaleas, the dogwoods, the wisteria vine climbing the clubhouse wall. Finally, there's the feel of that warm Georgia spring sunshine and the smell of freshly mowed grass. Today, I didn't hear any of that rippling of applause that always seems to ride up the hill on a warm gust of wind, but that's always there, too. It's an amazing place.

Brett led me over to one of the white metal tables that had been set out in the shade beneath the spreading arms of the ancient live oak trees behind the clubhouse, overlooking the ninth green. There were green-and-white umbrellas opened above all the tables. We sat down and took a moment to drink in the view.

"I never get tired of looking at all this," he said, sweeping his arm outwards. "Been here what, five, six years now? Never get tired of this."

I nodded in agreement, sat back, and waited.

Finally, Brett sat forward, leaning on his arms.

"I called you, Hacker, because I don't know what's going on," he said, looking intently at me. "My job is to present the image of Augusta National to the world, and I'm afraid I can't do that with this situation."

I waited.

"When they found that body here last week, it threw me for a loop," he continued. "Not only because of the publicity, even though we had nothing to do with the crime in any way. But the whole thing has been vacuumed up. It's like when they took that poor man's body away in the ambulance that morning, they took everything about him too. Who he was, who killed him, what he was doing here...They won't tell me anything."

"Who is 'they?'" I asked.

"The cops, mostly," Brett said. "I've asked the people I know down at city hall to find out what they can, and they come back with nothing. It's like John Judge has disappeared into a black hole in space. It's sucked him and everything about him in and it's like he never existed."

"Nobody here at the club can find out anything?" I asked.

"Nope," Brett said. "And that's what scares me a little. Maybe he did have something to do with this place, and I just don't know it. You remember I said that there are people who seem to have it in for us, because of who we are or what we supposedly represent. I haven't been able to sleep the last week because I'm thinking that there will be something that links this murder to Augusta National, and they're waiting until the entire world is looking at us next week before they spring the trap."

"So you want me to try and nose around a little and see what I can find out?" I said.

"You seem to have a knack for it," Brett said, a wry smile playing at his lips. "From what I've heard."

I was frowning. "I dunno, Brett," I said, doubt creeping into my voice. "I'm a damn Yankee in these parts. Trying to get friendly with the local redneck gendarmes in a week's time is gonna be tough. Are you sure they're just not sitting on the investigation for a couple of weeks, at least until the circus gets out of town? Maybe they think that's what you guys want."

He shook his head. "If that were the case, at least they'd tell us something about what they think went down. But nobody is saying anything about anything. All we get is the 'case is under investigation at this time' stuff."

"Not even the chairman of the Augusta National Golf Club can get an answer?" I was incredulous.

He shook his head. "He is, as you know, fairly new around here," Brett said. "I probably have better contacts locally than he does."

Now it was my turn to stall a little, looking out at the sun-soaked vista of grass and trees. This sounded very fishy. If what Conn had said about Augusta National—that nothing in town happened without its knowledge and involvement—was true, then Brett's story of a police freeze on information didn't make sense. From the picture Conn had painted, someone at the club could pick up the telephone and get anything he wanted from the city, including at least an idea of how the murder case was progressing. If not from the police themselves, then surely from someone at the mayor's office or the city government.

I turned back to Brett. "You must know something about what happened," I said.

He shrugged. "Claydon Marsh, our superintendent, went down there after the body was discovered early that morning. He waited until the cops arrived and watched while they uncovered the body. The guy was buried pretty deep, which must have taken some time. And it was done neatly, not in a rush, not haphazard. He heard the medical examiner say that the man had been shot once, in the back of the head. They spent most of the morning down there—we had to close the back nine, which didn't make some of the members very happy. Then, they took him away."

"Was he shot here, on property?" I asked.

"We don't really know," Brett said.

"How did the killers get into the grounds?"

"We don't know."

"I thought you guys had all the latest X-ray, super-duper spy gear to protect this place," I said.

"Well, we have video cameras all along the property perimeter," Brett said. "Our security guy ran the tapes for the cops. Nothing. No one coming in. No one going out. Very strange."

"Indeed," I said. "And nobody here knew anything about the guy?"

"Nada," Brett said, shaking his head. "As far as we know, he never set foot on our grounds in his entire life. No relationship whatsoever with Augusta National."

"Motive for the killing?"

"Dunno."

"Suspects?"

"Dunno," Brett said. He looked at me and shrugged apologetically. "I asked all those questions," he said. "Got nothing from the cops. Zip. 'Case is under investigation until further notice.' When I heard that for the umpteenth time, I figured I needed someone on the outside to do a little digging."

"So you thought of me," I said. "Thanks a bunch."

"It's not so much that they're not talking," Brett said. "I can understand if they've got some kind of case building and they don't want to let the cat out of the bag. But I really want to know why they're not telling us anything. That's what keeps me up at night, worrying."

"Which implies that there may be something that does connect Augusta National with the killing, and that implies some kind of blockbuster announcement," I mused.

"And with the tournament coming up next week, I want to know what that thing may be, so I can at the very least prepare some kind of public answer," Brett said. "I don't like to be blindsided."

"Who does?" I asked, and wondered if it was going to be me.

"C'mon," Brett said, standing up. "We've got to go see Grosvenor."

He stood up. I remained seated. He looked at me and smiled.

"Hacker," he said, "You know that nothing happens around here without approval from the top guy. It's the way the place was set up under Cliff Roberts and there hasn't been a chairman since that hasn't micro-managed this place. He knows why you're here and what we want you to try and do. He just wants to meet you in person."

"Okay," I said and followed him back into the clubhouse.

Charles McDaniel Grosvenor was a distinguished and patrician figure who had been universally acclaimed as an excellent choice to head Augusta National when the last chairman had keeled over with a heart attack about 18 months earlier. Unlike most of the chairmen appointed to the job after über-leader and club co-founder Clifford Roberts, all of whom had been Southerners, Grosvenor was a Yankee, from the Main Line of Philadelphia. From a family corporation in the import-export business, his wealth went back at least four or five generations. He had already served a two-year term as president of the United States Golf Association, was a member of at least a half dozen of the finest golf clubs in the land, from Cypress Point to Pine Valley, sat on the board of directors of numerous corporations, had been talked about as a possible candidate for the U.S. Senate—Republican, of course—and was expected to both maintain the hallowed traditions of the club and at the same time, shepherd in some much-needed changes. Like inviting a woman to join an all-boys club, and getting rid of that particular public relations nightmare. In his mid 60s, Grosvenor was seen as erudite, articulate, dignified and experienced, and everyone expected that he would carry on as chairman with a firm hand for at least the next ten or twelve years.

We in the press had met him for the first time at last year's Masters, and found him to have a sense of humor, a rare commodity on Washington Road. At the same time, he had left no doubt in anyone's mind that he adhered firmly to the belief that the Augusta National Golf Club was a private organization and that, despite the fact that they invited the world of golf onto their grounds one week a year, what they did and how they did it was nobody's business but their own.

Because of that, nobody outside the club really knew what went on inside the gates. Grosvenor had continued the constant tweaking of the golf course, the annual effort to find a few more yards of length and other subtle ways to make the course a wee bit harder for the modern professionals who came in every year armed with new technology that threatened to turn what Bob Jones had envisioned as a stern test of golf into a birdie-filled theme park no different from any course on the PGA Tour. But none of us on the outside were aware of any major organizational changes at the club. We just showed up once a year in April and watched the usual assortment of self-important, white-haired old farts in green jackets running around pretending they were princes.

We went back upstairs and down the hall. At the end, the hallway widened out and a secretary sat behind a mahogany desk, guarding the entrance to the chairman's office. She smiled at us, picked up the phone and announced us, and waved us through the thick door.

Charlie Grosvenor stood up behind his huge desk as we walked in. He came around to shake my hand, a journey which seemed to take several minutes. His desk was monumental, yet did not seem to overwhelm the décor in his office, which itself was huge, running the entire depth of the building, it seemed, with three windows overlooking the golf course and two more on the side. The desk itself was some kind of deep reddish wood, with an unusual grain that was polished to a mirror-like finish.

Charlie Grosvenor was in his mid-sixties. His hair was silver, but he seemed to still have most of it. His face was tanned in that just-back-from-the-islands tan that never seems to fade from the rich. He wore dark tan khakis, Docksiders, and a pink Oxford shirt, open at the neck. He moved with grace, and his handshake was firm. He looked me in the eye.

He saw me eyeing his desk as we shook hands and he motioned for us to take a seat in the seating area—love seat and twin upholstered chairs—in front of the huge desk.

"It's snakewood," he said, gesturing at his desk. "Very rare, comes from Guiana. Only Brazilian rosewood is more expensive, and you can't import that anymore. They're trying to protect the rainforests." He frowned as if that were a personal problem.

It probably was. I knew that Grosvenor's family business, the Grosvenor Group, had extensive operations throughout South America over the decades. His great-grandfather had competed with John D. Rockefeller to acquire that continent's natural resources, and had corralled enough coal, bauxite, tin and other goodies to amass a fortune almost as huge as the Rockefeller clan. These days, Grosvenor Group was deeply into oil, with operations in southeast Asia, shipping, and pipelining natural gas across the Siberian tundra. Which meant Charlie Grosvenor could easily afford his aircraft-carrier desk made of rare snakewood and have enough left over to gild it with solid gold if he wanted.

I looked around the office as Grosvenor asked if we wanted any coffee. Brett thanked him, but said we'd just had breakfast. The walls of the office were hung with photos of Charlie Grosvenor with various heads of state, world political figures, presidents and kings. Many of the photos had been taken here in Augusta, usually down on the 12th tee, with that damnable little hole perched on the edge of Rae's Creek in the background.

"So, Mr. Hacker,' Grosvenor began in his deep baritone voice that spoke of polished hallways of power and generations of wealth, "Mr. Jacoby here has explained to you what we want you to do?"

"Yes, sir," I said. "And I've explained to Brett that it's going to be hard to pry anything loose if the cops don't want it pried."

"Hmmm," he nodded. "There are always challenges when one deals with the authorities. But Brett has assured me that you seem to have a knack for overcoming such challenges."

He fixed his grey-blue eyes on me. I figured this was the point in the conversation when I was supposed to leap up and shout "Yes, O Master! I will do what you bid!" I resisted the impulse.

I shrugged. "I used to be a crime reporter," I said. "And I've had a few episodes where that background came in handy. But I'm frankly a little doubtful I can be much help here."

Grosvenor frowned. He didn't like being told he couldn't get what he wanted.

"Is it a question of remuneration?" he began.

"No," I said firmly. "There is no remuneration. I've been asked for a favor by an old friend of mine..." I nodded at Brett ... "and I'm happy to try and help. I can't ethically accept any money from you anyway. My hesitation is that I'm just not sure I can find out what you want to know, and that I think you guys probably have way more influence locally than I'll ever have."

His frown deepened and his eyebrows scrunched together. He didn't look happy.

"Well," he said. "I'm disappointed that you don't want to accept the assignment ..."

"No," I said, "I didn't say I wouldn't do it. I just said you need to realize that I'll probably be unable to deliver the goods. I will ask around. I'll see what I come up with. I'll tell Brett what I find out. I just want you to understand that I probably won't find out who killed John Judge, or why. And next week, I'll be just another reporter covering the golf tournament."

Now his lips were pursed, to go along with his knitted brow. "I see," he said, and looked over at Brett, who had turned an interesting shade of red.

"It's about all we can expect," Brett said, holding his hands out plaintively.

"Very well," the chairman said, heading back to the business side of his mammoth desk. "Brett will take care of the arrangements."

I sat there while the other two began to rise. Grosvenor noticed and sat back down.

"Is there anything else?" he asked.

"Yes," I said. "Do you know of any reason why someone might want to bury a body in one of your bunkers?"

His eyebrows began twitching up and down. "I'm not sure I understand what you mean," he said.

"I mean, do you have reason to believe that you or anyone at this club has an enemy" I said. "If John Judge had no connection personally with Augusta National, and if we temporarily discount the idea that this killing was entirely random or coincidental, then the young man's death or the placement of his body might indicate a warning. A message to someone here at the club to do, or not to do, something that the killer wants. Can you tell me if there is any reason to believe that someone is being warned here at Augusta National?"

Grosvenor leaned back and smiled. "I see," he said. "No. I am not aware of any situation involving any of our employees or members that might have led to this tragic event. Do you know of anything Brett?" He looked at Brett with arched brows.

"No sir," Brett said.

Grosvenor looked back at me. "There. Your question has been answered," he said. "Anything else?"

"I guess not," I said, and rose.

"Thank you, Mr. Chairman," Brett said, and tugged on my sleeve to follow him out of the room.

"One more thing, Mr. Hacker," Grosvenor said as we began to walk away. I turned.

"I don't want any dirty laundry splashed over the pages of any newspaper," he said. "Whatever you learn is to come to us and no further."

"Anything that's public record is public," I said. "Anything that I can dig out of the cops, I'll pass on to Brett first. If there's a problem, we can discuss it then."

"Fine," the chairman said, and waved his hand. We had been dismissed.

I did not back out of his office, bowing low.

Chapter Seven

After meeting with Brett, I drove aimlessly down Washington Avenue, thinking. Nothing seemed to be adding up. John Judge, white Southern boy, Bell South accountant, native of the area, is shot twice and buried in a bunker at Augusta National Golf Club. That by itself didn't make much sense. From all outward appearances, Judge was a nobody. Nobodies usually aren't executed Mob style, whether in Augusta, Georgia, or in South Boston, Mass., for no reason at all.

Then, the local authorities seemed to have clammed up tighter than Sergio Garcia with a major title on the line. I didn't know when the next municipal elections were scheduled, but if this had been Southie, the chief of police, the D.A. and the mayor would all be shoving each other aside to get in front of a TV camera and pontificate for the voters on how they would soon be bringing to justice the heinous perpetrator of this vicious crime. Instead, it appeared that someone had decreed that an iron curtain be dropped over the entire case, and so far, nothing was getting out. Judge's own folks back there in Blythe couldn't learn anything, which was strange enough—the cops are usually a bit more forthcoming and sympathetic to the families of murder victims. But then there was Brett Jacoby's claim that not even the high mucks at Augusta National could find out anything about the Judge murder. And it happened right in front of their suddenly non-seeing eyeballs. That really did not compute.

Brett had given me the business card of the detective in charge of the case, and some directions down to the Richmond County jail, where the sheriff's offices were. I found my way to the ugly municipal yellow-brick tower on the edge of downtown. It took up most of a city block, and it looked like the jail part of the building occupied the top three or four floors of the six-story structure. You could tell because the windows were narrower than the arrow-slits they had once built in medieval castles in Europe.

I parked my rental car, made my way up to the third floor, and asked to see Lt. Travis Kitchen, Homicide. Brett Jacoby wanted me to fly somewhat under the radar, so I told them I was a reporter for the ***Boston Journal***, in town a bit early for the Masters and doing a little groundwork on the Judge murder for a possible take-out for the Sunday paper. All of that was mostly true, so if they strapped me to a lie detector, I would pass with flying colors.

After some hemming and hawing, during which I got to read three back issues of ***Police Work and Detention*** magazine cover to cover, I was ushered into the office of Lt. Kitchen. He sat behind a standard-issue metal desk with his back to a window overlooking the city, with a tiny glimpse of the Savannah River in the distance. A large plate-glass window looked back into the squad room cubicles, which seemed to be mostly empty. Kitchen's desk was neat as a pin, holding only a blotter, a telephone and a coffee cup.

He stood up when I walked in, shook my hand and motioned me into the standard-issue metal armchair, black naugahyde seat, in front of the desk. I sat. He was in his mid-fifties, with flecks of grey hair beginning to blossom at his temples. He had a thin mustache, strong arms bulging out of his white short-sleeved dress shirt, and his striped necktie was held in place with a sterling silver clip. His eyes were dark, almost black, and he stared at me with the appraising and slightly disapproving look that all cops have.

"What can I do for you, Mr. Hacker?" he asked.

I went through my spiel, while he leveled those eyes at me. I don't think he ever blinked. When I finished—my story sounded lame even to me—he nodded once, reached over and pulled open his left-side desk drawer. He reached in, took out a slender file folder, put in on his blotter, and shut the drawer. He flipped the file open. There appeared to be one piece of paper in it. Kitchen peered at it as if it were the first time he had ever seen it. I pulled out my reporter's notebook, sat there waiting and listened to the silence. Finally, he looked at me.

"Judge, John H., aged 26," he began to read in a toneless voice. "Resided at the Talmadge Apartment complex on Western Boulevard in Grovetown. Not married. No criminal record except for two speeding tickets in the last four years. Employed by BellSouth Corporation as an accountant in their construction division, also in Grovetown. Victim last seen when he left his office after work on 29 March, approximately 5:15 p.m. Body discovered by employees of the Augusta National Golf Club on the morning of 31 March. Victim had been shot twice in the upper chest. Ballistics reports the weapon was a 9 mm Norinco 77B. The weapon has not been found."

He flipped the folder shut with the finality of death, while I scribbled notes. "That's all I can tell you," he said. "The investigation is continuing. I'm afraid I can't release any further details. Thank you for coming in."

"That's it?" I said in amazement. "No leads? No speculation as to why the body was dumped at the National?"

"I don't deal in speculation, Mr. Hacker," Kitchen said, looking at me coldly. "We will release facts on this case at the appropriate time. Which is not now."

"Because the investigation..."

"...is continuing," he said, finishing my sentence. I thought I saw a slight twitch at the corner of his lips. It might have been a smile.

"You know, sometimes the public can be helpful in providing information," I said. "Freezing us out might be counterproductive to finding out who actually killed this guy."

"Our investigators are following up all leads," Kitchen said, glancing at his watch.

"Why is it that your department has not been communicating with Augusta National?" I asked. "Are the local powers here trying to protect someone over there?"

Kitchen stood up, his face turning red. "My job is to find out who killed John Judge and bring them to justice," he said, his voice cold and angry. "I will do that, just as I do for every murder that occurs in Richmond County, in the best, most efficient, and most professional way I know how. And nobody will tell me how to do my duty, whether it's those fancy pants out-of-towners over on Washington Road, or some smart-ass reporter from Boston. You got that?"

I stood up too. "Yeah," I said. "Loud and clear. Thanks for your time." I felt his eyes burning a hole in my back as I walked out.

Chapter Eight

Out in the warm sunshine on the sidewalk outside the sheriff's office, I thought about all the things I didn't know. Making it worse was that I had no one locally I could call on for help. In Boston, I had lots of sources who could help flesh out the details of whatever I needed to know. But here in Augusta?

Well, actually, I did know someone. I asked a police officer coming out the door where the offices of the ***Augusta Chronicle*** were. He told me how to navigate the four blocks or so, and within a few minutes I was riding up the elevator to the newsroom. I asked around and found my luck had turned. Graham Dodd was in his office, rocked back in his chair, feet up on the desk, reading the Atlanta newspaper.

"Hacker!" he said when he saw me standing there. "You're early! Show doesn't start until next week."

The ***Chronicle*** is much too small of a newspaper to employ a full-time golf writer—as are most dailies in America. Graham Dodd's title was associate sports editor, which meant he was just waiting until the sports editor, the 80-year-old Morris Williams, either died or finally forgot where his office was. Williams was one of those ancient figures who began writing sports back in the depths of the Depression, and despite his growing senescence, could still crank out a column that mentioned Warren G. Harding, Barry Bonds, Mickey Mantle, Red Grange and Mikhail Gorbachev, yet still make some kind of sense.

But Graham Dodd did most of the work. During Masters week, Dodd would organize the others in the sports department to crank out reams of copy on the golf tournament, with sidebars and take-outs and backgrounders on all the players, while Morris Williams would park his skinny butt in one of the lawn chairs under the oak tree and hold court for four days. The rest of us working sportswriters, who all had some kind of similar situations back in our own newsrooms, empathized with Dodd.

Graham Dodd had an encyclopedic knowledge of the Masters tournament, and many of us learned to double-check our facts with him. He was gracious, willing to share, and we all looked forward to seeing him every year. But that was the only time we ever saw him—he never attended any of the other major tournaments. I once asked him why, and he gave me a wink. "Paper's owned by a cheap bastard," he said. Enough said.

He seemed genuinely glad to see me. "C'mon," he said, "Let's go get some lunch."

We went back down onto the street and he led me through a side alley and into a dark, wood-paneled tavern. It wasn't quite the noon hour yet, so the place was mostly empty, except for two off-duty soldiers in green T-shirts, camo pants and boots sitting at the bar drinking beer. A tired-looking woman with gray hair stood behind the bar wiping glasses down with a towel and stacking them on the glass shelves. A TV set in the far corner blared the day's news from CNN.

"One of Augusta's finest establishments, I see," I said.

Graham laughed. "Naw, it's one of Augusta's finest dumps," he said. "But it's the closest to the newspaper office and we've kept the place alive for generations now. Besides, they make a good burger."

We sat down at a rickety table for two, the top stained with cigarette burns. Graham looked over at the woman behind the bar. "Hiya, Doris," he called. "Two burgers all the way and a coupla Buds." Doris nodded and trundled off to the kitchen in the back.

"So, Hacker," Graham said, "What the hell are you doing here?"

I looked at him. He was an avuncular sort, with a shiny balding head and narrow spectacles that kept slipping down the end of his nose. His eyes were alive and intelligent. I could tell he knew something was up. Call it the newsman's sensibility.

"I came up to nose around a little on that murder thing," I said. "Trying to see if there's a story in there or not."

"Ah," Graham said, leaning back and nodding sagely. "The body in the bunker. Sounds like P.D. James, doesn't it? I figured it was only a matter of time before someone came down to do a little digging. What have you found out?"

"I found out that the local cops aren't saying anything," I said. "I just went to see some guy named Travis Kitchen. He gave me nothing and tossed my ass out the door."

Graham chuckled. "Yeah," he said. "I've heard Kitchen can be a hard case. But he isn't one to be pushed around. Some people have tried through the years. Most of them are doing time now."

"So what the hell is the story?" I asked. "Has your paper run anything?"

"Naw, not really," he said. "Reported the facts when it happened, of course. Our crime-beat guy tried to do a follow-up and got the same treatment as you, apparently. The official word is there is no official word."

"And?"

"And our crime guy's job is to walk in that building every day and find out who's been arrested for what," Graham said. "He ain't gonna get very far with the job if he rocks the boat. So he's laying low, waiting until the cops decided to tell him something about the case. They will, eventually."

"What about trying to actually do some reporting?" I wondered.

Graham laughed a little, softly, to himself. "Hacker," he said, "You always forget that the ***Augusta Chronicle*** ain't the Boston Whatever-the-Hell-your-paper is. Or the ***New York Times***. One, we don't have the budgets to do major investigative stories. Two, our owners don't really want us to rip the seamy cover off anything. They like it when everything is nice and peaceful and quiet and they can sell lots of ads and nobody is mad at anybody. We're a little Podunk town newspaper, Hacker. Go along, get along."

Doris came over with a tray, from which she unloaded our burgers and two frosty longneck bottles of Budweiser. She reached over to the table behind us and slapped bottles of ketchup and mustard down. Then she turned and shuffled away. Service with a smile.

"Doesn't anybody care why that kid got shot?" I wondered. "Isn't there any gossip on the street?"

"Ah," Graham said, pouring ketchup liberally over his fries. "The street gossip. Now that's different. There's always talk on the streets. Lots of it." He took a big bite from his burger, which told me that he wasn't going to talk anymore until he'd finished eating. I wasn't that hungry after my breakfast at the National, but I took a big bite out of my sandwich anyway. Dodd was right—it was good.

"So what is the street saying?" I asked when we had both semi-demolished our lunch. He took a swig from his beer bottle and smiled at me.

"Well," he said. "I've heard several theories. One, it was a drug deal gone bad. Kid was shot in the chest. Dealer says 'you've been cheating me: Boom, boom.' End of story."

"Are we talking about the same event?" I protested. "From what I've heard, the kid was lily white and pure."

Graham shook his head. "C'mon, Hacker," he said. "You live in a big city. You should know that drug runners can be anyone, white, black, green or blue. And they often think they're smarter than the bad guys. Usually, they're not."

I took another sip of beer. I had to admit, he had a point. I really didn't know that much about the Judge kid, other than what I'd heard in the diner in Blythe. I made a mental note to fix that.

"Another version I've heard is that the kid was just in the wrong place at the wrong time. Maybe someone was trying to rip him off, and he fought back." Graham frowned. "But while we do have a lot of car jacking and petty theft here in beautiful Augusta, that doesn't really make much sense."

"Nor does it explain why whoever killed him decided to drop the body beneath six inches of silica sand on the 10th fairway," I noted.

"Then there are those who believe that it was someone over at the National," Graham said, smiling at me. "Maybe one of the Pinkerton guys got a little trigger happy, caught the kid trespassing, and accidentally shot him."

"Which might explain why none of their vaunted security cameras caught anything that night," I said. "They went back and erased the tapes. Difficult, but not impossible."

Graham raised his eyebrows. "Where did you hear that?" he asked.

I shrugged. "Hey, I've been doing a little nosing around," I said. "Got my sources. But why would they shoot him twice?"

He thought a minute, chewing on his lower lip. "Still doesn't quite fit together," he said finally. "Besides, with all the local mojo they have around here, the guards could easily claim self-defense or accident and nobody, really, would think twice about it."

"Okay," I said. "That one is doubtful, but possible. What else?"

Doris came over and took our plates away. Graham asked me if I wanted some of their peach pie, but I declined. Doris made a cursory wipe of our table with a dingy gray cloth and disappeared.

"Well," Graham said, "It's nothing you can really pin down, but there has been some talk about the new chairman out there at the National."

"Grosvenor?" I said, disbelievingly. "You're telling me Charlie Grosvenor, the chairman of Augusta National shot and killed some local kid?"

He held up his hand in a stop sign. "Slow down, Hacker," he said, laughing at the expression on my face. "All I'm telling you is that I've heard a little whisper of gossip that Charlie has been rubbing some of the old guard out there the wrong way. Nothing definite, nothing for attribution, ever. Just that in the last year, since he took over, some noses have been put out of joint. I don't put much stock in such things. I mean, Charlie is, what, the fourth or fifth guy to run that place since I've been around? And every new guy has his own way of doing things, which usually means somebody doesn't like something he does. It's the nature of the beast. I mean, Augusta National does not do change well."

"You can say that again." I muttered.

"But I've heard the same grumbling maybe three or four times in the last nine months," Graham said. "From three or four different people. What it means, I don't have a clue. I'm just telling you what I've heard."

I thought about that for a minute. Graham's information was interesting gossip, and it backed up what Conn Thackery had told me, but I couldn't see how it affected the murder of John Judge.

"Well," I said finally. "Maybe the murder weapon will turn up on eBay like Cliff Roberts' gun, and we can trace it back to Charlie." I was referring to the gun that Clifford Roberts had used to kill himself down by the pond on the Par-Three course at Augusta back in 1977, when he was dying of cancer. Years later the gun had turned up at a classic firearms auction. It had been traced back to the official photographer for the club. There had been hell to pay on that one.

Graham winced and laughed. "That's cold, Hacker," he said.

"Speaking of the murder weapon, that Kitchen guy mentioned a gun I've never heard of," I said. I pulled out my notebook and flipped through the pages. "Yeah, here it is. He said it was a 9 mm Norinco 77B. You ever heard of that?"

Graham laughed. "Hacker, I'm a sports writer for Pete's sake. I can't even keep up with golf technology. But I'll ask our crime guy if he knows anything about it. He's a gun freak anyway."

He had to get back to work. I had more dead ends to beat my head against.

Chapter Nine

I decided to try finding out more about John Judge. I drove back out to I-20, headed west a couple of exits and turned off at the Groveland exit. Immediately, I found myself in American suburbia. I could have been on a road in southern California, northern Iowa, western Michigan or eastern Florida. It was a four-lane road chockablock with brand-name stores and restaurants. Taco Bell next to the Target next to the Burger King next to the Barnes & Noble next to the McDonalds next to the Wal-Mart next to the Home Depot next to the Ford dealer next to the Best Buy next to the Toys R Us. Squeezed in between were strip centers with karate studios, dry cleaners, liquor stores, grocery stores, cellphone stores and sub shops. It seemed to stretch onward for miles, this soulless, visually polluting, spiritually empty stretch of American capitalism that we've all become far too used to, and dependant upon.

In a mile or so, I saw a fire station. With all the merchandise stacked, boxed and stored along this stretch of highway, it figured the town fathers would make sure they could protect the town's lifeblood. They probably even made some developer pay for it in return for a tax abatement. I went inside and asked the uniform behind the desk where the local telephone company office was. He told me how to get to a nearby office park, set back off the four lanes of commerce.

When I got there, I spotted the BellSouth office. I parked outside and went in. Behind the reception counter was a young woman, maybe 18, with pink-streaked black hair, heavy mascara and lots of silver dangly things hanging from various parts of her body. She was painting her nails a brilliant shade of pink. She looked bored.

"Hep you?" she asked, barely looking up.

"I'd like to speak to the manager," I said.

She raised an eyebrow at that. "Of what?" she asked. She held up her fingers and peered at the paint job.

"Of the late John Judge," I said. "He did work here, didn't he?"

She looked at me then. Gave me the full up-and-down body scan.

"Another cop?" she said, almost to herself. "Ain't you guys finished with that?"

I slid one of my business cards across the desk. "Not a cop," I said. "Reporter."

She didn't look at it or pick it up. Probably didn't want to smudge her nails. "Oooo," she said, batting her blackened lashes at me, "You gonna put me on ***Inside Edition***?"

I fought back the impulse to leap across the desk and choke the very life out of her. "Sorry," I said. "I deal with printed words. In a newspaper. The kind you have to actually read."

She scrunched up her nose as if she suddenly smelled something foul. "Don't know anyone who reads newspapers," she informed me archly. She pronounced the word 'newspaper' as if it were the thing she could smell.

"Which could be why the republic is in grave danger," I said. "The manager?"

"Who shall I say is calling?" she asked.

"Hacker," I said. "***Boston Journal***. Just like it says on that card." I pointed to it, still lying on the desk where I had laid it. She sighed once, as if the stress caused by my expectation that she might actually pick the thing up and look at it was too much for her to bear. She picked up her telephone handset and pressed one of the intercom buttons, careful not to smudge her new paint job.

"Mack?" she said. "A Mister Hackman from the ***New York Times*** is here to see you." She paused and listened. "I think he wants to ask about Johnny," she said. She listened again. "OK," she said and hung up.

"If you can wait five minutes, he'll try to work you in," she said. "That'll give him time to shut off the online porn stuff he likes to watch during the afternoon."

I reached over and picked up my business card. She didn't try to stop me.

"Been working here long?" I asked.

"Fourteen weeks, six days and five hours," she said. "Give or take."

"You know Johnny well?"

She shrugged. "Just to say hello in the morning and goodbye in the afternoon," she said. "He was pretty quiet. Seemed nice."

"Any idea who it was shot him?"

She shrugged again and picked up the bottle of pink polish. "Somebody who doesn't like nice, I guess," she said and started in on the other fingers.

I sat down in the guest chair and passed on the chance to read that month's copy of ***The Linesman***, which looked like the inhouse newsletter for BellSouth employees. Instead, I folded my hands in my lap and went into a deep meditative state, which others might call a nap with my eyes open.

It wasn't long before a gentleman came out from the offices behind the reception desk, stuck his hand out and said "Mack Hutchinson. Would you come in?" He was about six feet tall with a pleasant face, slightly graying hair, glasses, pens tucked away in a plastic pocket protector in his dress shirt pocket. Tie, suit pants, well-polished shoes ... he was deep into the corporate environment.

I stood up, shook his hand, introduced myself and gave him the business card that the receptionist had ignored. He led me back through the warren of cubicles to his own office, which occupied the back corner of the office suite. He had a nice view of a parking lot. He indicated where he wanted me to sit, which was in his only guest chair. He sat behind his desk, took off his glasses, folded his hands, glanced at my card and said "How can I help you, Mister, er, Hacker?" Hey, at least the guy could read. We were making progress.

"I'm working on some background on the killing of John Judge," I said.

He stopped me, holding his hand up like a traffic cop.

"I'm sorry," he said, "But all media inquiries on that tragic situation are being handled by our Atlanta headquarters. I can give you the name of our public affairs officer, and he would be happy to try and answer whatever questions you may have."

He began to thumb through a Rolodex on his desk.

"Look," I said. "This is just a background conversation. Everything that's said here will be off the record. I just have a few quick questions and I really don't want to have to waltz around with your public relations people. Can't we just try to talk a bit?"

Hutchinson looked at me, then smiled and let the Rolodez flop shut. "Shoot," he said.

"How long did Judge work here?" I asked.

"Five years," he said sadly. "John was a fine young man. I had hopes that he would one day be ready to take over my position. I'll be retiring in another five years."

"He was in the construction division?"

Hutchinson nodded. "This community is one of the fastest growing in all Georgia," he said, a hint of pride evident in his voice. "Our division has laid the third highest number of miles of new line in the southeast in the last two years. John handled purchasing, coordination with the contractors and receivables. He did good work. He was dependable, honest, diligent. A fine young man." He shook his head. "His passing is a tragedy. It really is. He had a bright future. We all will miss him."

"Any idea who killed him?" I asked.

Hutchinson shook his head sadly. "Do you know how many times I've been asked that question in the last week or two?" he said. "I haven't the slightest idea. It had to have been just a random act of violence. He was such a nice young man. Quiet. Hard-working. In addition to his job here, he did a little freelance accounting work to keep some extra money coming in. He volunteered in his church. And in the community—he was always helping raise money for some worthy cause."

"Married?"

"No, John was not married," he said.

"Girlfriend?"

"I really couldn't tell you," he said, frowning. "I never met any, um, friends. But we weren't socially close. He seemed to me to be entirely devoted to his job, his church and his community."

"That normal around here?" I wondered. Healthy twenty-somethings are usually trying to get themselves laid, with whatever gender floats their boat.

Hutchinson frowned at me, disapprovingly. "I'm sure that many in this community, unlike perhaps in Boston--" he sneered when he said the name—"choose to live their lives along the model that John did. He was not unusual in the least."

"Except he ended up shot and buried in a bunker at Augusta National," I pointed out. "That strikes me as unusual. Even for Boston."

His frown deepened. He said nothing. I thanked him for his time and said I could find my way out. I stopped at the front desk where my friend in the pink hair had moved from painting to applying some sparkly designs to her nails. She glanced up at me.

"Did John Judge have a girlfriend?" I asked.

She smiled an evil smile. "Si, senor," she said in an exaggerated Spanish accent. "Hola...theees es Maria Sanchez..." she dragged out the syllables. "Eees Johnny there?"

"She called him here a lot?"

"Si, senor."

"How do you know she wasn't calling on business?"

She looked at me like I was an idiot.

"You tell the cops this?"

Her you're-an-idiot expression deepened. I seemed to be getting that a lot in this office. "They never asked," she said.

"Do you know anything about her?" I asked. "Where she lived? Worked?"

Pinkie shook her head and went back to working her nails. Normally at this point I would have left my card and asked her to call me if she thought of anything. But I had already plumbed the shallow depths of this girl's brain and knew that what I had just learned was all she knew. So I left. She didn't say goodbye.

Chapter Ten

In the car, driving back towards Augusta, I put in a call to Conn Thackery.

"Hey," he said. "I was just about to call you."

"About what?" I asked.

"Whether you wanted to play some golf on Thursday," he said. "I managed to get us into the Devereaux Milburn."

"The who?"

"Devereaux Milburn, my friend," Conn said. "Where is your knowledge of golf history? It used to as famous as the Crosby Clambake."

"You mean the AT&T Pebble Beach National Pro-Am?" I said.

"No, I mean the goddam Crosby Clambake," Conn said testily. "Why do they insist on taking everything that's good about the game of golf and selling it off to the highest bidder? Anyway, the Milburn has been held at the Palmetto Golf Club over in Aiken for years and years now. Used to be a pro-am format and all the boys going to the Masters would come into town the week before to play the Milburn. Hogan used to claim that he could make more money on the Calcutta at the Milburn than he could winning the Masters."

I zipped around a trailer tractor grinding smokily down the highway with a full load of pine logs.

"Any of the boys coming in this year?" I asked.

"Naw, it's been pretty much a local event for a long time now," Conn said. "Still has a good Calcutta, though. But I thought you'd enjoy meeting some of the locals. And I know you'll like playing Palmetto. Place is older than God. Mackenzie did some work on the course while he was in town doing the National, and Rees Jones recently fixed it up nice. You'll like it. It's old-fashioned, like you."

"Sounds good," I said. He gave me the details and said he'd come pick me up Thursday morning.

"So," he said, "How's the investigation going?"

I told him what I'd learned, or rather, not learned, that day.

"Lotta questions," he said. "Not many answers."

"Which reminds me," I said. "I want to track down this Maria Sanchez, who may or may not have been John Judge's girlfriend. Who's the leader of the Hispanic community around here?"

He laughed. "Hacker," he said, "I don't think we have a Hispanic community around here. The blacks would never stand for it!"

"Oh," I said. "I thought everyone had a Hispanic community. Aren't they supposed to be taking over the country?"

"Yeah," Conn said. "I guess you're right. Actually, now that I think about it, there have been a bunch of new Mexican restaurants cropping up around town. Hey! How cool is that? Augusta has a Hispanic community! Man, we've hit the big time!"

I laughed. "So how do you recommend I look for Maria?" I asked.

"I might call Father Jillson down at Holy Trinity," he said. "It's right downtown, near the river. I'll bet most of our so-called Hispanic community worship there. Tell him I sent you. I did a favor for him not too long ago."

He did a quick Google search while I waited and read me the telephone number for the church office. We rang off.

It was getting late, but I had nothing better to do, so I drove back into Augusta's downtown and spotted the gray stone steeple of the church. I parked in the side lot and followed a sign directing me to the office. I walked down the basement hallway. It smelled like most churches—a blend of piety and dust, wax polish and hope. I could hear someone practicing an organ piece in the sanctuary above. Whoever was playing had the grand bourdon stop going along with the pedal bass and was making the walls shake a little.

At the end of the hallway, a young woman sat behind the reception desk. She was dark haired, with shiny black eyes, dressed conservatively in a plain blue dress with a grey sweater tossed over her shoulders against the chill of the air-conditioning. I asked to see Father Jillson. Before the woman could say anything, we heard a deep voice call out "Come!" from the office on the right. The young woman smiled at me, her cheeks forming pretty dimples, and she nodded.

I walked in. Father Jillson was standing behind his desk, loading some papers into a tan leather briefcase.

"You just caught me," he said. "I'm getting ready to go home."

He was tall, well over six feet, and looked fit and trim. He looked to be in his forties, with neatly trimmed brown hair that was beginning to recede from his temples. A pair of gold-rimmed glasses hung on a halyard around his neck, dangling in the front of his black shirt and white clerical collar. He looked up at me and smiled and held out his hand.

"Roger Jillson," he said. "What can I do for you?"

I introduced myself and said that Conn Thackerey had suggested I come see him. He smiled at the name.

"Good old Conn," he said. "He's not one of the faith, but he's a damn good lawyer. Handled a tricky estate case for us couple of months ago. With the money he got for us, we're expanding our inner-city youth programs. Good man. Sit down, sit down."

I sat. I told him who I was and what I was doing. He nodded.

"I'm trying to find a young Hispanic woman," I said. "She is supposed to have known the young man who was murdered a couple of weeks ago and buried out at Augusta National."

Father Jillson crossed himself. "Awful thing," he said. "I remember reading about it."

"The people where he worked said this woman might have been his girlfriend," I continued. "And Conn said you might be able to help me locate her."

The priest nodded. "Perhaps," he said. "We do have many from the immigrant community worshipping here," he said. "More and more all the time, in fact. Our vestry has considered hiring a Hispanic priest and conducting services in Spanish. But there's the question of cost, as always. The Lord always seems to have needs and never seems to provide the budget to deal with them."

I murmured something that I hoped sounded sympathetic.

"What is this woman's name?" he asked.

"Maria Sanchez," I said.

He began to laugh, a deep, reverberating belly laugh.

"The Lord works in mysterious ways," he said, chuckling to himself.

"Amen," I said. "So you know her?"

"You do, too, Mr. Hacker," he chortled, "You do too."

He rose from his chair, grabbed his bulging briefcase and his suit jacket, made a crooked-finger gesture at me to follow him, and led me back out into the reception area. The young woman behind the desk was also getting ready to leave, shutting down her computer and pushing papers into neat piles.

"Maria Sanchez," Father Jillson said. "This is Mr. Hacker. He would like to ask you some questions."

We both saw her eyes widen in fright. One hand reflexively went up to cover her mouth.

"Now, don't worry, Maria," the priest said. "He's a reporter doing some story on the death of that young man a week or so ago. Your name came up and he'd like to ask you a few questions. You can answer them, or not. It's up to you. Here in America, the press is allowed to ask questions and we are allowed to tell them to go jump in the river." He looked at her. Color was beginning to return to a face that had gone ghostly white. "Would you like me to stay and, ummm, referee?"

Maria Sanchez looked at Father Jillson and smiled. "No, *gracias*," she said. "I will talk with him. I would like to help find the killer of my friend Johnny." Her voice was soft and lilting, with just a hint of an accent. She finished clearing off the desk, grabbed a large over-the-shoulder bag, and gave the room a final look. "Let us go," she said.

I shook hands with Father Jillson, thanked him for his time and followed her down the hallway. I was beginning to think maybe I should go back onto the Tour, the way my luck seemed to be running. First was the chance meeting in Blythe with Johnny Judge's folks and now this with Maria. It was like pull hooking two tee balls deep into the gunch, only to see them hit a rock or a branch and end up sitting pretty in the middle of the fairway. I told myself to remember to go buy a lotto ticket.

Outside, she took a deep breath of the fresh air. "We will go sit in the park," she said. "We can talk there."

She led me across the street and into the Riverwalk park. Finally realizing that the waterfront could be an asset, the city fathers had created the park a few years earlier on a bluff overlooking the Savannah River. Where once cotton factories had been piled cheek to jowl, there was now an open space with curving paths, bricked-in performance spaces, and tree-shaded areas with benches and picnic tables. It made for a nice spot for coffee, lunch or just a green space to relax and watch the river slowly drift by on its way to the sea at Tybee Point, many miles away.

We found a bench in a quiet corner with a nice view of the river. The setting sun sparkled on the fast-flowing water. Maria stared at the water for a moment, lost in thought. I studied her face. She was young, but had a worldly countenance. Her features were soft, but there was a toughness in her face.

"Where are you from?" I asked.

She started slightly, then glanced at me and smiled, blushing a bit. She had been far away.

"I am from Colombia," she said. "From the city of Cartagena. I came to this country with my family seven years ago. My family still lives near Miami, but I came here to Georgia to attend college. I decided to stay. There is much work to do to help others who are coming to the States."

"Is that what you do?"

She nodded. "Yes. I work at the church part time and help Father Jillson. He is a good ***padre***. Together, we try to help those who come to this city to find work, find a place to live, to find schools for the children." She sighed. "It is difficult. There are many who come to work in the farms, and they have many needs."

"How did you meet John Judge?"

She smiled, remembering. "He had volunteered to work with us at the holidays last year," she said. "We were distributing packages to those without food. He drove his pickup truck and I rode with him out to the fields. He was very nice, very funny. He wanted to help the poor, and asked if he could continue to work with us after that one day."

Her eyes were wide and glistening. "He was a very nice man," she said softly, haltingly. "I liked him very much."

"Was he your boyfriend?" I asked.

She ducked her head and gave a quick shake of the head. But she colored and she stopped looking at my eyes. Either she was embarrassed to discuss it, or she didn't want this line of questioning to go any further.

"No matter," I said reassuringly. "When was the last time you spoke to Johnny?"

She looked out at the river again. "It was the day...the day he died," she said in a soft whisper. "I talked to him at his office in the afternoon. He was going to meet me that night. We had some materials to sort through. Things to prepare. Office work, mostly."

"Do you have any idea what happened to him?"

She didn't answer for several long moments, but continued to stare out at the dark water flowing past. I let her look. When she finally turned to me, her eyes were filled with tears.

"No," she said. "I do not know anyone who didn't like Johnny. But I also cannot forget that afternoon, and something Johnny asked me."

"Can you tell me?" I asked.

She looked down at her hands, and the tears began to flow down her cheeks. They dripped, one after another, onto her folded hands.

"He asked me if I knew someone, if I knew anything about him," she said, voice quavering.

"Who?" I tried to keep my voice level and calm. But this was the first solid lead I had come across.

"Enrico de la Paz," she said.

"And he is...?"

"A very bad man," she said, looking at me with frightened eyes. "He, too, is from Colombia. He is one of the ***hibridos*** who works with the drug cartels. He is well known in Medellin. He is a killer with the blood of many on his hands."

"Do you know why John asked about him?"

She shook her head. "No, no," she said. "I asked Johnny 'Why are you asking me about this bad man?' He wouldn't tell me. He told me not to worry. He said it was just a name he had heard someone mention. He wondered who it was. I begged him to tell me more, but he just said he'd see me at the church later. I...I never saw him again."

She lowered her head and began weeping in earnest. I reached out and touched her shoulder, and let her cry. This was interesting. John Judge, mild-mannered and likeable accountant for the telephone company, had somehow come across the name of a noted killer in the Columbian drug cartels. After which he had turned up shot in the head execution style. Coincidence? Doubtful. Did that mean Enrico de la Paz was in Augusta? And if so, for what reason?

"Did you tell the police about this," I asked when she had calmed down a bit. She fished around in her bag for a tissue, and blew her nose and dried her eyes with it.

"No," she said. "I have not talked to the police."

"Don't you think you should?"

Her eyes grew wide again. "No!" she said forcefully. "I cannot. If I do, they will come to kill me. You must not tell anyone what I have told you. They will come to kill you, too."

"I don't know," I said. "This is the United States. You can generally tell the police something without getting killed for it."

She laughed. It was a bitter, sarcastic laugh. "You do not understand," she said. "There is nowhere they cannot reach. There is no policeman they cannot buy. There is nothing they cannot discover. If I tell the police about Johnny, I will not live another week. If you tell the police, you will not live, either."

She looked around the plaza. It was empty save for a wino sleeping on a bench about a hundred yards away.

"I must tell you something more," she said. "In the last week, I have been watched. I have been followed."

"What?" I was surprised. "Are you sure? How do you know?"

She shrugged. "It is nothing I can point to. But it is a feeling I have. A feeling that someone is watching me, watching what I do every day. I cannot look behind me and say "there—there he is,' but I know someone is there."

I looked at the wino, who seemed to be snoring away peacefully. I looked at the windows of the buildings across the plaza and up and down the riverfront. There was no one I could see. But someone could be there watching us. It was a creepy feeling.

She reached over and touched my arm. "Please," she said. "Do not go to the police. I beg you. It would be my death sentence. And probably yours as well."

Now it was my turn to look at the river. This was getting out of hand. There was a difference between nosing around a little to find out what officialdom was hiding from regular citizens, and getting involved with the Medellin cocaine cartel. And the difference was getting rousted by an overworked civil servant like Lt. Kitchen versus getting two in the hat from Enrico de la Paz. I certainly wasn't ready to volunteer for the latter, and I don't think that Brett Jacoby would expect me to, either.

On the other hand, I wasn't quite ready to hurl John Judge over the side, even though I had never met the man. He was on the verge of being forgotten. Dropped into that great vat of invisibility that catches so many. His mother would remember him, but she would eventually die. Maria would remember him fondly, but she would move on. His boss, Mack Hutchinson would find another to train as his successor, and go off to retirement giving nary a thought to the nice young man who once worked for him. The days would peel off the calendar, week after week, month after month, and before too long, no one on the planet would remember that once there was a nice, funny, likeable, earnest, hard-working young man named John H. Judge. Who had stumbled into something, or showed up in the wrong place, or whatever...and his life had come to a sudden, brutal, end. His life, and all the potential that it represented, taken away in a blink.

There was injustice there. No one deserved such a fate. Could I do anything about it? I didn't know. But I suddenly realized that I had to try.

I looked back at the young woman beside me, who was gazing at me with an expression that was equal parts fear and hope.

"Okay," I said. "I won't go to the cops. For now."

She reached out and touched me again, softly. "***Gracias***," she said. "God bless you."

"Thanks," I said. "I believe I'll need it if I'm gonna get through this one alive."

Chapter Eleven

Have you completely lost your mind, Hacker?" Mary Jane was being contrary. She began to list the reasons why.

"One: You don't even like Augusta National.

"Two: This doesn't concern you.

"Three: You're messing around with people who kill people like the rest of us eat peanuts.

"Four: This doesn't concern you. Oh, did I mention that already?

"Five: You could get killed."

"I think you mentioned that already, too," I said. "How about: 'I'd miss your rock-hard abs and the way you make my body sing?'"

"Don't make jokes," she scolded. "I'm serious. You need to tell the police what you've learned and get the hell out of there. You're a golf writer, not Sam Spade."

She was right, of course. I hated that. It was about nine in the evening, and I was sitting uncomfortably in the Victorian settee in my suite in the Olde Magnolia. Did the Victorians have different shaped bodies than we do now? I've never been able to figure out how to sit in the convex shape of their furniture without sliding off slowly towards the floor. They must have been perchers back then, instead of lollers.

I had called Mary Jane and filled her in on the day's events. She had listened quietly through my entire dissertation until I finished. Then she exploded on me.

"Look," I said when she had finally stopped analyzing my need for excitement and my compulsion to save the entire world, "I agree with almost everything you've said. But Maria Sanchez is afraid that if I tell the police what she told me, that her life will be in danger."

"That's crapola..." Mary Jane started up again. I cut her off.

"Wait a sec," I said. "That may or may not be the case. But I promised her I wouldn't go running to the authorities...yet." I emphasized the last word. "I just need a day or two to kick this thing around a bit more and see what else I can learn. There are still a lot of loose ends floating around. I don't even know why this Judge kid mentioned the name of that cartel guy. Maybe he read something in ***Time*** magazine or something."

She blew out her breath in an impatient "phew," which sounded like a preface to the beginning of another lecture.

"And," I said quickly, "I really need to find out if there is any connection other than the coincidental with Augusta National. Why did someone go to the trouble of dragging the kid's body out to the 10th hole and digging a hole for it? That doesn't sound like something the Medellin cartel would bother doing."

"Unless it was a warning," Mary Jane said.

"Exactly," I agreed. "A warning for what? To whom? See? These are all things I'd like to find out."

"Even if it means you get shot?" her voice was quieter, and I thought I heard a bit of a quaver.

"I'll try like heck not to get shot," I said.

There was silence.

"Victoria said today she misses you," she said.

I was silent.

"I miss you, too," she said.

"I'll be careful," I said. "I promise."

She was not happy when we bid each other goodnight and hung up. Because of that, I was not happy, either. It was different being in a relationship. Before Mary Jane, I could make decisions about what to do, and not do, and no one was affected by those decisions except me. Before Mary Jane, I could pull on the end of the string I found myself holding, and follow it to wherever it might lead. Even if it led to a shallow grave in the bunker at the 10th hole at Augusta National. But now, if I did that, Mary Jane would be affected. Victoria, too. Which meant I had to factor them into my decision making. I wasn't used to that. It made me uncomfortable. And it made me feel good at the same time. Someone cared about me, thus my life was no longer truly my own. That was the trade off, in a nutshell. So, in addition to trying to find out who killed John Judge while avoiding Enrico de la Paz, if indeed he was in the neighborhood, I had to worry about the feelings of Mary Jane and her daughter. How was that supposed to work?

For now, it meant I had to get out of my Victorian suite, the walls of which were suddenly closing in, the flocked chintz grabbing for my throat. I slid off the settee and decided to go down to the inn's lounge. Maybe there would be something to watch on TV, or one of the other guests to chat with. Anything to keep from thinking about my problems.

I walked downstairs and into the sitting room, on the opposite side of the mansion from the breakfast room. It was a pretty space, built in a faux rotunda with large windows, a curving series of window seats following the arch of the wall, two card tables in the center of the room, and a conversation pit arrangement against the near wall, with two large upholstered pieces set at an "L" facing a large-screen television.

To my surprise, the room was crowded with people, all of whom seemed to be talking golf while they sipped cocktails or coffee. I remembered that Conn had said the National used the Olde Magnolia for some of its VIP international guests. It looked like they were all here.

One of the other guests spotted me, and approached, holding out his hand.

"Wilkommen, wilkommen," he said heartily. He pumped my hand up and down. He was avuncular, with thinning hair and a bushy walrus-like mustache, wearing a tweedy jacket with leather patches at the elbows, some kind of gold club pin in his label and a necktie with the official colors of some organization. "Hans Kleiber," he said, introducing himself, still pumping my hand up and down. He apparently was going to do that for the rest of the evening, or until water poured out my nose. "You are English?" he said in a heavy, Germanic accent.

"Nein," I said. "Ich bin ein American." I thought that was pretty good for someone who pretty much flunked Spanish in high school.

Hans was delighted though, and laughed out loud. "Gut! Gut!" he almost shouted at me. "Come und meet der fellows!"

He led me into the middle of the room, put two fingers to his mouth and issued an ear-piercing shriek of a whistle. The room fell instantly silent. Hans threw his shoulders back importantly. I listened for the heel click, but was disappointed.

He turned to me, smiling. "Vat is your name?" he asked *sotto-voce*.

"Hacker," I told him.

He looked at me to see if I was kidding. But when he realized I was not, he burst out laughing raucously. He was still holding my hand and began pumping it up and down again. I waited until his grip loosened a bit and yanked it away.

"Mein herren und damen," Hans announced to the room. "I have the honor of presenting Herr Hacker to you." He brayed out another burst of laughter. "Hacker! Is that not vunderbar?" He turned to look at me. "Ve are all hackers, here, Herr Hacker. Every one of us! Ve are golfers and golf officials from all over zee world. Hackers ... every vun!"

Everyone seemed infected by Hans' gaiety, and they all began to laugh as the buzz of their conversation picked up and again filled the room. Hans led me around introducing me to some of them. Hans, it turned out, was director of the Swiss Golf Association, based in Epalinges, just outside Lausanne. He himself was a banker from Zurich, of course. In the next half hour, I met golf officials from Denmark, Luxembourg, Finland, South Africa and the Seychelles. There were people there from countries where I had no idea golf was played. All, apparently, had been invited by Augusta National to come witness the Masters as the worldwide establishment of golf. And, I learned, they all looked forward not only to the tournament, but to the endless parties, dinners, cocktail events and rounds of golf that made up their fortnight of fun. They all thought my name was hilarious, and once they found out I was a golf writer, they were filled with questions. Was Tiger Woods a nice man? Had I met his lovely wife Elin? Did I think Ernie Els would ever win at Augusta? How did the Europeans win the Ryder Cup so many times? And so forth.

Someone slipped a drink into my hand, which I discovered was fine single malt, with just one ice cube and a splash of water to open up the bouquet. As I wandered around the room, being led from group to group by Hans and others, the drink would mysteriously get refilled without any request from me. I'd be deep into a conversation about possible British Open sites in the future—Wentworth, no; Sunningdale, maybe—and suddenly my drink would be full again. These guys were good.

An hour or so later, I excused myself from a gripping discussion about whether or not Colin Montgomerie had deliberately taken a bad drop during a weather delay at the Hong Kong Open, and went to find the men's room. I splashed some water on my face and left my mostly full cocktail glass in the bathroom.

I came out intending to make my exit and go to bed. Instead, I came face to face with Charlie Grosvenor, who was chatting with a pleasant-looking woman with dark black hair pulled back in a bun. The Masters chairman was in casual mode, wearing an open-neck polo under a blue blazer. He caught my eye and waved me over.

"Mister Hacker," he said. "I hope your accommodations are satisfactory."

I smiled noncommittally.

"I'd like to introduce you to Beatrice Samper," he said, motioning to the woman standing beside him. "She is the executive director of the Federacion Colombiana de Golf, based in Bogata." He spoke the Spanish words in a flawless accent.

I turned and shook the woman's hand. "I didn't know they played much golf in Colombia," I said.

"Oh, yes," she said, her deep voice distinctive with its Spanish lilt. "We have many fine courses in the larger cities. It is one of the favorite games of the upper classes."

I turned to Grosvenor. "It sounds like you've spent some time down there," I said.

He nodded. "Oh, yes," he said. "I spent perhaps ten or fifteen years living in South America earlier in my career. Buenos Aires, Quito and Cartagena, which is a lovely city. Our firm has long had various operations throughout the continent and one of my first jobs was to oversee various companies."

Ms. Samper broke in. "His wife is from Colombia," she said with a proud smile. "She is a very lovely person."

"Is she here?" I asked. "I'd love to meet her."

"No, no," Grosvenor said with a small frown. "Marta does not come to Augusta very often. She prefers Philadelphia and New York. I'm afraid she feels Augusta is a bit of a backwater place."

"Which it pretty much is," I said.

He didn't say anything. But he gazed at me with a look of disapproval. I would have pressed my point—my thesis is not a hard one to defend—but I realized I would be arguing with the chairman of Augusta National, and figured that might not be wise. So I bowed to Beatrice Samper, mumbled something about a long day and an early start and made my escape. But as I walked away, with a last wave to my new best friend Hans, I caught sight of Charles Grosvenor and Beatrice Samper in a far corner, heads together, talking. Neither one looked very happy.

Chapter Twelve

The next morning, I called Brett Jacoby and asked if I could come over and look at the security tapes. He told me he'd call down to the office and tell them I would be there after breakfast. He sounded stressed, but asked if I'd learned anything. I told him I had made a little headway, but had a few more details to check out. He told me to keep in touch and quickly rang off. I imagined the pressure of preparing for an immense event of worldwide interest like the Masters must be fairly heavy. I did not envy him his position.

Instead, I went down to the breakfast room, grabbed a local newspaper and a table over near the windows, nodded at the two or three other guests – most of the heavy drinking international crowd were nowhere to be seen—and sipped my first cup of coffee of the day. A sullen-looking young black girl brought me a glass of orange juice and asked how I'd like my eggs. We settled on a bowl of oatmeal and some toast and jam, and she left me alone with a large pot of coffee.

The newspaper was full of the usual bad news from Washington and overseas, which I skipped over quickly. No sense in getting upset about things I could do nothing about. I was zipping through the front section, hoping to get quickly over to sports to see how the Red Sox were doing as they prepared to open the new season, when a piece at the bottom of the local news section caught my eye.

"Longtime Police Detective Leaves County Job," said the headline. I kept reading. "Lt. Travis Kitchen, head of the Richmond Sheriff's Department Homicide division for the last twelve years, has retired," the story said. "No reasons were given for Kitchen's sudden announcement. He had been with the county force for more than 25 years."

Well, I thought, that's interesting. I remembered the flush in Kitchen's cheeks when he told me nobody told him what to do or how to investigate a murder. Now, he had "retired." Took his pension and scrammed. I wondered if perhaps someone had tried to tell him what to do about the Judge murder, and he had quit in a funk. Or maybe someone had told him to quit. But who? Why? Stuff like that happens when a murder victim or suspect has some political connections and some higher-up is trying to keep an investigation under wraps. Was Augusta National—my erstwhile employer—trying to stifle any news of this case? And if so, why the hell had they asked me to investigate? The Judge kid didn't seem to have any heavy political connections. Just the opposite, in fact.

But then there was the scary presence of some Medellin drug cartel killer, who may or may not be involved. Maybe the cartel had gotten to Kitchen and told him to forget about the case or they'd find another bunker at the National for him. Maybe ...

I stopped myself. I could sit here all morning and come up with maybes. All I'd get out of that was a headache and no answers. I finished my breakfast and the sports pages, and decided to move on.

I was on my way to Augusta National when my cell phone rang. It was Graham Dodd from the ***Chronicle***.

"Wassup?" I greeted him.

"Same old," he said. "I just got a call from our crime guy down at the jail. He looked up that gun you told me about."

"Oh, yeah," I said. "The Norinco something or other."

"Right," Graham said. "He told me it is a Chinese make. Inexpensive. Heavily exported. Especially down in South America."

"Really?" I said. "The druggies like Chinese guns?"

"Apparently," Graham said. "Wonder if you get hungry again two hours after shooting somebody."

"Very funny," I said. "By the way, I just read in your paper this morning about that Kitchen guy quitting the cops. Sounded like it was unexpected."

"Yeah," Graham said. "Sounded like that to me, too. But hey, he's been on the force for a long time. No doubt he had to eat a lot of crap over the years. Maybe he just figured his time had come."

Yeah," I said, "Maybe. By the way, I'm supposed to play in some tournament over at the Palmetto Golf Club tomorrow with Conn. Any good?"

"The golf course is good, damn good," he said. "You must be playing in the Devereaux. I forgot that thing is this week. You'll enjoy it. Classic old course. While you're out there, look for an old geezer named Skipper Evans. He's got some great stories about golf in these parts. Knows a lot about the National, too. Spend half an hour with him, you can get four or five columns, easy."

"Excellent," I said. "I'll look for him."

Graham rang off as I entered the gates. I went through the same routine of dealing with the Pinkerton guards, drove in, left my car with the valet. Inside the door, the guard told me that Brett was tied up in a meeting, but pointed the way down to the security office and said they were expecting me.

It was in a block of buildings down past the clubhouse tucked between the parking lots and the first fairway. I passed the newfangled press building, which had been built about ten years ago replacing the homey old metal Quonset hut that had long sufficed for the Masters press corps, and came upon a series of low, one-story buildings that appeared to house offices. I knew the last one in the line was where the course superintendent worked, but there were no signs on any of the other doors, so I stood there a minute trying to decide which door led to the security offices.

"Hey!" someone shouted behind me. "What are you doing?" I flinched and turned around. Coming up at me fast, hand on hip holster, was one of the largest men I had ever seen. He would easily tip the scales at 300 pounds and it looked like 400 was a possibility. His head was proportionately small on that huge body, with blondish hair sticking up in a short, bristle-cut, and beady little eyes peering out at me. "This is a secure area," he said loudly as he came up to stand too closely to me. "You're not allowed here."

"Hi, PeeWee," I said. "Did ya miss me?"

He stared at me, befuddled. I should have been offended that he didn't remember me, but we went through a similar dance almost every year. Me and everybody else in the press corps.

PeeWee Reynolds was something of a legend, not least because of his highly ironic nickname. His job was guarding the entry to the press room during the Masters. He did it with such ferocity and dedication that he was hired to provide similar security services at most of the other major golf events around the country. I always wondered if he was regulation Pinkerton, or freelance. I suspected the latter, since I was reasonably certain that the Pinkerton company had some regulations about physical conditioning to qualify as a guard. PeeWee had no physical condition beyond immense, but he used it along with his natural orneriness to good effect. PeeWee either couldn't remember any of our names and faces, secretly enjoyed making us dig for our credentials every year, or he was as stupid as a rock. Every year, some of the guys tried to befriend him, encouraging him to talk about his background or his family or where he lived. But he refused to unbend. He'd sit there at the entrance to the press building, his arms crossed forbodingly across his massive chest, turning his no-neck head to peer at everyone walking in to make sure they had the right credentials, occasionally reaching out with a huge paw to stop someone whose badge he couldn't see. Someone claimed they had learned he lived in a double-wide in Easley, South Carolina, although that had never been verified.

But he was the gatekeeper at the Masters and almost every other big golf tournament during the year. I happened to be standing near the entrance to the press tent at the Ryder Cup in Brookline in 1999, where PeeWee as usual was guarding the gate when a well-tanned older lady with pouffy white hair started to stroll in.

"Hold on there lady," he growled at her, moving his bulk with surprising speed to block her way. "You cain't come waltzing in here. Who do you think you are?"

The lady had eyed him coldly. "I'm with him," she said, nodding behind PeeWee. He turned and saw former President George H.W. Bush walk up, surrounded by his retinue of Secret Service agents. The President smiled, took the arm of his wife, Barbara, and ushered her into the press room. Check and mate, PeeWee.

"Hacker, ***Boston Journal***," I said now as PeeWee stood there looking fierce. "Have an appointment in the security office to look at some tapes. Which door is it?"

PeeWee looked like he'd rather shoot me than tell me, but he grudgingly pointed out the door. I smiled, thanked him, and said I'd see him next week. He was silent, but he watched me warily as I turned and walked inside. He was probably trying to remember what he was doing next week. I figured I'd be selected for a cavity search when I showed up for the tournament in a few days.

I went inside. It was quiet and cool, the air conditioner humming softly in the background. After I introduced myself and went through the usual dance of identification and explanation, which only took one call over to Brett to get authorization, I was shown into a back office with a monitor and a player, and they showed me how to plug in the DVD disk and run it. "You want some coffee?" one of the Pinkerton guys asked me as he put the disk in the machine. "It's pretty damned boring, you ask me. Tain't nuttin' on it. We looked. The poh-leece looked. Nuttin'."

"No thanks on the coffee," I said. "How does this system work?"

He perched his rear end on the edge of the desk. "Your basic motion-sensor camera, hooked up to a digital camcorder," he said. "We got 'er rigged not to trip if it's just a squirrel or a skunk or a 'coon wanders in. But anything bulkier than a big dog triggers the camera to run, and sends an alert to the duty desk out front. We got 'em all around the perimeter of the grounds. If one trips, they all start recordin' so we can trace anyone comin' in or out."

"And the night before they found the body? ..."

"Nuttin'," the guard said. "Now, the funny thing was that one of the cameras tripped that night and started recording. But none of the other ones went off, and there warn't no alert here at the desk. The tape showed nothing but empty ground. That's what you got in there," he said, nodding at the DVD in my hand.

"Where was the camera that went off?" I asked. "Down by the tenth hole?"

"Nope," the guard said. "It was one way over to the west, near the boneyard."

"You got your own cemetery here?" I said, wonder in my voice.

He laughed. "Naw. The boneyard is what we call the junkyard." He looked around furtively. "'Course, they'd prolly fire my ass if they heard me say that. Ain't no 'junk' here at the National. It's the area where they store the stuff they use during the tournament—metal frames and wood boards for the bleachers, metal rods for the gallery ropes, all that kinda stuff. After the tournament is done, they stack all that crap out there and it looks like a bunch of dinosaur bones all stacked up."

"The boneyard," I said, shaking my head.

"But that's way over yonder," the guard said, pointing in one direction. "And they found that poor feller way over t'here—" He pointed in the other direction. "So even if someone had snuck in at the boneyard and tripped the camera, how'd they get all the way over to the tenth without nobody see'in 'em? Be awful hard. They'd have to cross the entire golf course draggin' that poor fella's body."

"Shore would," I said.

"Well," he said, probably trying to decide if I was making fun of him, "I'll let you get to it."

"How long is this tape of nothing?" I asked looking at the disk.

"'Bout an hour. Sure you don' want some coffee?"

I thanked him, but declined. He left me alone. I popped in the disk and hit the play button. At first, there was just visual static. Then the screen went black. In a few seconds, a fuzzy, gray picture appeared, with white numbers along the bottom that said "02:30:15." The seconds began ticking off. It was hard to tell what it was I was looking at, since the camera was shooting at night. Even with an infared night vision gizmo, there wasn't much available light to provide contrast or definition. I picked out what looked like a fence running top to bottom on the screen, and figured that the camera was up on a post, looking down the fence line. There were some barely distinguishable trees or bushes off to the left of the screen, which I figured was the outside of the property line. Inside the fence to the right on the screen, there was a fuzzy pile of something in the foreground. Maybe one of the piles of "bones."

I watched the screen for a few minutes. Nothing was moving. No shadowy figures dragging a body around. The only thing moving was the seconds and minutes ticking away on the counter. I hit fast-forward and let it run for a while, then stopped it, started over, hit play again. Same thing. Fuzzy, gray, silent and still. I hit stop and sent it back to the beginning. I hit play again and watched carefully. The video static was followed by the black. Then the picture came up again, showing nothing. Or did it? I rewound and did it again. And again.

I went out into the main office and asked my Pinkerton friend if he knew how to view the disk one frame at a time. He did, and showed me. He watched while I fiddled with the machine, until I had found the first ten or so frames that the camera had captured after it had tripped that night. I went through them one at a time.

"There," I said finally, stopping on the fourth frame. "Do you see that?"

"Son of a dad-blamed gun," the guard said. "I sure as hell do."

There was a shadow, almost indiscernible, in the top left corner of the screen. It lasted for less than five more frames, but there was definitely a movement of some kind. Someone—or something—had been there that night.

"I'll be damned," he said. "Ever one of us plus the Augusta cops looked at that thing six times to Sunday. Didn't notice a thing."

"You were looking for an intruder," I said. "But this was someone who knew where the system was and how to defeat it. I'm not sure how, but whoever it was managed to freeze the camera. Look at the trees and stuff..." I ran the fast-forward and got the usual gray picture of the fence. "You see? Nothing is moving. I mean, literally nothing. The leaves are frozen in place. I don't know what the weather was that night, but I'll bet there's usually some kind of breeze, especially at night."

"Son of a ..." The Pinkerton guy was beside himself.

"I don't know if they did something to the camera, or maybe hacked the software," I said. "You'd better get your tech guys to look at that. But at least now we're pretty sure that someone was on the grounds that night. Now all we need to do is find out who."

"Yeah," the guy said. "No problem."

I stopped off at Brett's office on my way out. I told him what I'd just learned.

"Really?" he said, amazed. "I thought everyone looked at that tape. Even the cops. Pretty amazing that no one else spotted that shadow."

"Yeah," I said. "Amazing."

He looked at me funny. "Do I detect a note of cynicism in your voice?" he said, smiling.

"Well, it is pretty strange that nobody paid enough attention," I said. "But then, a lot of things are getting pretty strange."

"Such as?" he asked. He wasn't smiling anymore.

"Such as the guy down at the cop shop, who's apparently been running homicide investigations for years around here, suddenly decides its time to quit. Right after he gives me a lecture about how nobody is going to push him around."

"You think someone pressured him?"

"As a matter of fact, I do," I said.

"Who?" he asked.

"I was going to ask you that," I said.

"How ...?" He stopped and looked at me. Not smiling this time. "You don't think anyone here ...?"

"I don't know, Brett," I said. "From what I've been told, the only real power group in Augusta is right here. What I see is a murder case, happened at Augusta National, cop in charge suddenly retires. That's a pretty direct connection if someone is putting pressure on someone to shitcan the case."

He sat there thinking. His phone began ringing. He looked at me, and for a second I thought I saw something in his eyes. Worry. Concern. Wariness. He looked at the ringing phone and sighed.

"Keep digging," he said. "Keep me posted."

Chapter Thirteen

Conn Thackery picked me up early the next morning. I transferred my golf clubs to the trunk of his Mercedes and we worked our way over to Washington Road and down to the Interstate, stopping for coffee at the Krispy Kreme. Then he headed east, over the Savannah River bridge and into South Carolina. The day promised to be clear and sunny, the few clouds in the sky painted a pretty pink in the early morning sun.

"How's your case going?" Conn asked as we motored along.

"Troubling," I said. "Things aren't adding up."

"Somehow," he said, "That doesn't surprise me. Those fellows at the National are a piece of work. Usually takes three or four passes before you can come within shouting distance of the truth with those guys."

I filled him in with what I had learned in the last day or two. He whistled at the news of Enrico de la Paz, the Colombian killer who may or may not be on the loose. And he laughed when he heard about the security tape.

"Those Pinkerton guys dress well, but they're not exactly your top of the line Dick Tracy crimebusters," he chuckled. "Whoever is involved in this thing is obviously way over their head."

"Maybe over the head of the Augusta constables, too," I said.

"Doesn't take much," he said. "Listen, we've got a great day here. Let's just go out and play some golf, have some laughs. Let's forget about all the bad stuff going on back there—" he motioned over his shoulder in the general direction of Augusta—"and have some fun."

"Sounds good to me," I said.

In a few minutes he pulled off the Interstate and followed a winding road through gently rolling hills and piney woods into the town of Aiken, South Carolina. We rolled slowly through the mostly empty grid of streets in the center of town. There were a handful of traffic lights, three or four impressive church steeples reaching into the blue morning sky, a couple of brick bank buildings and a street or two of shops. It all looked quaint, slightly upscale and well preserved.

"This old town used to be quite the place," Conn told me. "During the late 1800s it was what Florida is today—the place where the rich went to get away from the ice and snow up North. Railroad went right through downtown here, and from January to April, the trains were full every day. Rich people, their servants, steamer trunks full of clothes...it must have been quite a scene."

"What happened?" I asked.

"Well, Henry Flagler started pushing his railroad further and further south down into Florida, draining swamps and selling building lots along the ocean as he went," Conn said. "That kinda killed the tourist market around here. The Depression finished it off. But a lot of the horsey set stayed. In fact, Devereaux Milburn, the guy whose tournament we're playing in today, was a champion polo player and World War I hero. He was pals with guys like Tommy Hitchcock, Averill Harriman and the hoi polloi like that."

We headed south out of downtown, and I could tell that Aiken had once been a wealthy enclave. Huge brick mansions began to appear on both sides of the road, shaded by towering magnolias and waves of azalea hedges in full and colorful bloom. Some still had large barns and riding paddocks, with whitewashed rails and jumps; others fronted on grassy pastures where graceful horses grazed in the morning sun, snorts of warm breath flowing from their nostrils in the morning air.

Conn turned down what looked like a residential street and in a few hundred yards turned again into a long driveway that led up a hill and into some woods. I didn't see a sign. Apparently they liked to keep their golf clubs a secret here in Aiken.

He pulled into one of the spaces tucked between the thick stand of pine trees that made for a haphazard parking lot. There was a low, whitewashed bungalow to the left, a tee in front of it across the main drive and another one-story shack off to the right. After driving through the tonier parts of Aiken, it felt like we had arrived in some kind of backwoods clearing. Not only was there absolutely nothing remotely ostentatious about this place, it wouldn't have surprised me to find someone cooking up a fresh batch of hootch around the corner, eyes and ears cocked for the revenuers.

"This is it!" Conn said happily. "Welcome to the Palmetto. This place is the anti-National."

Conn popped open his trunk and an elderly black man materialized.

"Mornin' Mr. Conn," the man said as he began to unload our golf clubs.

"Hello, William," Conn said, shaking his hand. "How's the Missus and that boy of yours?"

William's lined face lit up as he smiled. "Fine, fine," he said. "Gerald has one more year to go at the university. He's doin' well, doin' well. Lookin' to go into the law school."

"Good Lord," Conn said, "I gotta talk him out of that! He'll take all my business away!"

The two men chuckled. Conn introduced me and I shook William's large hand, which was warm and solid and strong. He looked at me, eyebrows raised in question.

"Yore name shore nuff Hacker?" he asked. I nodded. He broke out in a soft chuckle. "Well, Mister Hacker, you have done come to the right place today. This be the world capital of hacker today." He shouldered our two golf bags and walked off, chuckling softly to himself.

Conn led me into the whitewashed building, which had been built in a shallow V shape. "This building was designed by Stanford White, the New York architect," he said. "That was before he was shot for fooling around with someone else's wife. I think he also designed the clubhouse at Shinnecock. This one is a whole lot less fancy."

Indeed it was. To the left of entry, there was a large function room, mostly empty of furniture. To the right was the locker room—men only—which featured a few rows of antique wooden lockers, some stuffed chairs, and a huge open hearth in which a bright fire was crackling. Beyond the lockers was a smallish bathroom area done in white hexagonal tiles with huge old sinks and lavatories with pull chain flushers. I felt like saying "Twenty-three skidoo" or something.

"Place doesn't even have a kitchen," Conn said with a hint of pride. "They bring in a caterer if they have an event here. If you're hungry, though, Tommy has a hot dog steamer in the back of his shop." He nodded out the window at the old clapboard shack. There was a wraparound porch on the far side of the building, which overlooked the last hole and had a dozen or so wooden rocking chairs. "Pretty cool, huh? This is your basic old-fashioned golf club," Conn said. "No pool, no tennis, no dining room. They do let women in, but they have to fend for themselves. It's pretty much drive in and tee it up. Just like it was back in 1892."

The place was beginning to fill up with golfers in pre-tournament mode. A long line of carts snaked away from the pro shop, and golfers were milling about, greeting one another in genial hubbub. I told Conn I was going to hit some balls for the first time in a week or two, and after finding my clubs, I grabbed a few and headed over to the nearby practice range. It was a shortish range, tucked in the bend of one of the fairways, with a tall wire fence to protect players from energetic practice shots. A sign asked that we not hit driver which was fine with me: I just wanted to swing a few irons and try to find a semblance of a rhythm.

I was happily whacking away when I heard a cough behind me. Someone said "Nice swing."

I turned. Travis Kitchen, the recently retired homicide cop was standing there, dressed in golf clothes, holding a handful of clubs, and wearing a Cheshire-cat grin. Even in a polo shirt and casual slacks, he looked neat and proper.

"Thanks," I said, grinning back at him. "Guess you retired codgers have nothing better to do than play golf, huh?"

"That's the plan," Kitchen said. "Beats the hell out of getting shot at."

"I would think so," I said. "I wonder what the rules are about former police officers talking to the press about cases they once managed if they're now retired."

"Well," Kitchen said, "While it would be both illegal and unethical to discuss any investigations that are still ongoing, if you want to buy me a beer after the round, maybe we can swap a few tidbits of information. I understand you've been busy, too."

I shrugged. "Just doing my job," I said.

He looked at me with a wry smile. "I think that's my line," he said.

He went to hit a few balls. I headed back up to the clubhouse to find Conn. People had begun to gather around the line of golf carts in anticipation of the shotgun start. Conn was sitting in the driver's seat of our cart, chatting with two guys in the next one. He grinned at me when I sat down next to him.

"We're going off the first," he said. "Had to slip Tommy a few bucks. But I thought you should see the course from beginning to end, like it was designed."

"Still gotta play them all," I said.

"Yeah, but a golf course, at least a good golf course like this one, has a rhythm to it," he said. "Start in the middle and it all gets out of whack."

"Whatever," I said.

A small man with a shaggy-dog mustache and round glasses mounted the three steps in front of the golf shop carrying a bullhorn. He pushed a button to make a high screeching sound that caused everyone standing around to turn and look.

"Howdy y'all," he said in the tinny amplified sound. "My name is Tom Bowen, and as the head professional, I want to welcome y'all to the fifty-third playing of the Devereaux Milburn Memorial."

There was scattered applause.

"There are rules sheets on every cart. Just to summarize, since I figure y'all can read, we're playing best-ball of two-man teams. We're also playing 'em down today, fellas." Scattered boos rang out. Tom ignored them. "We got a full house here, so let's try and keep play moving along. If you're out of a hole, pick the damn ball up. Any questions?" No one said anything. "Okay, then. Let's get started and good luck to everyone."

There followed the usual mad rush to the golf carts, as the golfers began to drive out to their assigned holes for the shotgun start. With a foursome beginning on each hole, and two assigned to the par-five holes, the entire field would begin and complete play roughly at the same time.

While the contestants scattered, I corralled Bowen. "I've been told to find a guy named Skipper Evans," I said. "Graham Dodd told me he's got some good stories."

Bowen smiled. "He does indeed," he said. "These days, he can't play anymore so he's in charge of getting lunch ready. I expect he'll get here a bit later. I'll make sure you two meet after the tournament."

I thanked him, grabbed my putter and strolled over to the practice green to get a feel for the speed of the greens.

Conn pulled our golf cart around next to the first tee, which occupied a flat space at the crest of a long and steep hill. The fairway began well below us and climbed away in the distance. I met the two fellows who'd be playing with us, and Tom the golf pro came out with an over-under shotgun and shot a couple of blanks into the air.

"I reckon that means we can start," said one of the other guys. At least, I think that's what he said—my ears were still ringing. We all launched our tee shots off the hill and down onto the fairway far below. There were two long thin bunkers bracketing each side of the fairway, so I aimed for the left one and tried to play a little cut back to the middle. I cut it a little too much, but it managed to stop before rolling into the right-side bunker. Conn pulled his a little into the left rough, and the other two guys were right down the middle.

I could immediately sense the old-fashioned appeal of the course at Palmetto. The first fairway, once we descended the long hill from the tee, sloped steadily upwards towards a green cut into the side of a hill, surrounded by sand and mounded hillocks. The second hole was similar, with a relatively easy tee shot through a stand of tall pines to another plateau green that dropped away steeply in front. Like many old courses that date from the 19th century, the golf holes seemed to fit the land, yet they demanded precise shots, especially coming into the greens. My pulse level rose a few beats. This was going to be fun.

We had to wait a while on the third tee while the fairway ahead of us cleared. "Hogan used to say that these next three holes were the strongest par-fours in a row he'd ever seen," said Conn.

"Yeah, but what did he know?" I said. Everyone chuckled.

As it turns out, Hogan was probably correct. The third was a monster hole of almost 470 yards, which meant that even after a good drive, we all had 200-plus yards to get to the green. And it was a small green, raised in front and terraced. I think my scrambling bogey was low score. The next hole wasn't much shorter, and called for a long carry over some rough, bush- and sand-filled terrain to a steeply sloping fairway. That left a long iron shot to a narrow plateau green that fell away on the right. Conn's bogey was our best score when I left my approach under the lip of the front bunker and couldn't get it out.

Then there was the fifth, yet another long, long par-four, with thick piney woods on both sides of a narrow fairway, with yet another multi-tiered, raised green at the end. I made a good up-and-down from in front and salvaged a par. But Hogan's three toughest holes had eaten my lunch, and I knew it.

Conn and I were playing fairly well, but neither one of us was grinding very hard. It was a gorgeous day, the golf course was in good nick and the company was fun. One of the other players in our foursome, Bennie McDougall, filled me in on some of the background of the tournament. "From right after World War II until the late 50's, all the pros came down the week before the Masters to play in the Milburn," he said. "With all the money around here, the betting got pretty heavy."

Bennie hit a shot and continued. "It was quite the scene," he said. "It was a pro-am, three-day event, and there were parties every night. Sam Snead used to stay up until three in the morning, dancing with all the girls. He loved to dance, Sam did."

He went on talking about the history of the course. The rich polo players who founded the place back in 1892 had just laid out four holes, and soon called in Herbert Leeds, who had recently built the Myopia Hunt Club north of Boston, to bring the course first to nine holes, then 18 in 1895. Leeds had installed the hard-pack sand greens that were used throughout most of the South in the old days. When Alister Mackenzie was in Augusta to work on the National in 1932, he had been hired to come over to Aiken and see what he could do about the Palmetto course. He added some length and showed the locals how to install grass greens, and sent over the construction superintendent and some material from the National to help. More recently, the club members had hired Rees Jones, the famed "Open Doctor" to tweak the layout a bit, modernizing it where necessary. He hadn't done much to change the course, Bennie told me, but the infrastructure he added had helped conditions improve.

But it was mostly the Mackenzie influences I noticed as we played our way around the old course. Like many courses from his era, the holes were not overpoweringly long, but all had tricky green complexes that punished a wayward shot. A couple holes were built around redans, or diametrically slanting mounds and bunkers that created a kind of risk-reward situation.

We made the loop of the old holes that wrapped around the clubhouse and finally came to the last tee, tucked back in the woods. There was a bit of a backup on the tee, as one unfortunate foursome had suffered the indignity of four awful tee shots: two out-of-bounds to the left, and two more lost in the woods to the right. By the time they had finished looking for the lost balls and returned to play again from the tee, two foursomes had backed up.

I saw that one of the players waiting to play off the last was Travis Kitchen. I sidled up to him.

"How're you playing?" I asked.

"Not too bad," he said. "My partner has come through with some great putts. He's made about everything he's looked at all day."

The fairway finally cleared and Kitchen's group prepared to tee off. The tee box for the 18th at Palmetto is tucked back on a platform at the edge of the woods, falling away steeply at the rear to a wetlands area far below. The hills and dense woods rose up in the distance beyond the little pond. The hole itself wasn't one of the more daunting ones, except for the low cedar fence marking out-of-bounds down the left side, and the woods lurking on the right. But if you could knock a three-wood relatively straight, the fairway was open and the approach would be a simple flip of a wedge.

Most of us were standing off to the left of the narrow tee when Kitchen bent over to tee his ball. He took a step or two behind the ball and lined up his shot. He stood there for a moment, looking down the fairway, visualizing the flight he wanted the ball to take. Then he walked forward and took his address position. Just as he was about to swing, someone on the nearby seventeenth green made a long putt and all the golfers in that foursome began yelling in excitement. The sudden noise startled all of us, and Kitchen broke from his address posture and took a step back away from the ball.

There was a sudden zipping sound followed immediately by a dullish thud. I thought I saw a tuft of dirt fly up into the air. I also saw Travis Kitchen's shoulders flinch defensively. He knew exactly what had happened. Someone had just fired a rifle at him. Instinctively, he took two running steps and threw himself off the tee to the right, down the slight embankment and into the bushy growth. There was another zip sound when he was in the air, and I heard him grunt moments before he hit the brush and rolled behind a medium-size oak. There was a third zip and a chunk of bark flew off the tree.

"Everyone get down!" I shouted, and nobody had to be told twice. The whole thing had taken maybe four or five seconds. Everyone either flattened themselves on the ground, or ducked behind one of the golf carts parked next to the tee. Three guys had whipped out their cell phones and were dialing 9-1-1.

I took a chance that whoever had fired the shots was by now getting the hell away, and, after taking one deep breath, made a dash across the tee and down into the brush after Kitchen. I rolled behind the same small tree. There were no more zips.

He was lying on his back, his face pale and sweaty. But his eyes were open and he was breathing in short, throaty gasps. "I think he got me in the leg," he said, his voice thin with pain. I bent down and pushed him over on his side to see. He groaned and said a few dirty words.

"No," I said. "I can confidently report that he got you in the ass," I said. "But I think you're gonna live." I could see that the bullet that had hit Kitchen in mid-dive had caught him in one buttock. But it looked like just a flesh wound that had grazed him. "He's OK!" I yelled over to the other guys. Already, dimly in the background, I could hear the wail of sirens approaching.

"I think you'd better tell my partner it's his hole," Kitchen said through clenched teeth..

Chapter Fourteen

Many hours later, as the sun began to sink behind the woods—the same woods from whence the shots had been fired—I sat myself down wearily in one of the old rocking chairs on the porch of the Palmetto Club. Needless to say, the attempted murder of Travis Kitchen had thrown something of a damper on the end of the tournament. Not to mention the peace and quiet of a perfectly nice day.

The Aiken PD had been the first to arrive, followed by several ambulances and fire trucks. Then the South Carolina Staties were there, in their impressive Gestapo-like uniforms with polished calf-high boots and Smokey Bear hats. There were some guys running around with SWAT jackets and blue jeans who came from I don't know where. Helicopters buzzed around the woods all afternoon, looking for the rifleman or men. The sound of police radios punctuated the afternoon air, with squelch squeaks, monotone female voices droning on about this and that, the usual traffic of official conversations that always to me sound fuzzy and indistinct.

I had taken a gaggle of police types back to the 18th tee and shown them where everyone had been and what had happened. Then we had all gone back to Stanford White's elegant little cottage and I had recounted the events over and over and over. Every time some new police jurisdiction had arrived, I had to tell the story again. By the end of the afternoon, I was starting to get hoarse.

The other golfers had come trundling in from the course after finishing their last hole to find the clubhouse area bristling with cops, EMTs and firemen. A catered lunch had been waiting in the one function room of the clubhouse, the wing opposite the locker rooms, and finally Tom Bowen the pro had asked for permission to have the food brought outside and placed on long tables so the golfers could get something to eat. Everyone made themselves a plate and grabbed a beer and stood around talking about the shooting of Travis Kitchen, recently retired homicide chief of Richmond County.

I never had time to eat anything. Conn Thackerey brought me a soft drink at one point in the afternoon, but that was about all I had during my endless repetitions of the story. So by the time I finally sank down into the rocking chair, I was hungry and totally exhausted. I closed my eyes and thought—once again—of the sequence of events. Kitchen's sudden move away from his tee shot had caused the shooter to miss the first shot, and his quick reflexes after that had saved his life. The guy who had made that long, cross-country putt on the 17th was hailed as the hero of the day, since it was the yelling and cheering from that event that had distracted Kitchen and made him step away from his ball.

I sensed someone come out on the porch and opened my eyes. Standing next to me was an older man, well into his 80s, with a round body, bright pink head with thinning white hair, and small narrow glasses perched on the end of a bulbous nose. He was smiling and carrying a plastic plate heaped with food. My stomach growled loud enough to be heard back in Augusta.

"Thought you might be a mite hungry," he drawled in a voice that cut like an axe through the air, a sharp baritone tinged with a Dixie drawl. "You ain't had time to think much the last few hours, have ya?"

I nodded my appreciation, too tired to come up with any kind of rejoinder, and gratefully took the plate and began wolfing down the food.

He pulled up a rocking chair and sat down next to me. "I'm Skipper Evans," he said. "Heard ole Graham told you to look me up." I nodded, my mouth too full to answer. "Yessir," he said, looking out on the golf course as the shadows began to lengthen across the last fairway. "This is a day that'll be talked about as long as they play golf here. That's for dead certain."

I swallowed and made myself stop shoveling long enough to thank the man. I asked how long he had been a member.

"Me?" he said, smiling. "I guess you could call me what that writer feller said...I'm the 'Oldest Member!' Hell, I been here so long I sign my chits in Roman numerals!"

He laughed aloud, a deep belly laugh that rang out over the fairways, echoed off the hills and faded into the piney woods.

"Yessir," he said, "I remember when the moonshiners would bring in their wooden barrels of hootch for the New Year's party. They came up through those same woods—" he motioned towards the 18th tee and the deep woods that lay behind it. "—Couple of good ole boys in coveralls, toting shotguns, their hound dogs runnin' around. I do believe they made a pretty good whiskey, because the New Year's Eve bash here was always a memorable event. Memorable."

He looked out again and sighed a little. Remembering the past. The cold December night. The glittering party inside. The orchestra. The beautiful people from Aiken and Manhattan and Chicago and Philly. Dancing into the wee hours, sipping some fine local hootch made in the deep dark woods beyond the golf course. Dancing and drinking and trying hard to forget the market crash and the soup lines and the clouds of war rising over Europe and Asia. It must have been easy to forget all that standing out here on the porch, the cold New Year's air washing away all the troubles and concerns of the day. It was easy, too easy, to look out upon that same scene today and forget that just a few hours ago, someone had fired a high-powered and silenced rifle at someone else, just missing. Easy to forget those "zip" sounds that had carried such malice at the time. I would have sighed, too, except my mouth was full of barbecue beef, sweet potato pie, cole slaw and honeyed grits.

Skipper sat there lost in his own thoughts while I finished my plate of food. He was nice enough not to comment upon my manner of shoveling it in as fast as possible. I'm sure he had been hungry before. Somehow, a cold can of beer materialized at my elbow. I didn't see him put it there, and nobody else had come out on the porch, so I figured the Gods had answered one of my unheard prayers and caused it to materialize at my side. I popped the top and took a swallow. Nectar.

"So, I said finally, belching softly to myself contentedly, "Never had a shooting before at the Palmetto?"

He chuckled softly, hooking his thumbs under the belt than ran across his broad, rounded stomach. "Nossir," he said, shaking his head. "Had quite a few fist fights over the years. Battles of one sort or another. Accusations of cheating on the course, or with one another's wife. But I can't say we've ever had a shooting. Man was lucky he moved at the right time."

"He has good instincts," I said. "But I guess a cop with his experience would have."

"Reckon that feller needs to look over some of his old cases, figger out which bad ole boy mighta just got outta jail," Skipper said, pushing his wire-rim glasses back up his nose. "This day and age, it's pretty doggone easy to get your hands on a rifle with a good scope, even someone who's just outta the slammer."

"Might not have been an old case," I said. "He was working on a new one when he quit the force—that body they found over at the National."

"Ahh," Skipper said, rocking back and forth. "Do tell? My, my. The chickens coming home to roost."

"Meaning what?" I asked.

"Hell young feller," Skipper said, "There's been a whole lotta water flowing under the bridge of the Augusta National over the years. Ever-body thinks that place was just born up all nice and pretty. They come up here once a year when the flowers are nice and the sun is warm and they watch them a golf tunnyment—and it's always sumpthin' to see, grant you that—but nobody knows nuthin' 'bout the history of that place. When you got a lotta cash in the till, it's easy to forget the days when you didn't."

"Well," I said. "I know they built that course during the Depression. But Cliff Roberts raised the cash, didn't he?"

"He tole people he had the cash," Skipper said, leaning forward and tapping me on the knee for emphasis. "He wasn't about to admit that he couldn't. His job was finance. He worked on Wall Street with all them big-money boys. But a lotta them boys lived and played over here. They knew what was goin' on. I remember them talkin' about the National all up until the War started."

He paused and laughed a bit to himself. "Why, I remember one feller here used to say that Adolph Hitler was the best damn thing that ever happened to Clifford Roberts," Skipper said, amusement in his voice. "When the war started, he had an excuse the shut the damn place down, and five years to raise more cash. If there hadn't a been a war, I expect they would have had to close the joint down, tunnyment and all."

"It was that bad?" I said, amazed.

"Oh, hell, yeah," Skipper said. "Most of the help was paid in chickens and pigs and bags of corn and rice. Heck, the prize money was crap, even in those days. Roberts had to go hat in hand to one of his Wall Street buddies and promise never to charge him dues in perpetuity if he'd cover the prize money for a few years. Only reason the fellows used to come play in the damn thing was because Bob Jones asked 'em to. Everbody loved Bob. That's why they came over here to Palmetto the week before—try and win a few more bucks. And they all showed up for the big Calcutta party at the Hotel Bon Air. Lord-a-mercy, the money that was being thrown around that ballroom Wednesday night every year before the Masters...could make your head spin. Hogan'd be sittin' there with a pencil, his beady little eyes watchin' everythin' and ever'one. He was always figgerin' the odds, tryin' to beat the pros. Snead would be out on the dance floor dancin' his fool head off, but he'd come over when his name was called and lay down a few hundred on hisself. The winnin' ticket was usually worth 12, 15 thousand. That was pretty serious scratch back then. And a hell of lot more than the official check for first place."

I took a sip of my beer. I had heard stories about the gambling at the Masters in its early years. It had continued, growing larger every year, until the U.S. Golf Association, worried about the appearance of impropriety with professional gamblers hanging about not only the Masters, but the other major golf tournaments, had issued its decree banning Calcutta or pari-mutuel wagering at golf events. But I hadn't heard that Augusta National had been hanging on by its fingertips financially at the beginning of the club's life.

"In fact," Skipper continued, "I believe that Cliff Roberts used to plan on winning enough cash in the annual Calcutta to keep the place running. He used to bet a load on Hogan every year. I remember the year after the war, '46 I think it was, he had a bundle riding on Ben. And little Herman Kaiser came along and was playing great golf, leading the tunnyment. Oh, my Lord, how they tried to booger that poor fella! Fired his caddie after two rounds. Sent Granny Rice out on the course to threaten him with slow-play. Had the marshals talkin' about how Hogan was birdiein' this hole and parrin' that one ... just trying to get ole Herman off his game."

Skipper guffawed with the memory. "Roberts even sent some Atlantic City roughs over to Herman's house Saturday night and tole him he'd better think twice about winnin'! It just put that ole boy's back right up, and he won the tunnyment and had to buy three wheelbarrows to carry his cash away. Ha!"

"Well," I said. "I guess Roberts managed to raise enough cash to keep the lights on."

"Oh, he did," Skipper said, nodding his head in agreement. "But the question is...how? Where did he find the money? The boys over here used to talk about it. Now you gotta understand, the members here used to be the cream of the crop. Rich? My Lord, you ain't seen rich like them. Family money, went back generations. Their damn wives were richer still! So they'd come up here, play them some golf, sit around of an afternoon right here on this porch, have a few drinks and talk about the National and that rascal Cliff Roberts."

"Rascal?"

"Oh yeah," Skipper said. "They knowed he was playing the odds somewhere to raise the money. Especially when he started building them cottages and things. Now here's a club that's been struggling to pay the light bills, cain't pay the help, and all of a sudden they're building houses and such? How'd he manage that? So the boys'd sit around and chew the fat and tell each other tales of what they'd heard."

"And what did they come up with?" I was fascinated.

"Oh hell, you name it, they figgured Roberts had done it, one time or 'nother. Like those bent-nose guys he sent after Herman Kaiser. How'd he know how to find them fellers? Well, he was a New York guy, wasn't he? Lotsa them Eye-talian types up there. La Cosa Nostra, you get my drift?"

"Cliff Roberts was tied into the New York Mob?" My voice was full of wonder.

"Oh, I'm sure he knew a few of them types," Skipper was nodding. "Roberts knew all the angles, and wasn't afeared of playin' 'em. He was a tough sumbitch. Smart one, too. He got hisself hooked up early with that Woodruff fellow over to Atlanta."

"The Coca-Cola guy?" I asked.

"You bet," Skipper said, nodding. "That was another smooth operator, let me tell you. Had more money than God and was always trying to double it. Though I have to admit, he gave a lot of it away later in his life."

"I heard that Woodruff gave Jones and Roberts a bottling plant down in South America," I said.

Skipper chuckled. Then he guffawed. Then he laughed aloud.

"Yeah," he said. "A bottling plant."

"It wasn't?"

"Oh, it was a helluva lot more than a goldurned bottlin' plant," he said, shoulders still shaking with mirth. "There's some of the old boys here used to say that bidness down there wasn't nuthin' but drug runnin'. Plain and simple."

"Oh, come on now," I said. "Bobby Jones and Cliff Roberts used to smuggle drugs into the United States from South America? Now I have heard everything."

"Well, Mister Smarty-Pants," Skipper said, giving me a friendly look over his spectacles. "You obviously don't know that one of the ingredients in that so-called secret formula of Co-Cola was actually cocaine. From the coca leaf. Hell, that's why they named it Coca-Cola! Gave it that little kick that people liked. And it was in the formula until the 1950s when the guvmint decided that cocaine was a bad thing. But all through the 30's and 40's, it was still legal and Roberts and Jones' little operation down there was just a plant for processing coca leaf. They'd fly that stuff up here all nice and legal and sell some of it to Co-Cola and ship the rest of it to Cliff's pals over in Atlantic City. Made them some nice money."

"The Eisenhower Cabin was built with drug money?" I was aghast. Delighted. Amazed. I wondered if I could verify any of this delicious gossip. Be a Pulitzer in it if I could.

"Hell's bells," Skipper said, "All that fancy equipment they got over there, the underground cables and air conditioning systems for their greens...how d'ya think they pay for all that?"

"I always thought they racked in with the TV contract and Masters sales," I said.

"Do the math, sonny boy, do the math," he said. "The tunnyment was always pretty much break-even. Ever'body knows the dues are kept low so nobody asks any damn questions. But that place is all the latest high-tech whiz-bang gizmos and such you've never seen the likes of! How d'ya think they pay for all of that?"

"Running drugs?"

"Well, they gotta get it somewhere," he said.

"But Jones and Roberts are long gone," I said. "What happened to that company in South America?"

"Ah," Skipper said, leaning back in his rocker, a playful Cheshire-cat grin on his red face. "Now that's an interesting question. I remember sittin' right here on this porch 'bout thirty years ago when a handful of our members from Wall Street asked the very same question. Couple of 'em went inside and made a few calls. Came back out with the answer inside of an hour."

He paused for dramatic effect. He probably wanted me to jump up and down and beg for the answer, but I just sat there and waited.

"You know the current chairman?" he asked.

"Grosvenor?"

"That'd be the one," he said. "You know about his company?"

"Yeah," I said, "Big import-export company." It suddenly dawned on me. The Grosvenor Group had a lot of businesses in South America. "Wait a minute," I said, excited. "The Grosvenor Group bought Roberts and Jones' bottling plant?"

"Yup," Skipper said, a satisfied smile playing across his face. "The bottling plant--" he held up his fingers to make a quotation mark around the world 'bottling.' "Also, a few hundred thousand acres of coca fields, the transportation company that shipped it up here and probably all the politicians and police that were getting paid off to look the other way. And remember—Clifford Roberts was the main fundraiser and campaign finance chief for Eisenhower when he ran for president. So he had him some friends in pretty damn high places."

I was stunned. I suddenly remembered a press conference at one Masters when Hord Hardin was the chairman. He had been moaning and groaning about the costs of everything going up—especially the prize money—in other major tournaments, and said he was worried that some day soon, even the Masters might have to sell naming rights to its tournament in return for sponsorship dollars. "If we don't offer the same purses as the British Open, the U.S. Open and the PGA, the players won't want to come here anymore," he had said. "But I can tell you that we'll stop having the Masters tournament before we have to call it the AT&T Masters or the Masters presented by Burger King."

Now, I was being told that Augusta National had long had a secret source of income, set up by Clifford Roberts and now controlled by Charlie Grosvenor. An illegal secret source.

"Did Bob Jones know about this?" I asked. I found it hard to imagine the great Bobby, renowned for his integrity and honesty as a golfer, agreeing to be part of a company that was running illegal drugs into the country.

"Well, Bob was a lawyer," Skipper reminded me. "Be hard to imagine he'd get involved in sumthin' without givin' it a long hard look. But on the other hand, he tended to let Clifford have his way with all things involving money. Bob just wanted to be left alone, play golf with his friends and have a good time. And like I said, Roberts was a pretty slick operator. He liked to play with fire sometimes. In fact, there's some who say he got burned."

"How's that?"

"There's some who say he didn't kill his own self," Skipper said. "But that someone did it for him. There was always parts of that story that never did quite add up."

"Such as?" Skipper was on a roll and I saw no reason to slow him down.

"The official story is that he was depressed and sick with cancer. So he walked out to that pond at 2:30 in the morning, in his jammies and robe and put a bullet in his head," Skipper said. "Now anyone who ever met Clifford Roberts knew that he would never go outside his cabin unless he was dressed to the nines. Coat and tie and spit-shined shoes. He was a fastidious man. So it never made much sense to me that he'd go kill himself in his pajamas. Then, it's said that earlier on the day of his death, he asked a Pinkerton guard for some instructions on how to shoot his pistol. Said he had heard some noises outside his cabin. This would be his cabin inside the gates of Augusta National, which is pretty heavily protected by those Pinkerton dudes. So that part doesn't make sense either."

"But if he had been threatened by someone, especially someone he knew to be dangerous, then he might have wanted to know how to defend himself," I said.

"Exactly," Skipper said. "Then, they say his suicide note was rambling and didn't make a whole lot of sense. Again, the man was pretty tightly wound, and never wrote anything that wasn't pretty damn short and to the point. Even if you think he was sick and despondent and ready to kill himself, if you knew Cliff Roberts, you'd be looking for a short, neatly written little note. You know, 'Dear World: Bye for now. Don't forget the nitrogen mix for the 15th green.' What they found wasn't like him at'all."

"But did Roberts still have any connection with the South America business?" I asked. "When did Grosvenor take over?"

"Jones and Roberts sold their interests, as far as I know, sometime at the end of the 1960s," Skipper said. "But I figure Roberts probably kept a minority position for himself. He knew how much cash that little operation was bringing in every year. But even if he did sell out completely, he still knew all about it, and that made him dangerous. Especially as he was getting older and sicker. And if he did still own a piece, knowing Roberts, he was probably a total pain in the ass as a partner, telling Grosvenor what to do and how to do it. Not hard to imagine them getting fed up with him and deciding to do something about it. There's lotsa fellers down there who will shoot somebody for a few bucks."

"My God," I said aloud. If what Skipper Evans was telling me was true—and it all sounded legitimate—then not only had Augusta National financed itself for decades with drug money, but Clifford Roberts might have been eliminated by a killer operating on orders from the cartel. The same cartel that quite possibly had sent another assassin north. One who had killed John Judge. Enrico de la Paz. Who might have been the unseen shooter in the woods earlier this afternoon here at the Palmetto Club. My head was spinning.

"Yessir," Skipper said. "Been quite the day here at the old Palmetto."

I couldn't disagree.

Chapter Fifteen

I found Conn in the pro shop, chatting with several other golfers, and let him know that I was finally ready to go. We bid goodbye to Tom the pro and headed back to the parking lot.

"Thanks for the interesting day," I said.

He snorted. "Just trying to show you the best of the Augusta lifestyle," he said. "Believe it or not, it usually doesn't involve gunplay."

The sun had set and the dusk of twilight was settling in. Given all that had happened earlier, it seemed eerily quiet and peaceful. The last rays of the sun lit the tops of the loblolly pines, and the sky was half pink and half gray with the encroaching nightfall.

We got in the car and Conn turned it on.

"What do you feel like eating tonight?" Conn asked. "I think I owe you a nice dinner."

"I don't know, but I'm starved."

We both just about jumped out of our skin. The answer had come from a voice in the back seat. We turned as one to look.

The dark figure who had been sitting there leaned forward. He was holding out a leather case with a badge and some identification. It was much too dark in the car to read. Conn reached up and punched the overhead light switch and the car was flooded with light. The man reached up and switched it back off.

"Wilcox," he said. "I'm with the feds. Not to worry. Maybe you could give me a lift back to Augusta and Mr. Hacker and I can have a little conversation."

"Are you FBI?" Conn asked, using his deep, impressive lawyer voice.

The man in the back seat leaned back into the shadows and sighed.

"Good Lord no," he said. "Let's just say I'm with one of the alphabet agencies and leave at that, shall we?"

"Is this an official inquiry?" Conn continued.

"Counselor," the man said, "I'm hiding in your back seat. Of course this isn't an official inquiry. I don't have a warrant. If anyone asks, I'm not even here. I just want to talk a bit with Mr. Hacker here. Can we go?"

"This is highly unusual," Conn said. "I'm within my rights to ask you for more information of the nature of this visit, or ask you to leave."

"Yeah," the man said, "You could. But I wouldn't recommend it. As one of our former presidents liked to say, 'Wouldn't be prudent.' Especially for Mr. Hacker, here."

I put my hand on Conn's arm.

"Let's go," I said. "Hear what the man has to say."

Conn shrugged and put the car in gear and we headed out of the Palmetto Club.

"What did you say your name was?" Conn asked, glancing back in his rear view mirror.

"Warren," he said.

"I thought you said Wilcox," I said.

"Wilcox, Warren, Wilson...who gives a damn?" he said. "I think Enrico de la Paz knows you've been sniffing around and that could be dangerous."

"How do you know that?" I said, astounded.

We were passing through downtown Aiken, and the streetlights cast their dim orange glimmer into the car. I turned around to look at Wilcox, or Wilson or whoever. He looked to be in his mid-forties. He was dressed in black slacks and a dark-colored long-sleeved shirt. His hair was dark and closely trimmed. I couldn't see his eyes, lost in the shadows of his face. He grinned at me.

"Sonny boy," he said, "I've been following Senor Enrico around for about a year now. I know everything about the man right down to what kind of underwear he likes. Boxer briefs, by the way. I think he likes the extra feeling of support in the ..."

"Too much information!" Conn yelled.

Wilcox chuckled. "Anyway," he continued, "We've got him under close surveillance. And let's just say his world and yours appear to have collided. That's not a good thing."

"Did he kill the Judge kid?" I asked quietly.

"Is that what this is about?" Wilcox said, wonder in his voice. "What do you care about the Judge kid?"

"I promised his people I'd try to find out what happened to him," I said.

"He got shot," Wilcox said.

I turned, furious. "Don't you dare be flip about it," I said. "I don't know who you are or what branch of our imperial federal government you work for, but you have no right to be flip about that young man. There are people who loved him and want to know what happened to him."

There was silence from the back seat. "I apologize," Wilcox said, quietly. "It's pretty easy to get conditioned to death in my line of work. You're right, the Judge kid is just as important as anyone else."

"So who killed him?" I asked again. "De la Paz?"

"I don't know," he said.

"I thought you said you've been following him for a year," I said.

"Well, yeah," he said. "But not 24/7. There've been some budget cuts."

"You're doing a heck of a job, Brownie," I said, mostly under my breath.

"How's that?"

"Nothing," I said.

Conn spoke up.

"I believe my friend Hacker is expressing some sense of dismay that yet another institution of our fine federal government is—how shall I put this?" He was speaking in courtroom cadence now, "About as useful as a third leg. That about right, Hacker?"

I nodded.

"What about Maria?" I asked. "Is she in danger?"

"Naw," Wilcox said. "We've had people watching her."

I made a harrumph noise. "Hope they do a better job than they did with Rico," I said.

"Well, now that we know Enrico is, umm, in active mode, we've added some resources," he said.

"Was that Enrico's active mode taking pot shots at Kitchen from the woods this morning?" I asked next.

"Very likely," he said.

"Why?"

"I think Lt. Kitchen was getting a little too close," Wilcox said. "Like you, he seemed somewhat adamant to find out who killed the Judge kid. We tried to dissuade him, but he kept on. Stubborn fellow."

"I think he feels it is his job to discover who is killing people in his county and put them in jail," Conn said from the driver's seat.

"Laudable concept," Wilcox said. "But his investigation was beginning to overlap a bit on our operations, so we had to close him down."

"How'd you do that?" I wondered.

"Well, first we tried being nice, in a meeting with Kitchen and his boss. He told us to, I think the phrase was, 'take a flying fuck from the fantail.' Colorful language. So then we stopped asking and told him to halt the investigation. Or rather, had the sheriff order him. Confiscated his case records. So he up and quit."

"And probably wasn't going to stop investigating," I guessed.

"Probably not," Wilcox agreed. "Which is probably why Rico tried to take him out today."

"How did Rico know where he was?" I asked.

Wilcox chuckled again. "Rico is pretty resourceful," he said. "He is known as '***L'Aguila Negron***,' the Black Eagle. He flies alone. He flies under the radar. He's in and out before you even know he's there at all. They give him the most important missions and he plans and executes them alone. He believes working with other people is just an opportunity for someone to screw the pooch. He's fluent in several languages, he knows how to use disguises. He's one of the better ones I've come across."

"And now he's after me?" I asked.

"Well, I'm not sure about that," Wilcox said. "I think he knows that someone at Augusta National has asked someone to look into the Judge killing. Right now, I think he's laying low and waiting to see what happens next."

"And what is the connection between this international man of mystery and Augusta National?" I asked.

"Ah," Wilcox said. "That my friend is an excellent question. But I'm still hungry. What say the U.S. government takes you gentlemen out for a steak? We can talk about all this over a nice T-bone."

I looked at Conn and he looked at me. We both shrugged. Why not?

Chapter Sixteen

Conn pulled into the parking lot of a strip shopping center back in Augusta and parked outside one of those Australian steak joints you can now find on every franchise row. As usual, it was busy and people were lined up outside waiting to be summoned for the opportunity to drop a lot of money on some over-cooked meat.

Wilcox told us to wait and went inside. He came out in a minute or two and motioned for us to follow. The people waiting in line gave us looks of equal parts envy and hatred. We walked inside and followed the hostess to a table at the back of the restaurant. Wilcox insisted on taking the seat with his back to the wall, where he could see the entire restaurant, especially the front door.

"How'd you do that?" I asked. "This place doesn't take reservations. It's part of its so-called charm."

Wilcox winked at me. "I believe you called it the imperial federal government," he said. "Works good at getting tables in busy restaurants and other things like that."

"Too bad it's not so good at foreign wars and hurricane relief," I said.

"Not my department," Wilcox said.

The waiter came with menus and started to go into his faux-Aussie shtick, with the throw another shrimp on the barbie stuff. Wilcox cut him off and said we'd have three steaks, medium rare, baked potatoes with everything, and a pitcher of cold beer. "And make it snappy," he said. "We're hungry."

"Yessir," the kid said, almost clicking his heels together. He must have been in the military once. He turned smartly and left.

"So what is this operation you're running and how does Enrico and Augusta National fit into it?" I said.

"What?" Wilcox grinned at me, "No foreplay? Right to the main act? Hacker, you disappoint me. I thought you'd want to ***do-si-do*** around a little first."

"Normally, I would," I said. "But after watching someone get shot at today, I'd much rather find out what the hell is going on."

He chuckled. "I guess I understand," he said. "Everybody reacts differently under fire."

"I've been under fire before," I said. "I just want to know what's going on and how it might affect my life."

"Do you know what a Judas goat is?" Wilcox asked, buttering a roll casually.

"No," I said.

"Isn't that like a goat shepherds used to train to lead all the others into the slaughterhouse?" Conn piped up. He'd been strangely silent since Wilcox invaded his car.

"Very good, counselor," Wilcox said, nodding in approval.

"By the way, how do you know I am a lawyer?" Conn asked.

Wilcox just looked at him across the table, expressionless.

"Oh," Conn said. "That's right, you're working for an alphabet agency."

Wilcox smiled at him as one would a child who suddenly grasped some obvious concept after a long struggle.

"These days, we think of a Judas goat as more of a decoy," he said. "We put one out there and see who shoots at it. Tells us a lot about the shooters, like who they are and where they are coming from. Useful in our line of work."

"And the relevance of this ...?" I let the question trail off.

"You're the decoy," Wilcox said to me.

"How's that?" I wasn't sure what he meant, but I was pretty certain I didn't like the part about being shot at.

"You've been asked to come down here and kick around a little, right? See what you could find out about the Judge kid?"

I was sure I didn't like the fact that Wilcox and his alphabet friends seemed to know everything about my life. But I let him continue.

"I think they already know everything about what happened to the Judge kid," he said. "They wanted to see what was coming next. So they trotted you out there to see who might come after you. Then they'd know exactly who was behind it and what to do about it. Cynical, perhaps, but effective."

The waiter came with our steaks, which gave me a chance to sit there and think. While the food looked and smelled divine, I was suddenly without appetite. The implications of what Wilcox had just said were blasting through my head.

Wilcox was practically rubbing his hands together in glee as the food was laid out in front of him. He poured out three glasses of beer, snapped his napkin onto his lap and picked up his knife and fork.

"Yum," he said.

Conn was looking at me strangely.

"Hacker?" he asked. "Are you OK? You've gone as white as a sheet.

I waved my hand weakly.

"You'd better start at the beginning," I said to Wilcox.

He nodded, mouth full, chewing furiously. "Eat," he mumbled. "Don't let it get cold."

I tried. It tasted like cardboard. I ate a few bites and mostly pushed my food around the plate while Wilcox and Conn shoveled it in like it was the Last Supper. Perhaps that's not the best analogy, but it's the one that came to mind as I watched them eat. I felt an itchy spot in my back, right between my shoulder blades, and kept looking back over my shoulder at the people in the restaurant, who were going about their business of dining and not paying me any attention. Wilcox must have seen me do this four or five times before he spoke up.

"Don't worry, Mr. Hacker," he said. "If Rico comes through that door with guns a-blazing, I'll yell for you to duck."

He must have thought that was pretty funny, because he started laughing uproariously. It took every ounce of willpower I had not to dump the remaining beer in our pitcher over his head. Conn smiled wanly, but looked like he'd like to bury his steak knife up to the hilt in the guy's chest. We waited until he calmed down.

Eventually, the waiter came back and cleared the table. Wilcox ordered coffee all around, and when it arrived, he sat back and heaved a satisfied sigh.

"Damn that was good," he said. "You can't get a good dinner like that in the jungles of Colombia. Though if you can marinate one of those agoutis in tequila overnight, they're not half bad roasted on a stick."

"I don't know what an agouti is," Conn said, "And I don't think I want to."

"Right, then," I said, "Let's get back to the present problem. Tell me what the hell is going on."

Wilcox held up a hand.

"I can't tell you everything I know, because some of it involves either national security or an ongoing operation," he said. "But we've had our friend Rico under surveillance for quite a while. He's a busy man."

"Who does he work for?" I asked.

"One of the major Colombian cartels," Wilcox said. "But that too doesn't really mean anything. The cartels themselves are not exactly independent organizations. There are alliances and relationships that extend in and out of Colombia like you wouldn't believe. For instance, we know Rico's group has some interesting connections with the government of Venezuela. That means they also have connections with Cuba, Nicaragua and probably Russia. Maybe Iran, but we haven't proved that yet."

"What kind of relationships are we talking about?" Conn asked.

"Basically, it boils down to safe haven to produce, store and transport narcotics in return for cash," Wilcox said. "We've managed over the years to put a pretty good dent in the traffic between Colombia and both the United States and Europe. So the cartels have been trying to pull an end-around. They move their stuff across the border into Venezuela, or Brazil, or Ecuador and then ship it from there. Or they take it over to Cuba where they can ship it easily into Spain and on to East Europe and Russia. If you've been paying any attention to the news, you know that Venezuela is not exactly a friendly anymore. And Cuba...well, Cuba has always been a problem. With the political situation the way it is these days, once they get the goods into either of those countries, we can't do much about it."

"Things haven't been going well with U.S.-Venezuelan relations, have they?" Conn said.

Wilcox shrugged. "We've got some people working on that problem," he said. "But for now, it's 'Yankee Go Home.'"

"But what has any of this to do with Augusta National?" I asked. "And why is Enrico up here shooting at people?"

"Ah," he said, "That gets a little trickier. And it involves some ancient history. Like back to the beginning of the last century. There was a little old company over in Atlanta just getting started up, called the Coca-Cola Company ..."

"I know, they imported cocaine from Colombia to put in their drink," I said. "I've heard that story."

"Well, it's more accurate to say that they imported the coca leaf," Wilcox said. "They used some kind of extract in the formula, not the street drug we know today. But they bought lots of the stuff, and created a pipeline to get it up here. And a company down there to buy from the farmers and prepare it for shipment to the states. Time goes by, the government makes the stuff illegal in 1914, so Coca-Cola has to find another secret ingredient to put in their syrup. Which they do. But that company down in Bogata is still there, and it still has an excellent transportation and logistics network into the states. On the surface, it's now a Coke bottling and distribution plant."

"But they kept shipping coca north," I said.

"Yeah," Wilcox said. "Frankly, no one paid much attention back then. We weren't really fighting a drug war, especially after they passed Prohibition. The feds were chasing bootleggers of booze and busting up speakeasies. So that little company in Colombia just kept loading and sending the stuff up. Nice little piece of business."

"You still haven't explained the Augusta connection," I pointed out.

"Getting to that," he said, sipping his coffee. "Okay, so now we get to the Nineteen Thirties. They repealed Prohibition in '33, probably because with the Depression and everything, they figured most Americans needed a stiff drink every now and then just to get by. Once that happened, the feds needed a new target, and drugs were at the top of the list.

"One day, some of Hoover's G-Men pay a little call on the head of Coca-Cola over in Atlanta and start asking him some questions about his little Colombian company. He sees the handwriting on the wall, and decides to offload what could become a problem for a squeaky clean, all-American franchise like Coke. And who do you think he sells it to?"

"Clifford Roberts and Bob Jones," I said. "The RoJo Company."

For once, Wilcox doesn't have a smart rejoinder. He looked at me with an amazed expression.

"How the hell did you know that?" he asked.

"I'm a trained reporter," I said. "Don't try this at home."

He nodded. "Very good," he said. "Now I know why Rico might be getting antsy about you. But you are correct. Roberts and Jones—it was mostly Roberts—took over the Colombian company and helped expand its bottling and distribution network throughout South America. In addition to Coca-Cola, RoJo started importing coffee beans to the U.S. They did quite well and made a lot of money."

"And the drugs?" I asked. "Did they shut that part down?"

"Officially, yes," Wilcox said. "I've seen the FBI files from those times, in which agents went down, inspected the plants, were shown the bottling operations, looked at the company records. The agents came back and wrote up a report giving RoJo a clean bill of health. Everything was hunky-dory."

"But it wasn't?" Conn asked.

"Of course not," Wilcox said. "That guy Clifford Roberts never passed up a chance to make a buck or three. He was a financial guy who knew his way around a balance sheet. He just moved the illegal part of the operation off the official books, and let the good times continue to roll. Coffee beans are a good way to get the stuff past the customs agents and their dogs. And with the political connections the guy had into the White House, he made sure he was told anytime there was going to be a crackdown at the border."

"And then he sold the company to the Grosvenor Group," I said. "Which is now run by the current chairman of Augusta National."

"You got it," Wilcox said, sitting back with a smile. "Small world, huh?"

"So you're saying that the drug-running component of RoJo is still operating today, under the aegis of Grosvenor?" Conn said. "And Charlie Grosvenor knows this?"

"Knows it? Hell, it probably makes more money than his tin, iron, gold and banana operations combined," Wilcox chuckled. "Oh, and the Coca-Cola plant, too."

"And you narcs haven't broken this thing up?" Conn said. "How come?"

"Not my department," Wilcox said again. "And as you might expect, some of these guys have connections. Roberts was Eisenhower's main man. That helped him. But he saw that if he got caught with his hand in the cookie jar, it might not help Ike. That's when he sold the company to Grosvenor's old man. Who later became the U.S. Senator from Pennsylvania and chairman of the Commerce Committee."

"And how does this Rico guy fit into the picture?" I asked.

Wilcox shrugged. "It's a dirty business," he said. "There is no honor among thieves as they say. Best we can figure, something went wrong, somebody cheated somebody, and Rico was sent up here to straighten things out."

"By shooting John Judge and trying to kill Travis Kitchen?" I asked.

"We figure the Judge killing was a way to warn Grosvenor that he'd better fix the problem or else," Wilcox said. "Today's thing? I figure Rico was shooting in self-defense. That Kitchen guy seems like a bulldog who wouldn't scare off easily."

"And so Augusta National brought me in me to ...?" I let the question hang.

"To muddle around a bit and see if Rico was still in town," Wilcox said. "And maybe to see if any of this story I just told might come out. So they could take steps to prevent that from happening. They got a lot of resources over at that club."

"You mean if Rico de la Paz doesn't kill me, then Charlie Grosvenor will?" I felt myself getting angry.

"Oh, I wouldn't worry about Charlie," Wilcox said. "He's connected and he's dirty as hell, in this deal and about seven others I know about. But he's not a violent person. More of a wuss. He prefers throwing money at problems to make them go away."

"Allright, Hacker," Conn piped up. "Sounds like your ship has just come in. With what you already know, I'll bet you can hold ole Charlie up for a few hundred thousand to shut up and go away."

Wilcox was nodding. "At the very least," he said.

I just looked at the two of them, amazed, and tried to figure out if they were serious.

"So you guys think I should waltz into Grosvenor's office and just ask for moolah?" I said.

"Why not?" Wilcox said. "He's got more than he'll ever spend."

"It would be tax-free," said Conn. "Don't think you can deduct graft and corruption. At least not yet. But if you get it in cash, no one will be the wiser. Unless Wilbert here decides to tell on you."

"Not my department," Wilcox said.

"And what about John Judge?" I asked. "After I get paid off and retire to the French Riviera or St. Andrews, whichever one I decide on, I'm just supposed to forget all about him? Who killed him and why?"

"If you don't, it'll probably be you stretched out in the morgue next," Wilcox said.

"I'm sorry," I said. "That's not a good enough reason."

He shrugged. "Your life," he said.

There was a buzzing sound. Wilcox produced a small cell phone, which he flipped open and held up to his ear. "Yo," he said. Then, "Right. OK. I'm ready."

He hung up. "Gotta go, fellas," he said, rising from the table. "Duty calls." He reached into his pocket and gave both us a business card. The only thing printed on it was a phone number. "Whoever answers this number can find me. Call me if Rico shows up or if you need me. If you can still dial the phone, of course. Ha-ha."

We followed him outside and watched as a black SUV with tinted windows pulled up in front of the restaurant, a long, whippy radio antenna draping back over the roof. Wilcox opened the door, gave us a final wave, and the car swallowed him and drove off. Conn and I walked back over to his car, parked in the side lot. We both peered into his back seat before getting in. We'd had enough surprises for one day.

"Well, that was interesting," Conn said as we drove away. "What are you gonna do next?"

"Beats the hell outta me," I said.

"Good plan," he said.

Chapter Seventeen

There was nobody behind the counter at the Olde Magnolia. I wanted to confirm my check-out date, when I would move over to the barren motel on Washington Road that is my home for the tournament week. The thought alone was depressing. I made a mental note to ask in the morning, and wearily climbed the stairs to my room. It had been a very long day.

I unlocked my room and walked in. Before I could flick on the light, my heart jumped up into my throat. ***There was somebody in my room.*** It was a presence, a sense. There was someone else in here. Fully expecting to come face-to-face with a pistol-toting bandillero from Colombia, I reached over in the darkness and pushed the light switch up.

The room was flooded with light from the overhead fixture.

"Umph," said a small, female voice from the bed. The comforter had been pulled back, the large decorative throw pillows were gone, and an S-shaped body curled under the blankets and sheets. The body shifted, then suddenly sat up.

"Hi, Hacker," said a sleep-tousled Mary Jane Cappaletti. "Surprise!"

She was wearing loose-fitting pajama bottoms and a T-shirt and her golden-brown hair was all mussed. She held out her arms and I stepped over to the bed and pulled her in close, sinking into her humid sleepy warmth. For several long moments, we stayed like that, unspeaking, letting the presence of the other seep into our pores, re-establishing the connection. After the day I'd had, I wanted to crawl in beside her, pull the sheets over my head and drink in her warmth and her love and her life force forever.

I really don't know how long we stayed there on the bed, wrapped in our embrace. Mary Jane might have fallen back asleep. Perhaps I did, too. But eventually, I moved, and then she moved and then we sat up and looked at each other.

"What the hell are you doing here?" I asked. But gently.

"Good to see you, too," she said, yawning. But she was smiling. "After we last talked, I called Victoria's grandfather and asked if he could take care of her for a while."

"That'd be the gangster who runs the North End," I said.

"I think she's safe with him, don't you think?" Mary Jane's blue eyes twinkled at me. Her former father-in-law—one of the main capos in the Boston area—doted on his only grandchild, spoiling her rotten, and we'd both imagined what might happen if something, anything, remotely dangerous threatened to break out around Victoria while the old man had her in his care.

"She'll end up eating pasta three times a day and turn into her grandmother," I said, smiling back.

"I told him you had run into some problems down here in Augusta and that I needed to come make sure you were OK," she continued. "He's sorta used to you getting into scrapes, so he understood."

Mary Jane's in-laws maintained close family ties even though their son-- Mary Jane's late husband--had been a ne'er-do-well wiseguy who ended up getting all shot up in the stairwell of a housing project over in Charlestown some years before. I think Carmine, the old man, knew his son had been a major loser, but his sense of ***famiglia*** dictated that he keep an eye out for Mary Jane and Victoria.

"Scrapes?" I said in mock indignation. "Who said anything about scrapes?"

"I heard on the radio driving over from Atlanta this afternoon that the former homicide detective for the county had been shot at by a sniper at a golf course in South Carolina," Mary Jane told me. "If you weren't somehow involved in that, I'll eat my pillow."

I didn't say anything, so she reached behind her, grabbed a pillow and began chomping on the corner. I reached out and pulled it away.

"Thought so," she said. "That's why I came. My man needs me. Someone's gotta watch your back."

I laughed. "You're gonna get my back if some crazed Colombian drug lord comes at me, six-guns blazing?"

She looked at me, her blue eyes serious and wide. I fell into those eyes and stopped laughing. It was suddenly serious. Very serious.

"Yes," she said, simply. "I am."

She meant it. She reached out and grabbed my hand. I reached back and grabbed her. We kissed. I stood up and went over to the wall and flicked the switch off. The room fell back into inky blackness. I went back to the bed and reached for her.

Somehow, miraculously, noiselessly, her pajamas had disappeared. Somehow, miraculously, my clothes fell onto the floor. And then we were very, very busy in the dark for a very, very long time.

Chapter Eighteen

We were both ravenous the next morning at breakfast. Before we stopped, we had loaded up on omelets, waffles, grits, home fries, bacon, ham with red-eye gravy, toast, and an ocean of coffee. Give her credit, our waitress said nothing, but kept bringing us food and refilling our coffee pot. I suspect she knew what had made us so hungry overnight, but had the class not to say anything about it.

Once we had satisfied our hunger, at least the food kind, we took our third or fourth cups of coffee into the sitting room, found a quiet corner in the sun, and sat. I filled Mary Jane in on the happenings of the last few days since we had talked. Instead of interrupting with questions and comments and asides, she sat there quietly and let me talk until I was finished.

"So what's next?" she asked when I finished. "Go over to the club and confront Grosvenor? Tell him we know he's a drug-running bastard? Or wander around town and wait for this Enrico guy to step out from behind a tree and pick us off?"

"Me," I said.

"Beg pardon?"

"I think it's me he'd pick off. You, he'd probably ask out for a drink. You are looking especially fine this morning."

"Afterglow and a good breakfast," she said, "And don't change the subject. What are we going to do next?"

"We?"

"Get used to it," she said.

"I'm not so sure what to do," I confessed. "I have to report something to Brett Jacoby over at The National. I have no idea what to tell him. I thought I might go see Travis Kitchen, assuming he's still in the hospital. Maybe compare notes. I also have to get ready to move over to the Motel 6 and prepare some Masters preview pieces for the Sunday paper. I'm still a golf writer, y'know."

"So what do we do first?" she asked, eyes bright with excitement.

"Drink some more coffee and maybe go back upstairs for a morning round of whoopee?" I suggested hopefully.

"Down, big fella," she said. "We've got work to do. Play is for later."

"If that's a promise, OK," I said.

Mary Jane went off to call back to Boston and check in with Victoria and her grandpa. As she left the room, Beatrice Samper, the Colombian golf official I had met the other night, walked into the sitting room, saw me and came over.

"Buenas dias," she said. "It seems to be a lovely morning."

I motioned for her to pull up a chair. "Indeed it is," I said. She told me that the group of international golf officials had been busy sightseeing and being wined and dined. While she was talking, Mary Jane came back, grinning.

"This is my inamorata, Mary Jane," I said. The two women greeted each other. I poured Beatrice a cup of coffee. "Senora

Samper is the director of the Colombian Golf Federation," I told Mary Jane.

"Are there many golf clubs in your country?" Mary Jane asked.

"Not so much," Beatrice said. "At the moment, it is mainly the wealthy and the businessmen who are playing. But we have a plan to build more courses and to encourage the children to play. In that way lies the future. We are very lucky to have Senor Grosvenor helping us fulfill our goals."

"He's donating money?" I asked.

"Oh, much more than that," she said. "He is very involved with our project. He has arranged for the golf companies in the USA to send equipment—the clubs, the balls, the shoes... everything! And now he is helping to find people to build some new courses for us. He is a very kind man. We could not hope to succeed without him."

Mary Jane and I exchanged glances.

"Well," I said, "That sounds like a good story. I will have to ask him to tell me all about it."

"Yes!" she said excitedly. "I'm sure that would help us very much! That would be so kind of you!"

I smiled and decided not to tell her that the chairman of Augusta National would probably choose to run naked down the 18th fairway on Masters Sunday rather than talk to someone like me from the media, even if it was for a good cause. I also wondered why Charlie Grosvenor was suddenly involved in helping youth golf in Colombia when there were all kinds of programs—like the First Tee—right here in the United States that needed help too.

"What are you doing today, Beatrice?" Mary Jane asked.

She glanced at her watch. "They have arranged a bus to come take some of us to a mall that sells ... how do you say ... out-takes ...?"

"An outlet mall?" Mary Jane said, her voice rising in excitement. "Hubba hubba ding-ding!"

"Would you like to come along?" Beatrice asked, smiling.

"You bet I would!" Mary Jane said. "Would it be OK?"

"I am sure there is no trouble with one more," Beatrice said. "You would be very welcome. We may be there for several hours."

"Is that all?" Mary Jane's color was up. "Hacker, you're on your own. I'll catch ya later. Gotta go put on some comfortable shoes and get my bag. Taa-taa!"

She bolted out. Beatrice and I watched her go, then looked at each other and laughed.

"Your woman friend enjoys shopping?" she asked, a sly look on her face.

"Apparently more than life itself," I said.

She tittered. "I believe I can understand," she said rising.

"Yes, I believe you can," I said. "Have a wonderful time."

In truth, I hadn't known that Mary Jane was a shopaholic. I'd never seen her get so worked up over a trip to the mall before. But then, in the short times I was actually home in Boston, we had other things to do together. More important things. I was a bit surprised, but chalked it up to yet another learning experience in our relationship.

Now I had the day free to do what I wanted. But I had no idea what. First, I found someone in the office of the Olde Magnolia and learned that my check-out was Sunday morning. OK, good. Then I got the number of the local hospital and called to check on Travis Kitchen. He was reported to be resting comfortably and would likely be kept for a few more days. Check. Be good to go over and chat with him some.

I knew I should call Brett Jacoby at the National to report, but I had to give some thought to what I wanted to say to him. I finally decided that I really hadn't found out anything more about the Judge affair that I could write up for the paper, so I could honestly report that I was still in the process of digging around.

I placed the call and was patched through to his office.

"Hacker!" he said when he came on the line. "Are you OK?"

"Why do you ask?" I said.

"I heard you were over at the Palmetto Club yesterday when that sniper started shooting the place up," he said. "What a world, huh?"

"Yeah," I said. "A small one."

"What do you mean?" It was his turn to be curious.

"There's a chance that the shooter yesterday might be the same one who killed John Judge," I said. "The, ummm, cops are looking into it."

"Really?" Jacoby said, amazement in his voice. "You mean it might be some serial killer with a thing against golf courses?"

"Something like that," I said. "I'm supposed to meet some people later today and hopefully get a few more facts. I'll call you tomorrow. You gonna be in the office?"

"Are you kidding?" he said wearily. "I'll probably be here until Thursday morning, when I might be able to go home for a few hours' sleep."

"That's why you make the big bucks," I said.

"Bite me," he said and hung up.

I only felt slightly guilty about dancing around the truth a bit with Brett. Then I thought about the fact that he had known where I was and what I was doing the day before. I recalled Conn's observation that everything that happens in Augusta goes through, back to or somehow involves Augusta National. Made me wonder why Brett hadn't commented on Mary Jane's arrival. It seems likely that someone at the Olde Magnolia had placed a call over to Washington Road about that. In any case, from what I had learned yesterday, the fine folks over at the

National apparently already knew the answers to the questions they had sent me out to discover. I was the decoy, intended to lead the bad guy out of the shadows. For whose benefit? And what if the bad guy decided to stay in the shadows and use the same high-powered rifle he fired from the woods yesterday at Travis Kitchen? In that case, I would very likely be toast.

The shopping bus was getting ready to leave and the lobby was bustling with excited women, and a few men, from several lands. I went out to watch the fun, careful not to get between the shopping-aroused women and the door. I didn't see Mary Jane until I went outside and saw her already in the bus, seated next to Beatrice Samper. They waved and smiled as the bus pulled away.

Back in the lobby of the Olde Magnolia, I came face to face with Hans Kleiber, the Swiss Golf Federation director I had met the other night. His face lit up when he saw me.

"Herr Hacker!" he exclaimed. "Guten morgen. Are you off to play some golf this fine morning?"

"No," I told him. "I have the morning free."

"Well, then," he said. "Why not accompany me? I am off to the local air field to meet another official from Europe who is flying in from New York. My good friend Christian Geer from Belgium is arriving within the hour. You would enjoy meeting him—he is quite knowledgeable about the history of golf in Europe."

I thought for a minute. I needed some quick filler pieces for the Masters preview section. Something on the European game as a way of previewing the European players competing this year might just work.

"That is very kind of you," I said. "I'd love to meet him."

"Excellent!" Hans said, pumping my hand. "If you are ready, I am just now going."

We got into his rental car and headed out toward Washington Road. From there, Daniel Field, one of the general aviation airports in the Augusta area, was just ten minutes. During the week of the Masters, Augusta becomes one of the busiest private aircraft destinations in the world. Not only do most of the top stars in the game own or charter their own private jets, but the high-powered contingent of "patrons" tends to eschew the usual commercial flights into Atlanta—a two-plus hour drive west on I-20—or the piddling service provided by puddle-jumping commercial jets into Augusta's Bush Field. Instead, every CEO, chairman of the board, network bigwig and a significant number of other out-of-town ticket-holders arrive on their Gulfstreams and Lears. The FAA assigns special air traffic controllers to the four fields in the vicinity of Augusta during the week, and landing and take-off slots as well as parking space on the tarmacs is almost as hard to obtain as a badge of entry into the hallowed gates of Augusta.

The players flying in—Tiger, Phil, Vijay and the rest of the big boys—get first dibs on the good spots. Everyone else fights for room, or adopts plan B, heading for Macon or Savannah or Columbia and driving into town.

As we pulled into the Daniel Field entrance, I could see things were already getting busy, even though the heavy traffic wouldn't begin until Sunday night or Monday morning. Because the one-story, nondescript cinderblock terminal was woefully inadequate for the arriving hordes, the city had begun setting up bright white tents on both sides of the terminal building. We parked and walked inside one of these tents and found the beginnings of a lavish hospitality area, with Astroturf floor, bright colored pennants, comfortable lounge chairs, a fully stocked bar and a long buffet food line with tables and chairs beyond. Delivery men were bringing in more stuff, and people were bustling around making preparations for the rush to come.

Hans wandered off to find out when his friend was arriving. I found myself a cup of coffee and wandered around watching all the activity. It always amazes me to watch people acting like mindless bees setting up for some big event. I wonder: What are they going to be doing next week? Or the week after? Is there a group of migrant event-workers, like fruit-pickers, that goes around the country setting up hospitality tents and laying out carpet and stocking the bars and marshalling the fleet of rental cars? Or are these all locals, who in the next weeks will be catering weddings, setting up tents for family reunions or handling some corporate grand opening? It all seems so temporary to me. Unlike, of course, producing a thousand words on the world of golf in the daily newspaper that later that day will be laid in the bottoms of bird cages all over New England. Hacker's deathless prose. At least it's absorbent.

As I was sitting there doing nothing, which is actually what I do best, I was startled to see Arnold Palmer strolling by, a big leather satchel tossed casually over his shoulder. I stood up and caught his eye and he came over to shake my hand.

"Hacker," he said, his huge mitts swallowing mine. "What are you doing here?"

"Oh, not much," I said. "I heard something about a golf tournament and thought I might come down and see if it was true."

"Wisenheimer," he said. But he was smiling. A couple of cute kids in the six-to-ten age bracket came running up and claimed their grandfather, grabbing a Palmer part for a hug. His tanned face creased with smiles. He looked over at me and winked. "Only thing I like better than playing golf," he said. "Spending time with these little monkeys."

"Well get to it," I said. "I'll catch up with you later in the week." Arnie would be around. He'll probably keep coming to the Masters as long as he can draw breath. And once he goes, don't be surprised if the dogwoods and the azaleas all die.

Arnie and family headed off to the parking lot. The rest of us in the tent all heard a high-pitched whine. It got louder and louder until everyone in the tent was sticking fingers in their ears for self-defense. It sounded like a fleet of 747s was pulling up outside. I ducked out the end of the tent and peered through the chain-link fence at the tarmac.

It wasn't a jumbo jet, but it was a large bastard. I'm not a plane freak, so I don't know whether it was a Gulfstream or a Falcon or a Hawker or a Lear. But it was big, white, shiny and loud as it pulled in close to the cinderblock terminal. The signalman guiding the beast into place gave it the crossed-X sign and the pilot finally cut the engines, which took several seconds to wind down so we could hear again. The bees inside the tent began buzzing again.

I continued to watch as the front door popped open on the jet and slowly unfolded from the top all the way down to the ground, with a set of steps magically popping up. One of the pilots, wearing a gold-encrusted cap and a white shirt with epaulets, and a young woman dressed in a slinky white dress, came down the steps blinking in the bright morning light and hurried into the terminal. Almost at once, a long stretch limousine pulled up to the plane. A man with slick hair, wearing dark glasses and a black sportcoat over a black turtleneck, stuck his head out of the plane's door and gave a nod. The driver of the limo, also all dressed in black, jumped out of the driver's seat, ran around the limo and opened the side door facing the plane. Then he stood at attention.

The guy with slick hair ducked back inside the plane after looking carefully up and down the tarmac. Within seconds, an older man with sharp, angular features and a mane of heavy white hair combed straight back so the ends danced in the wind at his collar, stepped out into the sunlight. He was wearing tan linen pants and an off-white guayabera, two-toned shoes and held a narrow black cane in his left hand. He eased himself down the steps of the plane, shadowed by the guy with the slick-backed hair, and folded himself carefully into the limo. The driver closed the door, ran around and got into the driver's seat, while Slick got into the front passenger seat. The limo pulled off past the far side of the terminal and I lost sight of it.

The pilot and the girl in white came back out of the terminal, in deep conversation with a pudgy uniformed person carrying a clipboard and waving his hands. The pilot stood at the steps and finished whatever he was saying to the pudgy guy while the girl reboarded the plane. The two men shook hands, the pilot got onto the plane, the steps folded back up and, with the high-pitched whine beginning to build again, taxied away.

I noted the numbers on the engine cowling: N8805C. Be interesting to find out who owned the ride.

I strolled into the terminal to find Hans, who had found his friend and was helping him collect his bags. He saw me and motioned me over.

"Herr Hacker, this is my very good friend Christian Geer. He is from Bruges, which is perhaps the loveliest village in all of Europe."

I shook the man's hand. He was short and stout, with thinning hair swept back across his head. His demeanor was reserved and he looked at me carefully with small black eyes.

"How was your flight?" I asked. "It's a long trip from Belgium."

"We actually arrived yesterday in New York," he said, his voice clipped and accented with French. "There are no customs officials here in Augusta, so we must arrive at a larger city first. Herr Kleiber tells me you are an American journalist, no?"

Geer looked like he'd just bit into something sour and distasteful when he said the words "American journalist." My uh-oh antenna went up.

"No," I said. "I'm an American golf writer. I'm not sure I'm qualified to call myself a 'journalist.'"

I was trying to inject some levity, but Geer continued to peer at me.

"I do not think I understand," he said.

Hans rescued me. "Come, come," he said, picking up Geer's bag. "Let us go." He shooed us ahead of him outside and into the parking lot.

"Yes," Geer said, glancing at his watch. "I have an appointment at two o'clock this afternoon with Chairman Grosvenor. I must not be tardy."

"Plenty of time, plenty of time," Hans said, as he packed the bag into the car's trunk and unlocked the doors. "We can perhaps stop for some lunch? I have fallen in love with the barbecue here. I have had this sandwich for three days in a row!"

As we drove away I turned to Geer in the back seat.

"So, what are you meeting with Grosvenor about?" I asked.

He fixed me with a steady gaze. "I am sure that the Chairman would not want me to disclose anything about our private meeting to the press," he said, ice dripping from the words. My uh-oh meter began to spark and smoke.

Hans, driving, felt the cold blast on the back of his neck. He waved his hand in the air.

"Oh, Herr Grosvenor likes to spend a few minutes with each of us from abroad," he said. "We talk about various issues in the game today. We share our opinions. It is good to learn what others think, especially over here in America."

"Building international goodwill and all that?" I said.

"Exactly," Hans nodded approvingly. "It is good of him to give us his time."

I heard Geer harrumph in the back seat.

"Well, I do not have time for such frivolities," he said. "Hans, would you mind taking me directly to the club? I have important matters to discuss with the Chairman, and it really can't wait."

Hans looked back in his rearview mirror with some concern.

"Is everything all right, Christian?" he said, concern in his voice.

"No," the man said, "It is not."

Nothing more was said. It was not a long way back to Washington Road. We pulled in, Hans negotiated his way past the Pinkerton gauntlet, and pulled up at the memorial turnaround.

"Please take my things back to the inn," Geer said. "I will get a ride back later from someone here."

"Of course, Christian," Hans said. "Is there anything else I can do?"

"No," he said. He turned on his heel and strode determinedly into the clubhouse.

Hans got back into the car and looked at me.

"Christian is quite a serious man," he said, "He is, after all, a leading banker in Belgium. In all of Europe, in fact. But he is not usually quite so intense. I hope there is nothing wrong."

There was nothing I could say, so I said it.

Chapter Nineteen

There was a message waiting for me from Conn Thackerey when we returned from our barbecue lunch at a place called Sonny's Big Boy. Hans had been ecstatic, but I found it a rather middle-of-the-road pulled pork and slaw kind of place. Good, but not in Hacker's Top Ten BBQ Joints, where the leader in the clubhouse remained a place between Dallas and Ft. Worth, the name of which I will never divulge because as soon as it becomes famous, it drops off my list. Selfish? You'd better believe it.

"Hack Man!" he said when I got him on the phone. "I've heard your lady friend is in town."

"How did you happen to hear that?" I asked.

"Hacker," he said chidingly. "Didn't I tell you that there are no secrets in this town? That everything that happens, especially anything involving the National, becomes instantly known by all?"

"I believe it," I grumbled. "Yeah, Mary Jane showed up last night."

"I have to meet this poor woman," he said. "Warn her to run, flee, escape with her life!"

"I've already told her that," I said.

"Well, I will try again," he said. "Meet me tonight at the Commerce Club around seven. We'll do cocktails and then see what Chef Bubba has whipped up."

"You've got a Commerce Club with a Chef Bubba?" I said. "That should be interesting."

"Ah, Hacker," he said. "Don't let stereotypes deceive you! I think you'll enjoy it."

"Where is the Commerce Club?" I asked.

"You know the tallest building in town?" he asked.

"That big white bank building that's always lit up at night?"

"That's the one," he said. "Eighteenth floor. I think they made the building that high to match the number of holes in a golf course. How sick is that? See you there at seven. Tell the lovely lady to dress for a business club dinner. Coat and tie for you, bub."

He rang off. I looked at my watch. Two o'clock. The shopping bus wasn't back yet. It was time to do some work, so I went upstairs, unpacked my laptop, blew the dust off it and began belting out pithy, penetrating and pungent prose previewing the coming Masters for the golf fans of New England.

Of all the majors I write about, Augusta is always the toughest. It's been played on the same course since 1935, even though that course has changed in character several times over the years. Most golf fans have watched the thing on television year after year, and know the course as well as their own. Every year, in the guise of reporting on the "tradition" of the Masters, we have to come up with the same hallowed and hoary facts about the place. Fruitlands Nursey, Amen Corner, Bobby Jones, Alistair Mackenzie, flopping nines, underground heating and air conditioning systems for the greens, ticket scalpers getting arrested, par-three winner never winning the big tournament, Gene Sarazen's 5-wood, Nicklaus in '86, Hogan's last round, Billy Jo Patton, Eisenhower's tree, Butler Cabin, and on and on and on.

Of course, I have to throw it all in there. My readers lap it up like starved kittens. I guess part of the tradition of the Masters is hearing the same old crap over and over, year after year, and believing that this somehow translates into something important we should all hold dear. Step away and look at it with fully open eyes, and you realize that it's just another golf tournament on a heavily tricked-up golf course that no one in his or her right mind would play more than once without significant financial incentive. All the beautiful azaleas and dogwoods and incredibly plush turfgrass in the world can't disguise the fact that Augusta National is a golf course that obscenely overemphasizes the importance of the short game. A well-balanced golf course will demand accurate driving, strategic and risk-reward iron shots, and a deft short game and a steady putting hand. If you can bust it long—and most of today's pros can—then many of Augusta's greens are approachable with short irons. When they had no rough to speak of, there was absolutely no penalty for trying to bash every drive as far as you could. And even in the last few years, with the addition of so-called "rough" that most nearly resembles everyone else's fairways after the mowers have been kept in the garage for a couple of days, the penalties for missing a fairway are minimal. So the tournament basically comes down to a putting contest on greens stretched to the outer limits of common sense. That's interesting, sure, but it's not really a complete test of golf.

The pros all gush about how much they treasure the place and what a fantastic tournament it is, but get them aside one-on-one in private with enough Guinness Stout in them to loosen their well-coached tongues, and to a man they'd admit that the golf course is ridiculous and the geezers that run the place are a bunch of humorless old farts.

But I kept all that in the back of my head while my fingers tapped out this year's preview stories, predictions, rundowns on the current crop of players who seemed to be on form, and whether any of them had a chance to defeat Tiger. They know, I know and Tiger knows none of them really do unless for some reason his game develops a spasm of some kind. But the truth is, if Tiger plays within 40 percent of his capabilities, he should win. There is no one else.

I was just finishing up the last piece, late in the afternoon, when I heard people clumping up the stairs. The door burst open and Mary Jane staggered in, under the weight of five or six shopping bags. She tossed them on the bed, looking at them with an expression of sheer satisfied joy.

"I gotta pee," she said, rushing off. "But wait until you see what I got!"

I thought about making a run for it, but figured I'd have to sit there and make expressions of amazement and wonder at her purchases some time, so I might as well stay and get it over with.

I ooh'ed and ahh'ed as she unpacked her purchases, most of which were admittedly cute things for the six-year-old Victoria. After the half-hour presentation, the bed and most of the floor were covered in tissue paper, shopping bags and assorted tops, skirts, sweaters and socks. It looked like the Christmas tornado had hit.

Mary Jane flopped herself down on the bed, crushing several of her new outfits.

"Wooo," she said. "I'm beat. What a day!"

"Don't get too comfortable," I said. "We have a dinner engagement."

I told her about meeting Conn for drinks at the Commerce Club. She glanced at the alarm clock next to the bed and heaved herself up.

"Gotta wash my hair," she said. "You don't need the bathroom for anything for a while, do you?"

"I'm good," I said. "Have at it."

She disappeared and I heard the shower power up. I went back to that last story and finished the last couple of graphs. Mary Jane stuck her head back out of the bathroom.

"Oh, by the way," she said. "I got some pretty good information out of Beatrice."

She withdrew and I heard her getting into the shower. She began to sing. I closed my laptop, went into the bathroom and sat on the toilet.

"Oooo, are you gonna come in and wash my back?" she said invitingly.

"In a minute," I said. "Tell me about Beatrice first."

"Well, once I got her talking, she didn't stop for most of the day."

"Is that why you were suddenly so hot and bothered to go shopping?" I asked. "To pump her for information?"

"Well, yeah," she said. "Duh. Of course, Victoria always needs clothes. Child is growing like a weed."

"So what did Beatrice say?"

"Oh, well. She told me all about Grosvenor's wife, Marta," she said.

"The one from Colombia."

"Yeah. She's his second wife," Mary Jane continued, speaking over the gushing water. Steam filled the room. "He met her on a business trip down there. She's quite a bit younger, and Beatrice says she's gorgeous. He divorced his first wife, the mother of his children, and took up with Marta."

"Where have I heard that before?" I said.

"Only in about a million other places," Mary Jane said. "I don't know what it is with you men and your trophy wives. Don't you eventually get tired of having sex with hot young babes with whom you have nothing else in common?"

"Soon as that happens, I'll let you know," I said.

A wet washcloth came flying over the top of the shower curtain on a trajectory towards my head. But I was expecting something, and I caught it and tossed it back.

"So that's the big deal? Charlie Grosvenor's a horn dog who goes for young babes?" I couldn't hide the disappointment in my voice. "Nine out of ten members at Augusta National probably have wives young enough to be their daughters. It's what your successful executive does these days. Make a pot of money, dump the old wife and give her half the stock options, and find some young hard-body hottie to cohabit with. It's the American way."

"Yeah, but Charlie's hottie is different," Mary Jane said. "Her last name was Obrador."

"Obrador?" I said, thinking. "Doesn't ring any bells."

"Don't you ever read the front section of your newspaper? He was the Colombian Interior minister who was secretly working for the Medellin cartel," Mary Jane told me. "Marta's father. He's now in prison, thanks to the United States and our war on drugs. And her brother has been a fugitive from justice for about the last ten years. He's supposedly working for the cartel too."

"And Marta?" I said. "Is she in the family business too?"

"Beatrice seems to think so," she said. "She said family ties are very strong in Colombia. You have to be very careful who you trust in that business, and so you usually do business only with relatives. Blood is thicker than water, and all that."

"So now we think that Charlie Grosvenor, or his company, and his wife are all drug merchants?" I said. "This is getting hard to believe."

"It might help explain why the hit man is in town shooting people, though," Mary Jane said. "Maybe there was a disagreement between Grosvenor's operation and the one run by the Obrador family."

"And Obrador sent Rico de la Paz up to send a warning. That's the first idea I've heard all week that makes any sense."

Mary Jane turned the water off and swept the shower curtain back.

"Your turn," she said.

"What about the back-washing part?" I said.

"I took care of it myself," she said.

I peeled off my clothes.

"Can't talk you into making sure you're all clean?" I said, getting into the shower.

"Gotta dry my hair," she said.

"How about me?" I said. "I have some parts that are very much in need of careful washing."

"I can see that," she said, grinning. "You'll just have to take care of that by yourself."

"Curses," I said. "Foiled again."

Chapter Twenty

The Commerce Club was dark, hushed and had the smell of old money. We had been shown into the express elevator in the building lobby by a smiling uniformed porter, and stepped out into restaurant's foyer. The semi-circular room was dominated by a tall mahogany counter. The large dining room lay to the right and the lounge was off to the left. A pretty girl dressed severely in black noted our names and motioned us into the lounge, where we found Conn holding up the end of the bar.

After introductions, he led us to a table against the windows that looked down on the sparkling lights of Augusta. From this side of the building, you could see the ridge that runs parallel to the river, and the rugged ground beyond, all hills and trees. Tables in the dining room looked more to the southeast, where the river began its long, flat, slow run to the sea.

We ordered drinks and admired the view and when the cocktails arrived, we all clinked glasses.

"So," Conn said to Mary Jane, "You're the woman brave

enough to take on our friend Hacker. Martyrdom is not required in this country, you know."

She laughed, her eyes bright and shining. "Don't tell anyone, but he's really a cupcake," she said. "Much better than 72 virgins, if you ask me."

Conn looked at her over the rim of his drink. I could see his lawyerly eyes sizing her up. He asked her a series of questions about her life and background. They seemed innocent and conversational, but I could tell he was doing a little light grilling. To her credit, Mary Jane answered his questions, chatting away happily about her life in Boston and her daughter Victoria. Finally, he smiled. One of his warm, from-the-heart smiles that I'd only seen used with people he really likes.

"Y'know what, Hacker?" he said. "I think she'll do."

"There you have it," I said to Mary Jane. "Conn's approval and a couple of bucks will get you anywhere in this town."

"It's pretty up here," Mary Jane said, gazing out at the twinkling lights of the city.

"Yeah, I've always thought this was the best view of the city," Conn said. "It tends to get uglier the closer to reality you get. But they did a nice job with this place."

"Who are the members?" I asked.

"Oh, your typical movers and shakers," he said. "Augusta's finest."

"Which one are you?" Mary Jane asked him.

"How's that?"

"Are you a mover or a shaker?"

He grinned at her. She grinned back. "Wouldn't you like to find out?" he said.

"Are you two flirting with each other right in front of me?" I said plaintively.

They laughed and I joined in.

Conn explained that the building had originally been built for the Augusta Mercantile Bank, one of the city's oldest financial firms, which, like most other local banks in the country, had been swept up in a series of mergers and acquisitions. At one time or another, it had been part of Citizens & Southern, Wachovia, Bank of America and now was part of some banking behemoth from Chicago.

"It's got some crazy name like the Fifth Third Bank or something," Conn told us. "Now if the First Bank is the best, what does that make the Fifth Third? Not someplace I'd want to put my hard-earned cash."

The hostess from the front came into the lounge and told us our table was ready. We followed her back through the foyer and into the main dining room on the other side of the building. It was a large space, with two tiers that provided excellent views out the window walls to the river and the southern part of the city. In the far corner, a tuxedoed piano player was doing something with a jazzy beat, soft and low. The tables were covered in white linens with candles burning in glass lamps on each table and banquette. Serving tables were scattered about, and the inside wall held old hunting prints and uplit sconces. For a businessman's dining room, it was pretty darn romantic.

It was busy, too. We wended our way to a table near the windows at the far end of the room. Our hostess handed us leather-bound menus and bowed herself away. Right behind her was the cocktail waitress from the other room with our half-finished drinks. Mary Jane and I looked out at the view.

"This side of the building has the best river views," Conn said, "But it also overlooks The Terry, down there to the right. I've always thought there was a certain ironic justice in that."

"What's The Terry?" Mary Jane asked.

"It's our ghetto," Conn said. "It's short for The Territory, and it's always been the black neighborhood."

"You don't mean they have to live there, do you?" Mary Jane said, aghast.

Conn laughed. "No ma'am, not since the end of the War of Northern Aggression, which I believe you Yankees call the Civil War. Like the rest of the South, it took us a while, but we finally got the message. But The Terry is still the only place the poor and the working poor can afford around these parts. Of course, it also is home to most of Augusta's lawless element."

"Does Augusta National donate money to charities like all the tournaments on the PGA Tour?" Mary Jane asked. "It seems to me with all the money they have over there, they could do something about places like The Terry."

"Not so you'd notice," Conn said. "It was just a few years ago that they started a charitable program. I think people finally realized that Augusta National was hording their cash, and shamed them into it. Now they donate money to national golf organizations, they support the First Tee, and they give a chunk of change to a local foundation that does contribute some to local charities, along with the Girl Scouts, Easter Seals and some local museums. But you're right; they don't exactly spread the wealth around. Of course, the club has always had a complicated relationship with its home town."

"How so?" Mary Jane asked, buttering a fresh yeast roll.

"Well, you have to remember that the club was founded, built and then visited by outsiders. In a small town like this, there are locals and then there is everyone else. Augusta National was never a local kind of place. The original members were either friends of Bobby or friends of Cliff. Neither of that group came from here. So people tended to look on the National as that uppity place that no one could join."

"That's not still the case, is it?" Mary Jane asked.

"No, they always invited a few of the more prosperous local fellows to join. The newspaper publisher, the mayor, the CEO of the golf cart company outside of town, a banker or two. But it's still pretty much outsiders, as the locals say. It's in Augusta, but it's not of Augusta"

"Tell her about the blacks," I said. I was perusing the menu. Chef Bubba had some interesting things cooking tonight.

"Well, of course, when the club was founded, Jim Crow was still the law down here in the South," Conn said. "Blacks could be waiters and caddies and groundsmen, but that was about it. My favorite story is about one member who actually came from Augusta had a manservant, a young kid really, who really got into the whole master-servant deal. So much so that Clifford Roberts noticed and told the member how much he admired his man Friday. Well, a few years later, the member dies and his widow, thinking that she'd do something nice for Cliff Roberts, wrapped the kid up as a Christmas wreath and sent him over to the National with a note saying 'To Cliff...Merry Christmas!'"

"Good Lord," Mary Jane said, shaking her head.

"Yeah. Roberts at least hired the kid and he eventually worked his way up to maitre'd in the clubhouse. But then, the club decided to allow the pros to bring their own caddies to the Masters back in 1983, and that meant all the Augusta caddies, who are all mostly from the Terry, lost the income they used to count on from Masters week. There was some rumbling and grumbling, but Cliff sent the Pinkerton guys over to the caddie shack to calm them down. Not much they could do—they're employees at will."

Our waiter came over and told us the specials for the night. Conn told us that while everything was good, Chef Bubba's southern fried catfish was renowned throughout Dixie. Mary Jane jumped on that, while I opted for the rack of lamb. Conn ordered the veal piccata and a bottle of Australian shiraz.

"What's ironic about the relationship with the city is that we really bailed out Augusta National in the early years when they were struggling," Conn continued. "Before the Masters become the worldwide spectacle that it is today, they had trouble getting fans to come watch the thing. So Roberts turned to the local business community for help. Right up until the late 1950s they gave thousands of tickets to local businesses to distribute to customers and friends. And even though the club has always been stingy spreading money around locally, Augusta realized that once a year they had a chance for a visitor bonanza."

"Didn't they used to have parades and stuff?" I asked. It was well before my time.

"Yeah," Conn said. "In fact, if you look over there against the wall, you'll see a white-haired lady in a white dress." Mary Jane and I sneaked a glance across the room. "That's Vera Phillips. She was Miss Golf back in the late 40s."

"Miss Golf?" Mary Jane said.

"Oh, yeah," Conn said. "It was Augusta's version of a debutante cotillion. Very chi-chi. And the whole city used to turn out for the Masters parade downtown. It was quite a spectacle."

"What happened?" Mary Jane wanted to know.

Conn shrugged. "I don't know. Combination of things, I guess. The tournament got bigger and more important once they started showing it on TV. Tickets became valuable. Money became paramount. Clifford Roberts either decided he didn't need good community relations anymore, or figured that the economic shot-in-the-arm that the Masters represented for the area ought to be enough for the town. And that they should be grateful for it. The fun kinda went out of it decades ago."

"But people do make a lot of money locally," I said.

"Oh, yeah," Conn nodded. "People have sent their kids to college from Masters money. The ones who rent out their homes for the week for ten or fifteen thousand dollars. The ones who sell their badges to the scalpers and brokers. A lot of moolah changes hands around here the first week in April."

"I understand that a lot of people around here still have badges from the old days," I said.

"And a lot of them turn around and sell them every year for a grand or two," Conn said. "When you've already seen Hogan and Palmer and Nicklaus over the years, and then some sharpie calls you offering some cold hard cash, and you figure you could go spend the week down on Hilton Head and still have some left over, it's not that hard a decision."

"Wasn't there a scandal a few years ago when somebody killed themselves over tickets?" Mary Jane said.

"Good memory," Conn said. "Yeah, there are always people trying to cash in on the Masters. Just like there are always people who'll pay anything to be able to say they went to the Masters. And the harder it is to get a badge, the more they want one. Anyway, that poor schlub had promised tickets to some heavies coming into town, and then at the last minute, his source bugged on him—probably got a better offer from someone else. So he shot himself in the head."

Conn scanned the room again. "There's a group over there...see the table with all those Japanese guys? The Anglo fellow eating with them is a ticket broker. He'll fly them in from Tokyo for a week, golf every day, nice condo, catered dinners and three or four badges, which they share. Some guys go on Thursday, some on Friday. I dunno what they do about Sunday afternoon. Probably arm-wrestle. Tell you the truth, I'd rather watch it on TV. You can get more of a sense of what's happening."

Our order of a starter of shrimp bisque arrived. We fell silent while we ate. I had to admit, Chef Bubba was pretty good. The soup was creamy, laced with sherry and had recognizable chunks of shrimp swimming around.

"So how do you like the Olde Magnolia?" Conn asked Mary Jane.

"It's lovely," she said. "Too bad we have to leave soon."

Conn was surprised. "They're throwing you out?"

"Not really," I told him. "Our deal was just for this week. Starting Sunday we move over to Hacker's Augusta address: Room 234 at the Motel 6. Same room has been rented by the ***Boston Journal*** for probably the last 25 years."

"That won't do," Conn said to me. "You can't take this lovely person to that motel hell. Heck, I feel bad enough thinking of you staying over there by yourself. You have to come stay with me. I've got the room—my cousin from Seattle usually comes over for the tournament, but he was too busy this year."

"That sounds nice," I said. "But we can't impose on you like that."

"Why not?" Conn said. "I invited you. That's not an imposition."

I looked at Mary Jane. She looked back at me as if to say "it's up to you."

"OK," I said. "That's very kind of you. Unfortunately, the paper prepaid for the week a couple of months ago, but I can maybe get them to send ..."

"Stop," Conn said. "Don't care about charging rent. You are my guests."

He held up his wine glass. We all clinked on it.

Chapter Twenty-One

When we got back to the Old Magnolia a couple of hours later, we found the place in an uproar. People were milling around in the lobby area, and a group had gathered in the sitting room. I saw Hans Kleiber and approached him. He was ashen faced, sitting in a chair with his head in his hands.

"What's up?" I asked.

He looked at me, shaken. "Christian Geer is dead!" he said, his voice hoarse. "the poor man had a heart attack while at the National this afternoon. It happened right after we dropped him off."

"My God," I said. Mary Jane made sympathetic noises next to me.

"Yes, it is a terrible thing," Hans said. "He was a very good friend. I cannot believe the news. But you saw how disturbed he was this morning. He was not himself at all."

"Did it happen while he was meeting with Grosvenor?" I asked.

"I do not know," Hans admitted. "We are trying to contact his family now in Belgium and make arrangements for sending his body home. Oh, this is a terrible event."

"Where have they taken him?" I asked.

"His remains were taken to the local hospital," Hans said. "There is nothing we can do until tomorrow."

We stayed and listened for a while as Hans reminisced about his friend. The other internationals filed in and out, offering condolences and talking about the tragic event. It was a reminder that golf is just a game, but life is real.

After some time, I motioned to Mary Jane and we made our exit. I grabbed her arm and led her out to the parking lot.

"Where are we going?" she wondered.

"To the hospital," I said. "I need to see someone."

In all my driving around town, I had passed the sprawling medical complex of the county hospital several times, so I knew where it was. We got there and parked in the near-empty lot. At the front desk, I asked for Travis Kitchen's room.

"He's on the fourth floor," the lady at the desk told us. "But visiting hours were over at nine. You can't go up now."

"This is official business," I said and dragged Mary Jane onto the nearest elevator. The lady protested, but I didn't really care.

On the fourth floor, there was another counter at the nurse's central station, with wings and corridors heading off in three directions. A middle-aged black nurse with a no-nonsense look on her face folded her arms across her chest.

"Didn't they tell you visiting hours were over?" she demanded.

"I need to see Lt. Kitchen right away," I said. "It's important."

"Life or death, I suppose," the nurse said.

"Could be," I said.

"Sonny boy, you have been watching too much television," the nurse said sternly. "This is the real world and our patients are resting. Go away."

"Now listen," I started in hotly. Mary Jane put her hand on my arm to stop me.

"No, Hacker," she said. "The lady is right. We can come back in the morning. It'd be smarter then."

I turned to argue with her, when I caught a look in her eye that made me stop. I heaved a sigh of frustration instead.

"Good boy," Mary Jane said. She leaned in and gave me a quick kiss and a hug. While we were in the brief embrace, I heard her whisper. "Be ready."

"Can I use the rest room?" Mary Jane asked the nurse as we broke our embrace. "He dragged me down here right after dinner, and ..."

The nurse was still glaring at us, arms folded. "Well, all right," she said. "Down the hall on the right." She motioned the way. "And you, Sonny Boy, you stay right here where I can keep an eye on you."

Mary Jane winked at me as she walked down the hall. I stood against the wall, arms crossed. The nurse went back to writing things on the charts in front of her. In a minute, there was a soft but insistent beep-beep-beep coming from the nurse's desk.

"Oh, what now?" the woman said, wearily heaving herself to her feet. "Mrs. Cathcart again?" She glared at me. "You stay right there, bub." And she hurried off down the hall.

Once she was out of sight, I leaned over the counter and looked at the charts. Kitchen was in 405. I followed the signs on the wall and quickly found the room. I pushed open the door and stepped inside. It was warm and dark in the room, all the lights were out. The only illumination was from the LED lights on a monitor that was keeping track of Kitchen's vital signs.

"Hold it right there," said a deep voice I recognized as Kitchen. "I've got a gun, it's loaded and it's aimed right at you."

I heard him as he sat up and leaned over. He flicked on the bedside light. It was true. He had a pistol in his hand and it was pointing at my belly.

"What the hell are you doing here?" he asked, surprised.

"They allow you to keep firearms in this hospital?" I said. "Seems counter-productive to me. I thought this was a place of healing."

"Yeah, well, you didn't get shot at yesterday," he said, lowering the gun. "I did. And until they catch the guy, I've gotta think he'll try again. So what the hell are you doing here? I know it's not a social visit because you didn't bring either flowers or candy."

"I think it's time we had a chat," I said. "And I need an official favor." Quickly, I filled him in on Christian Geer. How he had arrived, demanding to be taken to the National and Charlie Grosvenor, hinting that he had something very important and problematic to discuss. Whereupon he had a coronary and died.

Kitchen understood right away. "That sounds kinda fishy," he said.

"Will they do an autopsy?" I asked.

He stroked his chin, thinking. "Probably not," he said finally. "Foreign national. No apparent crime. Heart attack in front of witnesses? All of whose stories match? Nah, they'll probably do a quick embalm and ship him home."

"Can you still order one? Or don't retired homicide dicks have any pull in this county?"

"You really shouldn't insult an officer of the law," he said. "Especially one that's grumpy, has a sore ass and is armed. Not good for your longevity."

But he reached over for the telephone, pulled it onto his lap and began dialing.

A few minutes later, the nurse came in spitting fire and just about dragging Mary Jane by the scruff of the neck.

"All right, buster," she said. "Are you two going to leave on your own, or do I have to call the authorities?"

Kitchen pulled his gun out from under the covers. "Want me to shoot them, Cassie?" he asked dryly.

Mary Jane gasped at the sight of his pistol. The nurse glared at him, and then smiled. "No, Lieutenant," she said. "You'd better not. I think I can handle it."

I apologized, and so did Mary Jane, who had been the one to sneak into someone's room and trip the call button. Cassie the nurse was still angry, but she eventually accepted our apologies. But she also demanded that we get off her floor and fast.

Kitchen and I agreed to talk in the morning. His phone rang as we were leaving, and I heard Cassie berating him for being up so late, taking all these chances, not getting his proper rest ... Her voice disappeared as the elevator doors closed.

"That was a pretty neat trick," I said. "Where did you learn that?"

"Hacker, don't you ever watch sitcoms, soap operas or ER?" she said. "It's the oldest trick in the book."

"Oh," I said, feeling stupid. "Well, it worked pretty good. Thanks. Kitchen is going to try and get the medical examiner to do a quick autopsy tonight."

"What do you think they'll find?" Mary Jane asked as we arrived on the ground floor and began to make our way back to the car.

"I dunno," I said. "But I'll bet they find something."

Chapter Twenty-Two

What they found was atropine. Knowing the situation, the county medical examiner had done a favor for Travis Kitchen and run a down-and-dirty toxicology report on Christian Geer. Normally, such test reports take a couple of weeks to produce, at a minimum. But that's because the labs know they have to be careful and diligent and methodical because the results may very likely end up in a court of law in a homicide case. Kitchen had convinced the M.E. to just pull a blood and tissue sample from Geer and run some basic tests looking for a handful of agents that might have caused a coronary. If the tests showed anything suspicious, he said he'd go to court and get a warrant for a more complete examination before the body was returned to Europe.

Freed from the responsibility of doing the procedure by the book, the M.E. had quickly tested for a list of substances that he and Kitchen worked out. And he hit pay dirt on the third one.

"His blood levels showed an extremely high concentration of atropine," Kitchen told me the next morning when he called. "Doctors sometimes inject a few cc's to speed up your heartbeat if you've got coronary trouble."

"Are you sure he wasn't taking some other medications that contained atropine?" I asked.

"If he was, he was overdosing by a factor of fifty," Kitchen said. "The doc said atropine in that concentration meant that his heart pretty much exploded. I've heard that it has been used before to disguise assassinations. You can sneak up on someone, stick in a hypodermic and zap 'em, and they'll be dead within minutes. Nice and clean. Looks just like a heart attack, with the sweating, the pain in the chest, the gasping for breath, and then boom. You're down and out. Shoot it into somebody old and everyone will assume it's the big one. Like we almost did."

"We?" I said.

"Yeah, I talked to the chief about my resignation," he said. "I was pissed that they wanted me to stop on this case."

"Who's they?" I asked.

"The feds. They're tracking some South American drug lords and they feel this is all part of it. And that my investigation might ruin their case. I told them the citizens of Richmond County don't give a rat's ass about their case—they want justice. My chief backed them. So I quit."

"Can't say as I blame you," I said.

"I talked to the chief today, and told him what we'd found. That and the fact that they tried to kill me made both of us reconsider our positions. We also decided not to announce it publicly right away. I'm officially on medical leave for a few weeks. But in the meantime, I'm back on the case, unofficially."

"When do you get out of the hospital?"

"In about ten minutes, or I'm leaving anyway," he said. "As long as I don't have to sit down, I think I can function."

"What are you going to do?" I asked.

"First thing, I'm going to take a ride down to the Terry," he said. "I want to talk to Lester."

"Who's that?"

"He's our local criminal enterprise," Kitchen said. "He runs the prostitution, gambling, loan sharking and narcotics games in this town. If something bad is happening in Augusta, Lester is either the one doing it, or knows who is."

"Sounds interesting. Need someone to go along?"

"I got shot in the ass, not the head," he said, chuckling. "I can't take a newspaper reporter along on an official investigation. I can see the county attorney getting red in the face just thinking about it."

"You just said this was an unofficial investigation," I pointed out. "Plus, with your injured, um, quarters, you might need someone to drive so you can sit on a pillow or something. I'll try and miss all the potholes, too."

"We don't have potholes in the South," he said. "Maybe the occasional possum."

"I'll sign a waiver if you want," I said. "Promise not to hold Richmond County responsible if Lester decides he wants to shoot us."

I heard a loud woman's voice in the background that sounded a lot like Nurse Cassie complaining about something that Kitchen was, or was not, doing. He sighed.

"I'm too weak to argue with either you or Nurse Ratchet here," he said. "Where are you?"

"Over at the Olde Magnolia," I said. "Ready to rock n' roll."

"Okay," he said. "I'll be over shortly."

Nurse Cassie said something that sounded like "The hell you will..." before the phone went dead.

I told Mary Jane what was up. She whistled at the news about Christian Geer, but frowned at the idea of me going with Travis down to the Terry.

"What is it about you?" she asked rhetorically. "You always have to be right there on the front lines, don't you?"

"I might be able to ask a question to help find out something useful," I said. "You never know."

"And the danger?"

"I'm going with the chief of homicide for the county," I reminded her. "I doubt that we're going to get into a gun fight."

She was not happy, but when Kitchen showed up driving his county issue Chevrolet Caprice, she managed to smile at both of us. "Be careful," she said.

"I'll keep an eye out for him," Kitchen said, giving her a wink.

I got behind the wheel, while Kitchen eased himself into a semi-comfortable position in the passenger seat. I asked how Nurse Cassie was. He growled. "Good nurse. Total bitch," he said.

He gave me directions as we motored down the hill and into downtown Augusta. We talked as we drove. I told him about my talk with Maria Sanchez, who had been the first one to tell me about Enrico. I also told him about our dinner with Wilcox, the federal agent. He found that most interesting.

We passed the Medical College of Georgia where the Golf Writers Association once held their annual awards banquet during the Masters, and eventually passed through the downtown. I followed his instructions to head south on 7th Street. Once we passed Greene Street, the streetscape changed.

Here, we drove past ancient triple-decker tenements with sagging wooden porches and peeling paint. Back yards, if there were any, were wrapped in layers of chain link. On almost every corner, some seedy looking storefront attracted two or three black men, who lounged against the wall, drinking from something hidden in a brown paper bag, who stared at us as we drove past. It was like driving from America into some other world that most of us don't know exists, and the rest of us try to forget.

We passed a block-sized park with concrete basketball courts and playgrounds, and bare-dirt ball fields. A few brave-hearted trees along the edges of the park were beginning to produce a bit of shade as their spring leaves popped out.

"This is Dyess Park," Kitchen said. "At night, it's not someplace you want to be. But James Brown used to give away turkeys to everyone here at Thanksgiving."

"He grew up here, didn't he?" I asked.

"His aunt ran a whorehouse right over there, on Twiggs," Kitchen pointed. "He used to sing and dance for pennies and nickels when he was about 10 years old. No wonder he became the 'hardest working man in show business.'"

On the far side of the park, Kitchen told me to take a right and then a few more quick turns until we reached Dugas Street. It looked like most of the other streets—dusty, drab, occupied by sad-looking little houses, and mostly empty save for a couple of beat-up cars and one mangy looking dog napping on the sidewalk in the sun.

At the end of the street—it just stopped in a tree-shaded thicket—there was the usual group of men, gathered around a stoop. They looked at us without expression as we pulled up in front of a blue-gray house with brick steps and a narrow front porch. One of the men in the group peeled off and walked, slowly, inside.

"Reception committee?" I guessed.

"Just some of Lester's homies," Kitchen said. "I'll bet they knew we were in the neighborhood ten minutes ago."

I got out of the car and went around to help Kitchen ease his way carefully out of the seat. Once he was upright, he walked, with a slight limp and a wince or two, up to the house.

"Heard you done got shot," one of the men on the front steps said. The others sat there, impassive, silent, stone-faced.

"Right in the ass," Kitchen said, smiling. "Not convenient."

"You know thass right," the man said.

Travis put out his hand and the man, after a brief hesitation, shook it.

"How you doin' Chester?" Kitchen said. "The boss in?"

"Ain't he always?" the man said.

Kitchen nodded. We climbed the stairs and entered the front door across the porch. I looked back. The men still sat there, impassively, staring at the car as if they expected it to get up and fly.

Inside, there was a stairway leading up to the second floor along the left wall, and a narrow hallway that led to the back of the house. A front sitting room to the right was empty, save for a high-backed couch and two wooded chairs sitting on a round, woven rug. Another black man, broad-shouldered and buff, dressed in a gray suit that stretched tightly across his upper body, stood in the hallway, cracking his knuckles. He nodded at Kitchen.

"Lieutenant," he murmured in greeting.

"William," Kitchen said. "We'd like to chat with Lester for a minute if he's free."

"Umm, hmm," William said. "Who this be?" he said, looking at me.

"Name's Hacker," Kitchen said. "From Boston."

"Boston, huh?" William said, giving me the up-and-down. "I lost me a bunch of money on the Patriots last fall." He didn't look happy about that.

"You and me, both," I said.

William looked at Kitchen. "He packin'?" he asked. Kitchen shook his head no, but I held out my arms anyway. William gave me a quick, but thoroughly efficient pat-down. He stood up, shot his cuffs, and nodded for us to go on through.

I'm not sure what I expected the office of the head of Augusta's black criminal enterprise to look like, but it surely wasn't what we found after we walked through that hallway door. We walked into the back of the house which was entirely taken up by the kitchen and a breakfast nook of sorts beyond it. Old, peeling linoleum covered the floor, and the porcelain in the sink was worn down to the black iron beneath the veneer. An almond-colored refrigerator from Sears competed with a lime-green gas stove for attention. Open shelves lined the walls—some held melamine dishes and others various boxes and cans of food. A dirty window over the sink, the screen folded over in one corner, looked out on a scruffy back yard where a mean-looking, muscular brown dog ran around, chained to a metal post in the center of the yard.

There were two people in the room. One was a huge old mammy, wearing a kerchief around her ears, an old pink sweater over a flowered corduroy dress, battered old slip-ins that may, at one point, have been fuzzy slippers, and navy blue woolen socks pulled up over her calves. Her large upper body and thick arms nipped inward at the waist before shooting outwards again in an enormous pair of hips. There was a shelf around her middle that looked flat and sturdy enough to hold a cup and saucer. She was stirring a huge pot of something on the back burner, while a tin coffee pot bubbled on one of the front burners. She was singing softly to herself, a monotone hum, which every now and then sounded vaguely like a gospel song. I kept hearing the word "Jesus."

Beyond the kitchen, Lester was sitting in the eating nook, which contained a round, fake-wood table with three spindle-back wooden chairs. The table was covered with a lace-like cloth. There was an old radio on a shelf above his head, playing some rap. Lester had in front of him a cell phone, a notebook, and the Augusta newspaper, which he was slowly perusing when we came in.

He was a short, skinny man, with graying curly hair cut close to his skull. He was wearing blue jeans, a mock turtleneck and sneakers. He also wore gold-rimmed glasses, and had a pencil stuck behind one ear. Instead of a crime boss, Lester looked like he could be the head of shipping for an auto parts store. He did not look dangerous, deadly or even very scary.

Kitchen took the lead.

"Miz Johnson," he said bowing slightly to the huge woman at the stove. "How're ya doin'?"

She muttered something indistinguishable and gave her pot another stir.

"Lester," he nodded at the man. "Staying out of trouble?"

Lester finished the story he was reading before carefully folding the paper and putting it to one side of the table. He looked up at us without expression and motioned for us to take a seat at his table. I held out a chair for Kitchen and eased him down into it.

"Thass right," Lester said, watching. "I heard you got your ass popped. Mmm-mmm. That shore do smart don't it?"

Kitchen, teeth clenched, didn't say anything.

"Mama," Lester called over to the woman. "Is that Brunswick stew ready yet? Might let these white boys get a little taste. Best damn stuff in Augusta."

Mama grumbled something and reached up into a cupboard for some bowls.

"What can I do for you, Lieutenant?" Lester said, looking at Kitchen directly. "I don' believe any of my boys has been gettin' in trouble."

"No, Lester," Kitchen said. "I stopped by to see if you could give me a little help."

Lester's face broke out in a wide grin. "Is that a fact?" he said, chuckling. "Hey, Mama! You hear that? The poh-leece want ***me*** to give ***them*** a little ***hep***!" He leaned back, face beaming.

Mama dished out some stew in three bowls. She carried two bowls over to the table, the floor creaking in protest as she waddled. She made her way slowly back to the stove, picked up the third bowl, fished in a drawer for some spoons and brought that over to the table. She reached behind her and grabbed a box of Saltines on a shelf and plopped that down on the table as well. Then she waddled back to the stove.

"Thanks, Mama," Lester said. "Smells pretty damn good."

Mama shot him a look and shook her head.

"I'm sorry, Mama," Lester said. "Pretty daggone good."

"Thank you kindly Miz Johnson," Kitchen said. "It does smell wonderful." He picked up a spoon and dug right in. Lester opened the crackers and crumbled two of them into pieces on top of his stew, and began to eat. I followed suit. For the next few minutes, nobody said anything as we ate. Mama's Brunswick stew was amazing. Filled with chicken, corn and sausage, she had also thrown in carrots, celery, potatoes, tomatoes, the usual okra, and a blend of spices I'm not sure I could identify. But it was smooth, peppery and delicious.

When we had finished, we all three sat back in our chairs. Mama waddled back over and picked up the bowls and carried them heavily to the sink. Lester's cell phone rang, but he ignored it.

"What you need?" Lester asked Kitchen.

The police lieutenant reached into his jacket pocket and pulled out a sheet with a photo on it and showed it to Lester. "What do you know about this guy?" he asked.

Lester studied it carefully. Or pretended to, while he bought some time. "Uh-huh," he said to himself a couple of times while he looked at it. Kitchen waited patiently. I looked at the photo upside down. It was a grainy shot of a man with a mustache and long hair.

"Not a good picture," Lester said finally. "But it do look a lot like Carlos."

Mama, over at the sink, started when she heard that name. "Lord a'mercy," she moaned.

"And who is Carlos?" Kitchen said.

"Dude from South America," Lester said, still looking at the photo. "Seen him once or twice. He have somethin' to do with the trade in blow."

"He's a runner?" Kitchen pressed. "Delivers the goods?"

Lester shook his head. "Naw," he said. "He be more important than that. He come to town when things get a little messed up. Like y'all put somebody in jail or somethin'. Carlos come up and straighten things out again. Pretty soon, it's all back to normal. Product come in, product go out."

"Where does he come from?" Kitchen asked.

"Miami."

"How does he get things straightened out?"

Lester smiled, a rueful smile. "That be a real good question, my man," he said. "Carlos is one strange dude. You don't always know when he's here, but you shore do know when he's ***been*** here. People tend to get shot when he's in town. Ain't nobody I know messed with him still alive."

"And you get along with him?" I asked.

"I still here, ain't I?" he said, looking at me directly for the first time. "Who you be?"

"Hacker," I said. "From Boston." It worked before as an ice-breaker.

"Uh-huh," Lester said.

"Have you seen this Carlos around lately?" Kitchen continued.

"Last time was a couple months ago," Lester said. "But I have heard tell he's been seen around last few weeks. Like I said, you don't always know when the dude is about. He ain't come over for some of Mama's stew yet."

"You know anything about that boy that was shot over at Augusta National?" I asked.

"Sheeeeeit," Lester erupted. "Don' you be talkin' 'bout those white cracker boys. God-damn bigots, all of 'em. Racist mother-. . ."

Mama made a warning noise, deep in her throat.

"Sorry, Mama," Lester caught himself just in time. "I guess you can tell those white cracker asses not be my favorite people. No, I don' know who shot that boy. Far as I care, you can lock up the entire bunch o'them crackers. Do the world a favor."

"Thanks, Lester," Kitchen said, getting up. "Maybe if you hear where Carlos is or see him or something, you can give me a call. Like to talk to him."

Lester laughed. "Don' think Mister Carlos be interested in talkin' to no poh-leece," he said. "Shootin' one, maybe. Talkin'? Not so much."

"Well, I'd appreciate it a lot if you hear anything you'd let me know," Kitchen said. The two men nodded at each other. He turned to the old woman.

"Miz Johnson," he said, bowing slightly. "Thank you so much for the wonderful gumbo. You haven't lost your magic. It's still the best in the county, bar none."

I added my own thanks in as gracious a Southern manner as I could muster for a white-assed cracker boy. The woman grumbled something, but I thought I could detect a hint of a smile. We walked out past William, still guarding the hall, and continued outside. The group of men were still sitting on the front stoop. They watched us with silent, white eyes as we got in our car and drove away.

"Who is this Carlos person?" I asked when we were heading back towards downtown.

"His real name is Enrico de la Paz," Kitchen said. "Carlos is an alias. Got the photo from a friend at the FBI."

"Ah," I said. "Seems like Enrico is a popular guy around here. Everyone seems to know him."

"And doesn't want to cross him," Kitchen said.

"Wonder if that holds true with those white-assed crackers over at the National," I said.

"Maybe we should go ask them," Kitchen said.

"Capital idea," I said.

"Drive on," he said.

Chapter Twenty-Three

It was hard even for Lt. Travis Kitchen of the Richmond County Police Department to get inside the gates at Augusta National. The Pinkerton guards made us wait at the gate, and wouldn't open it until they had phoned in to the clubhouse and talked to about half a dozen people. I thought at one point that Kitchen was going to pull his service revolver and kneecap one of the guards who exhibited a little attitude.

Someone inside must have given permission, because they finally opened the gate, and we soon found ourselves waiting outside Charlie Grosvenor's office. Even though it was Saturday, the place was humming with life. The tournament started on Thursday, but CBS technicians were crawling all over the golf course, setting up the cameras and their satellite uplinks. The construction of all the bleachers and stands was finished, save for some last-minute touch ups by the painters armed with buckets of Masters green paint. The fairway ropes were being strung, the mowers were out clipping the grass down to the prescribed 1/32nd of an inch, and the food stations were getting ready for the hordes of patrons who would be lined up at the gate by 6 a.m. Monday morning. Even the tickets for a boring practice round are snapped up and highly prized.

Brett Jacoby walked into the foyer where we were waiting. Grosvenor's secretary picked up the phone and buzzed the inner office.

"Hacker," Brett said in greeting. "I didn't know you were coming over. What's going on? Charlie just called me into this meeting."

I introduced Brett to Kitchen.

"We've come to a point in the investigation where we can share some information," I said.

"We?" Brett said, looking at Kitchen.

"Yeah," I said. "Turns out the Judge case got a little more complicated."

"What do you mean?" Brett asked, sounding like he really didn't want to know.

I shook my head and nodded toward the door of Grosvenor's office. We waited in silence. After several long minutes, the door to Grosvenor's inner sanctum opened and the chairman walked out. He was dressed in casual weekend clothes, khaki's and a maroon golf shirt with the Izod alligator on it.

"Gentlemen," he said, and motioned us to come in. We filed in and took seats around the coffee table. Kitchen and I sat on the sofa, Brett pulled up a side chair and we let Grosvenor take the large leather armchair that faced the fireplace, which was filled with an arrangement of magnolia leaves.

Again, I introduced Kitchen. He and Grosvenor shook hands. Grosvenor looked at me.

"I thought you understood that your inquiries were to be somewhat confidential," the chairman said, his voice registering disappointment. "We wanted to know what was going on with the unfortunate incident of several weeks ago, but I don't believe you had authorization to involve the authorities beyond the scope of your brief."

"Mr. Grosvenor," Kitchen responded. "A serious crime was committed here at Augusta National and a young man was murdered. In the course of investigating that crime, my office found suggestions of further criminal behavior. Mr. Hacker, whom you asked to nose around, also discovered potential evidence of wrong-doing. It is my responsibility as a sworn officer of Richmond County to investigate serious crimes and bring those responsible to justice."

Grosvenor shifted uncomfortably in his chair.

"Lt. Kitchen," he said. "It is my understanding that you have resigned from the Richmond County police department. Under what authority, then, are you here?"

"I un-resigned," he said. "I'm still a cop."

"I see," Grosvenor said. "Well, let me state that we here at Augusta National—all our employees—have been instructed to cooperate fully with the authorities in this case. As far as I know, no one here at the club had anything to do with the unfortunate incident. And while we would certainly wish to continue our cooperation in any way, it is also the case that one of the major events of the year is planned to begin in two days. Everyone here at the club is rather preoccupied at the moment. Can this discussion be put off until next week when things are a bit less hectic?"

"No," Kitchen said.

Grosvenor stared at him. His eyes narrowed. He was not used to being refused.

"How can I help you?" he asked, his voice icy.

"Do you know someone named Enrico de la Paz?" Kitchen asked.

Grosvenor blinked. He looked at Brett, then at me, then back at Kitchen. "N-n-no," he stammered. "I don't think so."

"How about Jose Feliz Obrador?" Kitchen pressed.

"I don't think so," he said hesitantly.

"You don't think you know your own father-in-law?" Kitchen sounded incredulous.

Grosvenor leaped out of his chair. It was an almost involuntary movement, a reflex action. He realized, once he was standing, that he had jumped, and tried to make it seem natural by walking over to his huge desk and rooting around for a paper.

"I'm sorry," he said. "I must have mis-heard the name. Yes, Obrador is my wife's father. But we have not seen nor spoken to the man in more than twenty years. He is involved in some bad business down in South America."

He walked back over and sat down in his leather chair again.

"He is involved with the Colombian drug cartels, is he not?" Kitchen pressed on.

"I have heard that," Grosvenor said, "But I don't know personally if that's true."

Kitchen smiled slightly and began firing questions.

"Did you know that de la Paz has been seen in recent weeks here in Augusta?"

"No."

"That he is well known locally as the main connection to the drug trade from South America."

"No."

"That he is, in fact, Obrador's enforcer?"

"No."

"That he very likely is the one who shot and killed John Judge?"

"No." Grosvenor was sweating now, squirming, crossing and recrossing his legs. "Listen, what's the point of all this? I've told you that we have nothing to do with him. Haven't seen nor heard from him. My God, if this Paz fellow was the one who killed that poor lad, then go and arrest him."

"You'd like that, wouldn't you?" Kitchen said. "You'd like de la Paz to be put on ice, wouldn't you? Has he been here? Called? Has he threatened you in person?"

"No, of course not," Grosvenor said, wiping a hand across his brow. "Why would you think that?"

"Because Rico only comes to town when there's a problem," Kitchen said. "And I think you're the problem. I think the Judge killing was a warning. I think you're involved in some way in Obrador's business and he wants you out. And maybe because he's family, he wants you to get out before he has to take you out. How'm I doing?"

Grosvenor had turned an interesting shade of red. He kept silent.

"What happened with Christian Geer?" Kitchen continued.

"He came to see me two days ago," Grosvenor said. "We talked for a bit in this office, and then he left. Brett was here, he'll tell you. Apparently, he had a heart attack downstairs in the lobby. I heard the sirens of the ambulance arrive and that's when I found out what had happened."

"Did he show signs of illness?"

"Not at all," Grosvenor said. "He was in good spirits."

"What did he come here to talk about? He was heard by Hacker and others to say he had important things to discuss with you."

"That conversation was private and shall remain so," Grosvenor said.

"Do you or your corporation have business interests in Belgium?"

"I don't believe that is any of your business."

"Maybe and maybe not," Kitchen said. "We are investigating the apparent murder of Christian Geer. You will be asked to give a formal statement."

"Murder!" Grosvenor leapt out of his chair again. "The man had a heart attack! He collapsed downstairs in front of my staff. No one touched him at all. I've never heard such nonsense in my life."

"We have evidence to the contrary," Kitchen said calmly.

The two men stared at each other. "Perhaps you'd like to revise your story?" Kitchen asked.

"Absolutely not!" Grosvenor almost shouted. "This conversation is at an end. If you wish to speak with me again, I will be accompanied by counsel."

Despite his brave front, Grosvenor's voice was shaking. He turned to look at me.

"Mister Hacker," he said. "Our agreement has come to an end. I insist that you immediately discontinue your inquiry. I trust you will honor your commitment to not discuss or write about this matter with anyone. I ...we...Augusta National appreciates your efforts and we wish you well."

"You can't fire me, because I quit," I said. Kitchen chuckled. He stood up.

"Thank you for your time," he said. "You will be hearing from me again." He paused and looked down at Grosvenor, who was gripping the arms of his leather chair.

"Are you sure you don't want our help?" he said, his voice low and calm. "Rico is a dangerous man. Lethal. I wouldn't want him coming after me. Again. Tell us what you know. We can put a stop to this. You can get protection if you cooperate with us."

Grosvenor looked up at Kitchen, and for a brief moment, I saw fear. Part of him wanted desperately to ask for help, to spill the beans, to put an end to the entire thing. But the larger part of him was Charles Grosvenor, chairman of Augusta National, billionaire, man of power and distinction, who could get anyone from the President on down to return his calls. That Grosvenor was a man who commanded, and was not frightened of anyone or anything. That scared look I saw was there for just an instant, and then it disappeared.

He waved his hand. "No," he said weakly, resigned. "There is nothing I need help with."

Chapter Twenty-Four

Travis Kitchen dropped me off at the Olde Magnolia. I asked him for a copy of the picture of Enrico de la Paz, and he gave me his. He eased himself behind the wheel, moving carefully.

"Well," I said. "I guess that's that."

"For you, anyway," he said. "I still have to try and catch the bad guy. You get to go back to being a sports writer."

"Will you call the Judge kid's mother and tell her what you know?" I asked. "I promised I'd try to get them some information."

"I'll take care of it myself," he said. "Soon as I get home, take an Extra-Strength Tylenol and lie on my stomach."

"Good luck on catching Rico," I said. "Be careful out there."

"Yeah," he said. "Thanks for your help. You coulda been a good detective."

"Nah," I said. "I'm not good at rules and regulations."

He drove off, and I went inside to find Mary Jane. She was glad to see me alive and in one piece, and ecstatic to hear my part of the case was over. I felt a little disappointed, a little relieved, and more than a little interested in finding out what had actually happened with John Judge, with Enrico and the National, with the death of Christian Geer, and what might happen next. Mary Jane looked at my face and understood.

"You did the best you could," she said. "And you found out a lot of stuff. But you're a golf writer, and a damn good one, and you should be proud of that."

"I know," I said, "And I am. I just want to see how this thing works itself out. Are the feds or even Travis Kitchen going to be able to pin anything on Charlie Grosvenor? It doesn't look like it. Are they going to find Rico and take him down? Nobody has been able to yet. Who killed John Judge and why? And, most important..."

I paused. She waited. "I wonder who's going to win the Masters next week?"

She laughed.

The next day, Sunday, was a busy one, so I didn't have much time to fret or think about the case. I got up early, letting Mary Jane sleep in, and drove over to the National to pick up my credentials. Most of the media crowd would be arriving either later that afternoon or Monday, but I knew that Brett's staff would be on hand. On the way into the media center, I passed Pee Wee at his post at the door. He made no sign of recognition, but just stared at me with his little beady eyes.

I got my badge, tossed out most of the volumes of background material that had been prepared, and looked around the room. For years, the media had made do with a recycled Quonset hut left over from WWII days. Inside the old corrugated metal arch, the National had set up a few rows of tables and chairs, and the telephone company had run some wires in. There had been a big, hand-written scoreboard and some TVs stationed around the room. But the floor had been dirt that got pretty sloppy when it rained and the roof leaked, and the space wasn't heated, so in those years when the Georgia spring turned nippy, we froze to death. But we all felt a little nostalgic when they finally tore the thing down.

The new media center the club built for us was a fabulous facility, but not one that anyone would write poetry about. The press room had three tiers in a semi-circle, providing faultless sight lines to a big central scoreboard. There were large-screen plasma televisions everywhere. There was an almost equally large interview theater, spotless restrooms, and even our own canteen. All the comforts of home, and none of the warm feeling.

There weren't many people around. The notice board informed me that Tiger Woods was out on the course, getting in some practice; and that Phil Mickelson and Davis Love III were scheduled to go out later in the morning. But I didn't feel like chasing any of them around the hilly course today.

I went back to the inn and had a leisurely breakfast with Mary Jane. Afterwards, I called over to the Motel 6 and spoke to Billy Moore, the manager, whom I'd become friendly with after attending the tournament for the last umpteen years in a row. I told him he could release the fabulous Hacker suite, also known as Room 234, to someone else, as I had scored more comfortable accommodations in town. He was glad to hear it—he not only got to keep the ***Boston Journal's*** $1500, which had been prepaid months in advance, but now he could now rent the room again to someone else for just as much. Most of the motels located at the intersection of Washington Road and the interstate already had "No Vacancy" signs out for the only time all year. Billy told me he'd have no trouble selling the room. I said I'd try and find time to come over and say hello before I left town.

Mary Jane and I then packed up and drove over to Conn's house. He lived a few miles north of downtown, in the Stevens Creek neighborhood along the Savannah River, not far from the West Lake Country Club. His house was built on a bluff across the road from the river, surrounded by trees. It was quiet and private and peaceful. There was a deck that wrapped around the house, overlooking the river in the near distance. The sun was shining warmly. There were comfortable lounges on the deck, and Conn had a cooler filled with beer next to his fancy barbecue grill. There was a copy of the Sunday ***New York Times*** on the table.

"So what do you want to do the rest of the day?" he asked. "Go play some golf?"

I looked at him and the deck and the stuffed lounge chairs and the beer. "I think I'd like to do nothing," I said. I grabbed a piece of the paper and a cold beer and parked myself in the sun. Mary Jane and Conn started an intense but jovial conversation about something, but it wasn't long before my eyes were closed and the afternoon gone.

MARY JANE WANTED to do some more shopping the next day, so I had her drop me off at the golf course around noon. "Taa-taa, dahling," she said as she drove away, the color high in her cheeks.

Just for fun, I kept my media badge hidden as I approached the media center. Sure enough, Pee Wee, standing guard at his post outside the door, put a big beefy hand on my chest when I tried to walk in. I smiled brightly, showed him the badge and wished him to have a wonderful day. He blinked, grunted and turned to the guy behind me.

The press center was about half full, but no one was doing any work. Part of the routine at the Masters is catching up with old friends. There are probably less than twenty writers who attend every major tournament—the British and American Opens, the PGA and the Masters. Like me, they represent the biggest daily newspapers, along with the golf and sports magazines. Typically, the rest of the media horde comes from the area where the tournament is being held.

But the Masters is different, and not just because it's played in the same place every year. Just as in the early days Augusta National begged people to buy tickets, the club had to do some fast tap dancing to get media coverage. On the advice of the famous sportswriter Grantland Rice, one of the founding members of the club, the tournament had been scheduled in late spring in order to make it easy for the big-city writers who had been in Florida for baseball's spring training to stop off in Augusta on their way north with the ball clubs. In those early years, I'm sure the club offered to put some of the writers up in hotel rooms if they agreed to cover the tournament.

Maybe it was all they could get, but the Masters also invited sports writers from the second and third tier of newspapers to attend. Thus, the tournament has long been personally reported by writers for the ***Fayetteville Observer***, the ***Kankakee Daily Journal*** and the ***Allentown Morning Call,*** among about three dozen other tiny hometown newspapers. And those papers continue to send their writers and sports editors down to Augusta every year, mainly because they can. The main qualification for media accreditation at the tradition-bound Masters has always been "were you here last year?" If yes, you're in. If no, you have to jump through myriad hoops before getting turned down. Once those small-town guys got in, they made sure they stayed in by showing up every year.

Of course, the club's power in granting media credentials effectively gives Augusta National a high degree of control over the writers. Those who act up, misbehave or write something to offend are quickly removed from the approved list, never to get back to Augusta again. That's a powerful incentive, whether you earn your living writing golf daily, like me, or attend the one tournament a year as part of a springtime Southern jaunt, like most of the guys from the tiny papers.

Those who are approved, on the other hand, are treated like kings. The media center is nice, the food and drink are plentiful, they bring us the players for interviews, and then proffer printed transcripts a few minutes later, and they're just as nice as pecan pie. Up to a point, anyway. For years, the ***New York Times*** golf beat writer was the erudite and distinguished Lincoln Werden. He probably covered forty or more Masters in his long career. But time passed, as it does, and he finally retired. The next spring, he wrote Augusta National asking if he could get a media credential to come back and see his old friends from over the decades—the players, the members and the press alike.

"No," the club answered. "Working media only." Of course, the piece he had written in 1973, criticizing Augusta National for not inviting the black golfer Lee Elder to play even though he had met all the qualifications for other players, might have had something to do with their attitude. But that's always been the essence of Augusta—their way or the highway.

I spent—or wasted—a good hour catching up with guys I hadn't seen in a year. We swapped lies, exchanged gossip and debated who, if anyone, might present a challenge to Tiger this week. I set up shop at the cubicle assigned to the ***Boston Journal***, touched base with the desk back in Boston, and planned my coverage for the next few days.

The first piece I wanted to do was a profile on Bobby McCallen, the Rhode Island kid who had finished second in last summer's U.S. Amateur and was therefore invited to play in the Masters. Augusta National also invites the British Amateur winner and the U.S. Mid-Am champ. It's supposed to be a homage to Bob Jones' long career as an amateur. But that conveniently ignores the fact that the Masters used to invite the four quarterfinalists from the Amateur. They apparently decided that a smaller homage was good enough.

I had pre-arranged a time to meet with McCallen, and when I wandered over to the clubhouse, they told me he would be coming off the course shortly after an early morning practice round. He showed up about thirty minutes later, and he told me that he was going right back out again as soon as he could. I laughed and told him not to leave his game out there before the tournament started, reminding him of one of the British amateur champs who can come over a few years ago and played something like fifteen practice rounds before going out in the tournament and shooting 80-84.

"Where are you staying?" I asked him.

"They got us up in the Crow's Nest," he said. "It's pretty cool up there. Want to see it?"

I accepted his invitation because I had never been up there. The steep-pitched roof of the Augusta clubhouse, topped with a cupola, creates a dormer space on the third floor, under the roof. Up there, there are a few small bedrooms and a bath that create an intimate little dorm that can sleep four. During the Masters, they reserve that space for the amateur competitors, if they want it.

I followed Bobby up the stairs to the second floor. Just past the entrance to the Champion's locker room, a steep and narrow wooden stair led up to the garret. The space was square, small and the bedrooms were hidden behind partitions. And there weren't many windows, but light flooded in from the windows in the square cupola that opened up in the center of the ceiling, supported by strong beams. Bobby stepped into his room to get something, and saw me looking up at the cupola when he came back. He chuckled.

"You get the best views of the place from up there," he said, nodding upwards.

"How do you know?" I smiled.

Bobby got a conspiratorial look in his eyes and quietly shut the door to the stairway.

"C'mere," he said. "I'll give you a boost. If you pull yourself up to that beam, you can get a foothold on that one." He was pointing. "Then you can stand there and look out. Unbelievable!"

He bent over and laced his hands together. I shrugged. Why not? It's a sight that not many have the chance to see. I stuck my foot in his hands and he hoisted me upward. It was easy to place my feet where he told me, and my head reached about halfway up the window facing the golf course. It was pretty amazing. I could see all the way down to Rae's Creek, and even beyond to the fairways of the adjacent Augusta Country Club. Down below, there were excellent sight lines for the first tee, the ninth green, the eighteenth green and the tenth tee, all in a row across the top of the hill.

"Wow," I said.

"Yeah," Bobby said below me. "OK, try to land soft when you come down. If they hear a thump, they'll come up here and throw me out of here!"

I grabbed a beam and swung down slowly.

"That'd be a great place to watch the last round of the tournament," I said.

"Unless I'm playing in it," Bobby said with the unabashed ambition and bravado of youth. I liked that attitude. If you can't feel like a world-beater when you're barely twenty, when can you?

We went back downstairs and strolled over to the putting green. Bobby and I talked for about thirty minutes, and with plenty of good quotes, I went back to the press center and wrote the piece for the next day's paper.

Chapter Twenty-Five

Tuesday was routine for a major. The practice range, putting green and the golf course were busy all day with pros getting their game faces on. I stayed pretty close to the media center, conserving my energy for the weekend. Augusta National is one of the hilliest courses the pros play all year, and one can get tired pretty quick tromping around watching golf.

Every few hours, they'd parade in somebody for an interview. Colin Montgomerie, the senior statesman of Europe, still hoping he could win his first major title. Ernie Els, the genial South African, who may be too nice to be a worldbeater. Vijay Singh, who they probably had to drag kicking and screaming off the range for the interview. He was his usual untalkative self.

I listened with only half an ear as they answered our questions. In one way or another, they all bravely professed to be striking the ball well. Their conditioning programs and the way they had prepared for the Masters had gone well. They were ready, confident, hopeful. None of them said what they were really thinking—that maybe Tiger could come down with food poisoning, roll his car into a ditch or slip in the bathroom. Otherwise, they knew, and we knew, they were probably in for a long week of disappointment. Again.

After filing my piece in the early afternoon, I scrammed. Mary Jane and I went for a walk on a bike path that ran along the riverfront. It was a pretty spring afternoon. We held hands. The sun was golden. Birds were singing. We went back to Conn's house and insisted on taking him out to dinner.

"OK," he said. "I know a place. Bit of a drive, but different."

He wasn't kidding. It took a good 45 minutes to get there. We headed back west toward Atlanta on I-20, then turned off at Highway 78 and drove north through rolling Georgia farm country for a half hour. Finally, we reached the town of Washington.

It was like driving backward in time. As we neared the center of town, where five or six roads converged, elegant antebellum mansions began cropping up on either side of the road. Many had huge white, two-story fluted columns, brick stairs, heavy wrought-iron ornamentation, and gigantic old magnolias and live oaks.

"Welcome," Conn said, "To the Old South."

Mary Jane was agog. Most of the yards had hedgerows of azaleas ablaze in pinks, reds and whites, with the elegant sweeping arms of the dogwoods painting daubs of white against the green background. Children played innocently on the streets, chased by barking dogs, their bikes scattered across the broad green lawns.

"Ah do declare," Mary Jane drawled in her best Scarlett imitation. "We must be goin' to Miss Pitty Pat's for supper, Mister Wilkes."

Conn and I laughed. He pulled us into the central square, dominated by a large stone courthouse on one side, and a turreted, imposingly Gothic three-story building opposite.

"That's the Fitzpatrick Hotel," Conn said. "They got a new woman chef down from Atlanta last year, and I heard she's good."

We parked and went inside, where all was deep wood panelling, beveled glass mirrors, and rococo chandeliers. A matronly woman bade us welcome and asked us to come in and sit a spell. Mary Jane was delighted. I wanted to ask if the woman still owned slaves, but decided to go with the flow of the evening instead.

We enjoyed cocktails in the Victorian lounge, and then were shown into the elegant dining room, where the white-linen tablecloths, candles and dark wood paneling evoked the lazy, carefree days before the cannons boomed at Fort Sumter, before Atlanta was burned to the ground, before the Southern way of life was irrevocably changed.

"So," Conn said after we had ordered, "What's new at the National this year?"

"The usual tweaking," I said. "Tees moved back, mature trees planted to look like they've been there forever, another half-inch in the rough. Anything they can do to maintain relevance, they'll do it."

"Tiger really got to them, didn't he?"

"You'd better believe it," I said. "But to be fair, if Tiger hadn't shot that 18-under-par, someone else would have. But there's only so much they can do to stretch that course. The only other defense they have is the greens, and they're already close to impossible. If they shave them down any further, the tournament will never end—guys will be out there five- and six-putting until the sun goes down."

"They still don't have much rough," Conn pointed out. "What if they grew the rough like the Open?"

"Same thing," I said. "The tournament would never end. Those greens were made to accept only shots with backspin for control. Take away the spin, which is what happens when you hit the ball from deep rough, and they'll be missing greens, chipping over and back and over and back, and then three-putting. You'd be looking at eight-hour rounds."

"So what is the answer, oh Great Swami of golf?" Conn chuckled.

"There really isn't one," I said. "Of course, since the Masters is just an exhibition really, and since Augusta National seems to make up its own rules about most everything anyway, they could try introducing a Masters-only golf ball that doesn't go quite as far. A lot of people think the U.S. Golf Association should do that anyway, but those guys are gun-shy of being sued again by the industry. The Masters could maybe get away with it, since it's just that one tournament, one time a year. But I'd bet the players would kick and scream anyway. So my guess is they'll keep tweaking the course, the pros will keep making birdies, and eventually the National will just have to get used to seeing nothing but red numbers on the scoreboard."

"Are you guys going to talk about golf all night?" Mary Jane said, frowning.

"No," Conn said. "In fact, I was about to mention an interesting call I got in the office today. It was from Martha Judge of Blythe, South Carolina."

"John's mother," I said.

"Yup. She wants to talk to me about a wrongful death suit against Grosvenor and the Augusta National Golf Club."

"No kidding?" Mary Jane said. "Do you think she has a case?"

"Don't know yet," Conn said. "She's going to come up next week and sit down with me. Grosvenor would have to have prior knowledge for it to stick, I think. If the Judge boy was killed as a warning to Grosvenor, he probably didn't know it was going to happen."

"Which takes him off the hook," I said.

"Maybe," Conn said, nodding. "I got one of my associates doing some research on the law. Might be fun to tee it up against those guys."

"They'd probably go out and retain the Chief Justice of the Supreme Court to argue their case," I said. "Don't think money or connections are a problem."

"I always like a good fight," Conn said, his eyes alight.

"Men are so interesting," Mary Jane said. "Everything boils down to a fight, doesn't it? Did you ever think of maybe going to them and asking nicely if there isn't something they'd like to do for the poor boy's mother? You know, to make it right?"

Conn and I looked at her for a moment. Then we both burst out in laughter.

"What?" Mary Jane said, her face turning red.

"The bull elephant in full charge does not stop to talk things over, or consider a more reasonable course of action," Conn said. "The only way to get his attention is smack him in the head or put a bullet into his brain. Nature over nurture."

"But..." Mary Jane was not convinced.

"Conn's right," I said. "You can't expect a beast to change its stripes, nor can you expect Augusta National to roll over and play nice. They never have, and they never will. They're used to doing what they want and getting their way. And they have the money and resources to get whatever they want."

"In that case, why pick a fight with them? If they're going to win, anyway? It seems like a waste of time," she said.

"Because sometimes you have to pick the fight, even if the chances of winning are slim," Conn said. "Sometimes it's just the right thing to do. And in those cases, even if you get your head beaten in, figuratively speaking of course, you can sleep well at night knowing you've done the right thing."

"You sound like Hacker now," Mary Jane said. "He's always riding off into the sunset to save someone. Drives me nutty."

I smiled at her. "But it makes me more loveable."

"Well, no, it doesn't," she said. "It makes me nutty. But I understand that it's part of what makes you tick. I can deal with that. If you changed that part of you, even if you could, then you might not be the same Hacker. And I might not like that Hacker like I do the real one."

"Awww," I said. She blushed. Conn smiled.

"Glad we got that out of the way," he said. "If she had said that while we were eating, I might have been sick."

Chapter Twenty-Six

Wednesday is always one of the busiest days at the Masters. Tiger gives us his pre-game thoughts. The chairman of the club delivers his state of the Masters address. The Golf Writers Association holds one of the two annual meetings of the membership (the other is at the U.S. Open), and holds a banquet at night presenting the Player of the Year awards. And in the afternoon, there is the fun and frivolity of the Par-3 tournament. And, of course, the anticipation level for the main event ratchets up another notch.

Conn had some work to do at his office, so he gave Mary Jane his Masters pass. She was looking forward to seeing this holy of holies for the first time. I drove us over early in the morning and parked in the press lot.

"Wow," she said when we got out of the car. "This is the best parking lot I think I have ever seen."

"Stop it," I said.

We went through the entrance gate and I walked her over to the putting green. There were some players striking putts, getting ready for a morning practice round. Mary Jane recognized Ben Crenshaw and began hyperventilating.

"He's a bit old for you, isn't he?" I asked dryly.

"Maybe I could be his trophy wife," she said wistfully. "He's soooo cute!"

Of all the descriptors I had used with Crenshaw over the years, "cute" was a new one for me, so I said nothing. I showed some points of interest to Mary Jane—the famed wisteria vine, the first tee, and showed her where the tenth tee was, across the hill to the left. Glancing at my watch, I told her I had to go, and we arranged to meet for lunch in a couple of hours up by the old oak tree behind the clubhouse.

"Where's Amen Corner?" she asked.

"Keep walking downhill," I said. "If you fall into Rae's Creek, you've gone too far."

I peeled off for the media center. There was a line waiting to get in. Pee Wee was being more ornery than usual, because he had a lot more guarding than normal. Card-carrying members of the Golf Writers Association who aren't credentialed for the tournament are allowed onto the grounds for this one day so they can attend the general meeting. They are told they have to leave immediately after the one-hour business meeting, but that edict is generally ignored. Pee Wee will throw them out of the media center, but they're free to wander the grounds for the day.

The confab was thankfully brief. The order of business, as usual, involved our president's report on his meetings with the U.S. Golf Association, PGA of America and the Royal & Ancient to try and make our job even easier, arranging better and closer media hotels, better shuttle transportation to tournament sites, more access to the players and better working conditions. As if we have it tough anyway. Then, also as usual, someone got up to complain about the judging in the annual writing contest. I've always thought writing contests are silly, so I never enter, which is just as well since the same four or five guys seem to win every year anyway. This year, at least, we were spared the usual endless and ongoing debate about whether we were admitting too many or not enough new members.

Once the writers' meeting adjourned, the interview theater quickly filled up. Charlie Grosvenor walked in looking regal in his Masters green sport coat and gray flannel trousers. Some men can pull the look off, some can't. Grosvenor, who probably had a personal tailor, didn't look bad in dark green. He took his place at the table on the riser up front, and waited to be introduced by the press and publicity chairman, also green-jacketed.

Grosvenor's remarks were brief. He went over the changes to the course made in the year since the last tournament, why they were made, and how the club hoped that all changes were in keeping with the vision of the founder, otherwise known as His Holiness Bob Jones. I wanted to place my hand over my heart and start singing "The Battle Hymn of the Republic." Glory, glory hallelujah.

Most of us knew better than to ask any kind of tricky question. Grosvenor would, like every other chairman before him, always hide behind the old rubric: "Augusta National is a private club, and we prefer not to comment on that." But there is always someone who asks something about money, or who the members are, or when they're going to admit a woman, or if they were going to invite more Europeans or Asians or amateurs or green-eyed Martians with antennae. "We're a private club," he'd say, "And we prefer not to comment on that."

So I didn't ask Grosvenor if he was still worried about Enrico de la Paz sneaking up on him with a handgun. Or hiding in the blooming azaleas with a high-powered rifle, waiting for a chance to pick him off. Or what the problem was between him and the Colombian cartel. Or if Augusta National was still cashing in on drug running, like they apparently had been doing since the days of the High Priest Roberts.

I made sure he saw me, though. And throughout the press conference, his eyes kept flicking over to me. Maybe he was waiting for me to spill his beans. But I had promised to keep quiet, and I did. Not too many guys would have. I wondered if he was surprised.

Grosvenor then introduced Tiger as the defending champ, and he did his usual professional job of fending off questions about how many strokes did he think he'd win by this year. He went through the usual litany of taking it one shot at a time, good field of players here, had to earn every win, game was in good shape, had some good practice rounds and he just hoped to be in shouting distance by Sunday afternoon and then let the chips and putts fall where they may.

I wrote up a quick piece and sent it along to Boston, with a note telling the desk I'd file a more detailed preview story later in the day. That one pretty much writes itself. ***"The umpty-third Masters tournament gets underway today at the Augusta National Golf Club, with a field of 91 hopefuls chasing one man, Tiger Woods, and his quest to overtake Jack Nicklaus' record of 18 major tournament wins."*** Quotes from Tiger, Phil, Ernie and Veej, graph or two about the changes to the golf course. Then a page or two of notes and quotes I'd picked up over the last few days. Ain't exactly rocket science, is it?

I strolled back out onto the grounds and loitered around the grassy lawn where the game's movers and shakers meet and greet at the white metal tables shaded by the Masters-green umbrellas. The CEOs of all the golf equipment makers were out in force, hobnobbing with each other and with executives from CBS, U.S. Golf Association bigwigs and a handful of golf-crazy movie stars.

The grounds were packed with spectators today, and I noticed a line waiting to get into the pro shop to stock up on Masters logo junk. Every year somebody—usually a Japanese magnate of some kind—casually strolls into the shop and buys all the cashmere sweaters or the entire wall of golf shirts, dropping a few hundred thousand dollars or twenty zillion yen, with a smile and a bow. No wonder Marty Tinsdale, the head pro, motors around town in a brand-new Mercedes every year.

Mary Jane materialized out of the crowd, carrying a green plastic bag and wearing a big smile.

"I got Phil Mickelson's autograph," she said. "He seems like such a sweet man."

I grimaced. "It's all image," I said. "In real life, he kicks his dog on a daily basis."

"No!" she exclaimed, "Really?"

I laughed. "Have no idea," I said. "But I always distrust someone who appears to be quasi-perfect like him."

"You are such a cynic," she said, shaking her head. "I might not share this sandwich with you after all." She held up her bag. "Got a couple of those pimento-and-cheese things. And a couple of burgers. Finest lunch of its kind available anywhere on the planet."

"Stop it," I said.

"Where can we go eat?"

I thought a minute. The shaded tables were all full, and I didn't think the Pinkertons would let us in there anyway. One had to have some special dispensation or a billion-dollar net worth to get in there without an invitation.

"I know," I said. "Let's go over to the range, grab a seat and watch them practice."

"Oh, joy," Mary Jane said.

We walked around the west side of the clubhouse towards the range, which occupied a fairly short space heading back towards Washington Road. So short, in fact, that the club had to string netting across some tall poles to prevent balls flying out into the busy traffic. Back in Snead and Hogan's time, the range was deep enough for all but the really big hitters of the day. Now, even Fred Funk can knock a driver midway up the net. And in those years when John Daly shows up, the fans always encourage him to try and hit one over the netting. Which he does with apparent ease and his usual lack of regard for the consequences.

To get to the bleachers where I thought we could sit and eat, we had to walk past the circular drive at the club's main entrance, where people were taking photos of each other in front of the yellow-flowered Masters logo. As we made the circular walk, I noticed a large white limousine driving up Magnolia Lane. It looked familiar, but I didn't know why. I lingered a moment and watched as it pulled up. The passenger-side front door opened and the man who stepped out was the same guy I had seen at Daniels Field the other morning, the one from the huge private jet. He opened the back door, and helped the same old man with the cane out of the car. Together, they walked into the clubhouse with one of the Pinkerton guards holding the door for them.

"C'mon, Hacker," Mary Jane was impatient. "The sign says Camilo Villegas is hitting balls. He's another hottie."

"How do you even know who Camilo Villegas is?" I wondered.

"I pay attention, of course," she said.

I made a mental note to find out who the rich guy with the limo was. If I had whipped out my cell phone, the beefy hand of the National's law enforcers would have dropped on me like the plague. I'd have to wait until I got back to the media center. But I'd bet Travis Kitchen could find out who the guy was. I could give him the tail number of the jet as a good start.

We found a space in the last row at the top of the bleachers and Mary Jane passed out the sandwiches. There were a half-dozen players working on their swings, accompanied by their caddies, swing gurus and sometimes by an equipment company rep. At a normal pro stop, the equipment guys are more in evidence as they entice the pros to try a new driver or wedge. But here at a major, they know better. Nobody wants to use something new and unfamiliar in a major tournament.

Villegas was rifling three-irons down the range, where they either hit or one-hopped the netting 275 yards away. The youngster from Colombia was one of the brightest new stars on the Tour, noted for his unusual crab-like crouch on the greens to sight his putting line.

"Cute little tushy on that one," Mary Jane said, her mouth full of sandwich.

"How sexist," I said. "What about his excellent golfing form and prodigious ability?"

"Yeah," she said, nodding. "That too. But his tushy is world-class."

"What about Retief?" I asked, nodding at the South African who was hitting balls a couple of stations down the range from Villegas. "How's his tush?"

She glanced at him for a moment. "It's OK," she said. "But not in the same ballpark."

I was thinking that a top-ten-tushy ranking of the PGA Tour might make for an interesting future column, at least for the female readers of the ***Boston Journal***, but then I thought of Frank Donatello, my obese, obtuse and mostly brain-dead editor. He would spike something like that faster than a story that praised anything about the Yankees. "Whaddaya, gone gay on me Hacker?" he would mutter darkly, throwing the piece in his overflowing trash can.

My reverie was broken by the sound of squealing tires. I turned around in time to see the long white limo screeching away from the front door, its rear tires running up over the curb and across part of the grassy circle. The huge car swayed as it bumped over the curb and back down onto the driveway on the other side, and it peeled off down Magnolia Lane towards the exit at an unusually fast clip.

"Somebody's in a hurry to leave," Mary Jane said. "Good thing they didn't run over anybody."

Whoever it was in the limo apparently didn't want to stay very long. As soon as I could, I'd have to call Kitchen and find out who that guy was.

It was approaching 1 p.m., the starting time for the par-3 tournament, another Wednesday fixture at the Masters. The nine-hole short course, tucked in behind the "cabins" that extended down and behind the tenth tee, had been a late addition to the Masters, but the annual event had become extremely popular with players and fans alike. For one thing, both Arnold Palmer and Jack Nicklaus, who had given up trying to play in the Masters, both showed up for this one, often accompanied by a grandchild or two. The other players were in relaxed mode, playing just for the fun of it, letting their kids caddy for them, and perhaps hoping to make a hole-in-one and collect one of the crystal bowls that were awarded. However none of them really wanted to win because of the curse—no winner of the par-3 tournament has ever gone on to win the main event. More than once I had seen players deliberately dump a shot or two into the pond that surrounded the ninth and final green, to make sure that they wouldn't win the par-three tournament.

The "patrons" were extra rowdy, placing noisy bets on which player would get it closest to the hole, up and in, or make the longest putt, and hooting and hollering at every shot. The Pooh-Bahs in the green jackets might not like it, but the only word to describe the galleries at the par-three tournament is "mob-like." The club permitted such undignified behavior, mainly because there was no way they could stop it.

I led Mary Jane to the shady hillside that overlooked the eighth and ninth greens, and we managed to find an opening in the gathering crowd on the grassy slope where we could sit and watch the fun. The cheers, jeers and groans from the other holes came rolling through the piney woods, and soon, the play reached us. Arnie was in one of the first threesomes, and he was applauded every step of the way. Even though Jack Nicklaus won six green jackets to Arnie's four, it is Palmer who has always owned the fan's hearts. Jack is respected and admired, Arnie is beloved.

A few minutes later, Villegas' group played through. He made a routine par on the eighth hole, and after a short wait, teed his ball on the ninth. The tee is cut into the side of the hill we were sitting on, and the green is surrounded by water and slightly downhill, about 130 yards away. Villegas picked his club, waggled and swung.

"Woooo, great tush!" Mary Jane hollered after he made contact. The fans around us laughed and cheered. Camilo broke from watching the flight of his shot and glanced our way with a big smile. I tried to sink into the ground.

"Are you trying to get thrown out of here?" I asked.

"This would be the best place of its kind you've ever been tossed from," she said.

Chapter Twenty-Seven

I called Travis Kitchen when I got back to the media center after the fun and games of the par-3 tournament. I told him about the limo and the plane and gave him the tail number of the jet. Then I finished up my pieces, sent them off, found Mary Jane and we went back to Conn's house.

Later that night, as Mary Jane was assembling a huge dish of lasagna for dinner and throwing together a big green salad. Conn and I were working our way deep into a bottle of red wine and talking about the tournament when my phone rang. It was Kitchen.

"You'll never guess whose plane that was you saw," he said.

"Well, with the body guard and the limo, I'm thinking it must be someone important," I said. "And the old man was wearing a guayabera, so I'm thinking Miami. I don't know, some Cuban exile?"

"You're on the right track," he said. "The plane is registered to a company called Importeza Americas, based in Coral Gables. That company is run by someone named Juan Carlos Obrador."

"Obrador," I said. "Same name as the cartel."

"Yeah, isn't that a coincidence?" Kitchen said. "Juan Carlos is the brother of Jose Felix, the bad guy. Juan of course is originally from Colombia, but he's apparently a legitimate businessman and became a naturalized American citizen about ten years ago."

"What kind of business?"

"Import export," he said.

"Same business as Grosvenor," I said. "Isn't that a coincidence? What does this guy sell?"

"All kinds of things from South America from produce to cut flowers to indigenous Indian artwork. Donated a ton of money to the Miami art museum and has a wing named after him."

"Do you think he dropped in on Charlie to discuss a couple of tsotchkes for the office? If so, it didn't go so well. He was in and out of there in five minutes."

"I don't know," Kitchen said. "Could have been a meeting of old friends and competitors. Could have been a social call. Or it could have been Charlie's final warning."

"Is there anything that indicates Obrador is connected to the family business?" I asked.

"Nothing that I can find in the official records," he said. "But it does make one wonder."

"Anything new on the Rico front?"

"Naw, he's apparently gone to ground," Kitchen said. "If he's still in town."

"Well, keep me posted," I said.

"Oh, absolutely," he said sarcastically. "I have nothing better to do than make sure you're kept up to date and fully informed."

The TOURNAMENT BEGAN on schedule the next morning with the ceremonial drive off the first tee. Those duties used to be handled by old-timers like Jock Hutchison, Gene Sarazen, Sam Snead and Byron Nelson, but the Grim Reaper had taken care of all of those greats from bygone days, so the Masters had to find some past champions who are still upright and breathing. They had thankfully managed to convince aging former champions like Doug Ford and Billy Casper to forego their lifetime privilege of playing in the Masters, and talked Arnie into doing the honors of the opening shot. Those of us who found it painful to watch the old geezers trying to break 100 were thankful.

Tiger didn't have his "A" game on Thursday, but still managed to scrape it around in 69. The first day leader was the usual unknown who somehow managed to shake off the nerves and make everything he looked at. The young Irishman Casey O'Shea, one of the up-and-coming stars of the European Tour, posted a nifty 65 to take the first-day lead. In the media center, we began placing bets on how high he would go the next day. I put five bucks down on 79. I'd seen plenty of first-day wonders flame out fast.

But I was wrong. O'Shea came back on Friday with a nice 68 and was the leader by three, with Tiger right on his heels. Vijay, Jim Furyk and a couple of the Australians were not far back. Ernie Els was six behind, and Phil Mickelson, after splashing one in the creek on 12, and making a weak par on 13, had to birdie two of the last five to make the cut.

Friday night, we collected Conn and made the rounds of some of the parties that were held throughout town every night. We started with one up on the Hill for some of the locals who ran in Conn's circles, and then hit the famous Aussie party later in the evening. The first one was elegant, with ***luminarias*** in someone's backyard, mint juleps and some good snacks. The guests mostly stood around and talked golf.

The Aussie party, when we arrived, was close to being out of control, as it is every year. When we got there, Stuart Appleby, Robert Allenby and Geoff Ogilvy were singing karaoke in hideous off-key form in the family room, while out back a band was providing thumping inspiration for dancers crowded onto a temporary parquet floor that reminded me of the old Boston Garden. The beer was flowing in prodigious amounts, the sheilas were out in force, and someone who was pointed out to me as the director of the Australian Golf Union was staggering around with his necktie tied around his head like a Japanese shogun warrior. In other words, it was your typical Aussie gathering.

We didn't stay late, as we had in years past. Conn and I looked at each other and sighed. "I'm getting old," Conn said. "The idea of going home and getting some sleep is somehow more appealing to me than this." He motioned at the madness going on around us. I had to agree. But Mary Jane made me take her onto the dance floor before we left.

We dawdled on Saturday morning. The weather had turned ugly, as a cold front was passing through, accompanied by gusty wind and intermittent rain. It looked like it was going to be a tough day to be playing golf.

Mary Jane had been invited by Beatrice Samper to make the two-hour drive back to Atlanta for some serious department-store shopping at one of the upscale malls in Buckhead. Since she had already seen as much of the Masters as she could handle, she was looking forward to it. Beatrice picked her up at around 10. Mary Jane gave me a kiss and said she'd be home by early evening.

Conn and I waited another couple of hours, doing nothing much, and I drove him over to the course just after noon.

Saturday is moving day, when the players try to claw their way up the leaderboard to be in position for that Sunday final round. Anyone who could get to within four or five shots of the lead had to be considered a contender, as almost anything could—and often did—happen on Sunday when nerves are stretched taut and the tournament hangs on the outcome of virtually every shot.

The rain had mostly let up by the time we got there, but a quick glance at the morning scores told me that no one would be going low today. With the wind and wet conditions, making pars was a notable achievement for most of the field. The fans were unperturbed, however, and many had purchased one of those throwaway clear-plastic hooded ponchos to keep the rain off. One of the wags in the media center, watching a TV shot that panned across the plastic-wrapped fans gathered in the bleachers behind the 12th tee down at Amen Corner said "It looks like a bunch of condoms out there."

"Geez," I said, "Don't let that delicate flower Tom Watson hear you. He'll get you booted." It was Watson who wrote to the club to complain when CBS color man Gary McCord referred to the greens as being so slick it seemed they had applied bikini wax to them. McCord has not been heard at Augusta since.

The last group, Tiger and the O'Shea kid, went off at about two-thirty. The young Irishman, his flaming red hair peeking out the top of his visor, was still playing good golf, controlled and steady. He smiled a lot and seemed to be enjoying his time in the cauldron. Tiger made a nice birdie on the long second, and another on the eighth and was within one of the lead. Ernie Els made a nice run of birdies and inched up to within three. It was beginning to feel like the Masters again, exciting, tense and dramatic. Even if you don't drink the Kool-Aid, this tournament has a way of demanding your attention like a slap to the face. It was good stuff.

The leaders were beginning their back nine and I was sitting at my cubicle in the warm and dry media center watching it all on television when my phone rang.

"H-Hacker?" It was Mary Jane. She sounded a little funny.

"What's up, babe?" I asked.

There was silence on the line for a long moment. Then I heard a man's voice.

"Senor Hacker?" someone said in accented tones. "I have your pretty little friend. Her life is now in your hands. You will, please, do exactly as I say."

My heart sank and simultaneously began to race in my chest.

"Who is this?" I asked. "Rico?"

"Si," he said.

I muttered a curse or three. "What do you want?"

"You and I must have a conversation," he said. "But we must be alone or the woman dies."

"If you touch one hair on her head, I will hunt you down and kill you with my bare hands," I said, trying to keep my voice even. Quigs Quigley, sitting next to me, watching the tournament in rapt attention, turned and looked at me with a raised eyebrow. I ignored him.

"This is not the time to be a hero," the voice said softly. "These are my instructions. You and I will meet tonight at 7 p.m. After our conversation, I will release your friend."

"OK," I said. "Where?"

"I am in Atlanta. I will meet you at the Oaklawn Cemetery. It is just to the east of downtown and right off the Interstate Numero Twenty." He gave me the exit number and told me to take a left at the first light and I would see the entrance to the cemetery. Once inside the gates, I was to follow his instructions to make my way through the park. I wrote down the instructions, my mind racing.

"And Senor Hacker," he continued. "A word of warning. If I see the slightest sign of the authorities, and I will be looking, the girl is dead. Do you understand?"

"Yes," I said.

"You had better leave at once. You have three hours. Until six." He rang off.

I sat there thinking, trying to quell the feelings of fear for Mary Jane that suddenly rose up and took over my entire body. I could feel the blood running through my veins, pulsing with the beats of my heart.

I called my office back in Boston. Luckily, I had already filed my Sunday column and a couple of pages of notes. When I got the desk editor on the line, I told him a sudden emergency had come up and I had to leave the tournament. He must have heard the stress in my voice, because he didn't ask any questions, but told me he'd pick up the AP wire story. "What do you want me to tell Frank?" he asked.

"Nothing," I said. "I'll check in later tonight." ***I hope***, I thought.

I grabbed my cell phone and the directions and got up and left. I tried to act as normal as possible, even though I wanted to run like hell. As I came out of the media center, I saw Pee Wee arguing with Conn, whose face was red. He saw me and threw up his hands.

"Would you tell this Nazi that if he lays his fat paw on me again, I'll file a suit as big as his ass," he said.

Pee Wee looked ready to put a whomping on Conn. I grabbed Conn by the arm and almost dragged him away. "C'mon, Hack," he said. "I was just getting warmed up on that lardbutt. I mean..." He suddenly looked at me. "What's wrong?" he asked. "You look like you just lost your best friend."

I filled in the basics as we quick stepped it out to the press lot. When we got to the car, Conn started to get in.

"You can't go," I said. "He said he'd kill her if he saw anyone else."

"He won't see me," Conn said. "You can drop me off before you go inside the cemetery. I'm not letting you go by yourself. C'mon, let's get moving."

Reluctantly, I agreed. I was actually glad to have him along for the two-hour drive over to Atlanta. We pulled out onto Washington Road and entered the thick traffic. People were just driving past the golf club to try and catch a glimpse of the excitement. The cars were moving at an interminably slow pace in both directions. I sat on my horn, but it still took a good ten minutes to inch our way the mile or two to the interstate. When we finally got onto the highway, I took the car up to 80 and kept it there.

I fished in my pocket and found the card that the fed had given me. With shaking hands, I managed to dial the number. It rang three times, and then someone answered.

"Speak," a voice said. I told him I needed to speak with someone I only knew as Wilcox who had given me this number.

"Your name?" I told him.

"Hold." He went away for about five minutes. There was no elevator music nor a recorded voice repeating the message "Your call is important to us, please hold the line ..." I guess the federal government is too cheap to pay for that kind of system.

Finally, I heard a soft click, and Wilcox' voice.

"Mister Hacker," he said. "How nice of you to call. How are things at the golf tournament?"

"Shut up and listen," I barked. I told him what had happened and where I was going.

"Hmmm," he said when I had finished. "That's right in character. Rico likes to make his hits in graveyards. I think he has a thing for it. No matter, we'll organize a reception."

"No!" I almost shouted. "He said he'd kill Mary Jane if he saw any cops lounging around."

"No, really?" Wilcox said, his voice dripping with sarcasm. "I'll tell the boys to turn off their blue lights, then." He chuckled. He was the only one who found it funny. "You go do the meet," he said. "We'll be there. You won't see us. Trust me."

"If you mess this up and Mary Jane is hurt, I will kill you with my bare hands," I said, for the second time in one afternoon.

"I believe that would constitute assault on a federal officer," he said. "But don't worry. We are actually pretty good at these things."

Chapter Twenty-Eight

I'm not exactly sure how, but I kept the speedometer between 80 and 90 most of the way to Atlanta and didn't see a solitary statey the entire way. Conn tried to keep me relaxed by keeping up a steady conversation, but I could not tell you a word of what he said during that ride. I answered in monosyllables, nodded in the right places and maybe even laughed once or twice at his jokes, but my mind was elsewhere. I saw Mary Jane, bound and gagged. Saw a menacing figure lift a gun to her head.

I must have started and groaned a little. Conn put his arm on my shoulder. "You OK?" he asked gently.

"Not really," I said. "I don't think I've ever been less OK."

He nodded. "Well, you're doing fine so far. Try to keep it together."

"What do you know about this Oaklawn place?" I asked.

"It's a pretty historic cemetery," he told me. "I think they started planting people there before the Civil War. I know they've got a section where they buried a lot of the Confederate Army. But it's got all this ornate Victorian stonework, and the rich families built huge mausoleums, trying to outdo each other. Lotta famous Atlantans are buried there. Margaret Mitchell for one."

"Gone with the Wind?" I asked.

"That's the one," he said.

"Frankly my dear, I don't give a damn," I said.

"Good one."

He set off on a long and rambling discussion of why some people like to spend their hard-earned money on gaudy memorials after they die and how the Victorians liked to take the entire family to the cemetery on Sunday afternoon for outings with the dead people. I tuned him out and kept driving. I was making pretty good time until we reached Lithonia, a town about fifteen miles due east of Atlanta and the unofficial beginning of the sprawling metropolis of Atlanta. The traffic began to get heavier and slower, and there wasn't much I could do about it. Atlanta is world-famous for its traffic jams, and I prayed silently that we wouldn't get caught behind a pileup.

I kept one eye on the exit numbers and soon we were approaching downtown Atlanta. "Okay," I said. "What's the plan?"

"When we get near, we'll find a place where you can drop me off," Conn said. "I'll keep an eye on the entrance to the place, and if any cops show up for a normal patrol, I'll try and keep them away."

"Good," I said. "And if you see Wilcox and his Keystone Kops, tell them to keep the hell away."

"Right," he said. "I'll just step in the way of the SWAT team and tell them to please keep their voices down."

A sign told me that our exit was two miles away. I glanced at the clock on my dashboard. It was 6:40. Thanks to Daylight Savings Time which had kicked in a few weeks ago, it was still light.

I got off the highway, eased onto Boulevard—that's the name of the street—and turned left at the first light. The cemetery appeared off to our right, and I could see what Conn meant. Looming over the low brick wall that surrounded the park, I could see granite monuments piercing the Atlanta sky. Some were obelisks that resembled small versions of the Washington monument. Others looked like pint-sized chapels.

We saw the entrance a half block ahead. Conn pointed across the street from the arched entry to the cemetery. "There," he said. "Perfect."

He was pointing at a small storefront restaurant. The sign above the door, framed by two Coca-Cola logos, read "Six Feet Under."

"You gotta have a sense of humor if you open a restaurant across the street from a graveyard," Conn said. "I'll go in there, and keep my eyes open."

I pulled over to the curb and Conn got out. He was halfway out of the seat when he leaned back in. "Good luck," he said. "Don't do anything stupid. You gotta be calm."

I nodded. I couldn't speak. My heartbeat was approaching liftoff speed. Mach 1. I turned into the cemetery, passing under the red-brick arch. It was full of mature trees shading the many fanciful sculptures and mausoleums. Off to the right, a large cherry tree, in full impressive bloom of pink and white, spread its limbs next to a structure that looked like a magnificent European cathedral with stained-glass windows, gargoyles and a slate roof, built in 1:25 scale.

The narrow road came to a circle and I followed it around to the right as it climbed a hill. The impressive glass-and-steel structures of Atlanta's downtown loomed in the near distance, poking up into a darkening sky. Dimly, in a back corner of my brain. I noted the irony of the bustle and hustle of this modern commercial center within sight of the quiet, shaded and elaborate resting places of the dead. On the far side of the hill, the road descended and split apart again at another circle. As I drove slowly along, I saw a small green-lettered sign with an arrow pointing the way to Margaret Mitchell's grave. On the left, I caught sight of a massive granite lion, draped in a battle flag, eyes shut in either pain or death. The plinth was carved with the words "Our Unknown Dead." The brutality with which the Civil War had been fought must have resulted in thousands of grey-clad soldiers left in death without any distinguishing characteristics.

Following Rico's instructions, I turned off on a narrow sand road and crept along it to where it ended at the brick boundary wall, about five feet high. I cut the engine and looked around. The place was empty, save for the rows of headstones, many decorated with weeping angels, soldiers in battle dress and other stonework representations of grief and death.

I got out of the car. The only sound was the faint humming of the cars on the nearby interstate, and a few birds singing mournfully in the trees as twilight deepened..

"Hola, Senor Hacker." The voice from the phone came from behind me. I turned around and saw a man, about five-six and slender, walking towards me. One of his hands was holding the arm of Mary Jane. She was bound and blindfolded with a kerchief that covered her face. In his other hand, he held a stubby black pistol, pointed at me. I held my hands up and watched as they approached. His hair was jet black and his features contained elements of a mestizo: an oval dark face, broad flat nose, and a thick mustache.

They eased around me so Rico was standing with his back to the brick wall. He wanted to keep an eye on the park behind me.

"I take it you are alone?" he said.

"Yes," I said. Mary Jane's head moved, once, when she heard my voice.

"You have been asking about me," he said. "Maria Sanchez. Lester Johnson. Now, here I am. You can ask me what you want to know."

"Let Mary Jane go," I said. "This doesn't concern her."

"No." he shook his head sadly. "That I cannot do. She is my ticket to freedom. You will be driving me from this place. I need to go back to Augusta tonight. There is still unfinished business there."

"What kind of unfinished business?" I asked. "More people to kill?"

He smiled. "You tell me what kind of business. You seem to have learned a great deal."

"I believe you killed John Judge," I said. "Somehow, you managed to breach the club's security system and bury him in the bunker. I believe it was a warning to Charlie Grosvenor, but a warning for what, I don't know. Then, you tried to kill Travis Kitchen at the Palmetto club, but you missed. I know Juan Carlos Obrador has come to Augusta, and I know he has met with Grosvenor. I know you work for the Obrador family. I know Grosvenor is pretty dirty. I think this whole thing is because of some arrangement between Charlie and Juan Carlos that went wrong. How'm I doing?"

"I would say you were almost entirely wrong," he said. "To begin, I did not kill that young man."

"Liar," I said.

Lithe as a cat, he stepped behind Mary Jane in a fluid motion and brought his gun up to the base of her skull.

"I would suggest, Senor, that you be very careful about your words. I do not lie."

I held out my hands in supplication. "Don't," I said, my voice rising. "She is not involved in any of this."

"She is your woman," he said. "That makes her involved." But he lowered his gun and stepped away from Mary Jane again.

"So what do we do now?" I asked.

He shrugged. "As I have said, you will drive me back to Augusta. The woman, too. When my business is finished, I will let you go. Her as well."

"How do I know that?" I asked. "How do I know that you won't kill both of us when your business is done?"

He smiled again, showing his teeth. "You must have trust, Senor Hacker."

"I'm supposed to trust you? You're a hired gun, an assassin. That is not the most trustworthy type of person I can think of."

He shrugged. "Then don't trust me," he said. "And life will happen as fate decrees. Your fate may be good, or it may be bad. We will find out which one together."

There was a sudden noise to our left as something crashed loudly high in the branches of a tree. Rico pushed Mary Jane to the ground, crouched in a shooter's position and pointed his gun in the direction of the sound. We heard something heavy hit the ground. At almost the same moment, someone leaped over the brick wall. It was Conn, wielding an aluminum baseball bat.

He turned towards Conn, gun raised. I took two leaping steps and grabbed for Rico's gun hand, forcing it up into the air. I managed to knock him slightly off balance, and Conn, taking advantage of the element of surprise, was able to land a hard blow across Rico's back with his bat. It made a hollow sound, and I felt the reverberations as it hit. Rico arched backwards in pain. But he wrenched his arm free from mine, shoved me away with his other hand and jumped backwards and to the side in front of a waist-high granite headstone. Again, he moved with the stealth of a cat. Conn had his bat raised for another strike, but de la Paz had regained the upper hand and was bringing the gun down to the firing position.

Until he stumbled on something underfoot. His feet seemed to spin out from under him, he gave out a startled cry and both his arms went up in the air as he tried to regain his balance. Conn stepped forward and took a full swing, the bat landing on the back of Rico's head with an awful sound, like a cantaloupe dropping on the sidewalk. Rico groaned in pain, took a half-step, lost his footing again, and fell. He dropped the gun and I quickly kicked it away. But Rico was not moving. I jumped over to Mary Jane, who had stayed on the ground when Rico pushed her down. I yanked the kerchief off her face, pulled her to her feet and wrapped her in my arms. She began to sob quietly, her body racked with heaving breaths. Conn stood over the prostrate figure, bat held high to strike again if Rico moved.

In the next instant, the cemetery seemed to explode. We were suddenly enveloped in bright flood lights from about four different directions. What seemed like an entire division of soldiers materialized out of the ether, all dressed in black jumpsuits and helmets with black faceguards, and all carrying impressive-looking automatic rifles, with barrel-mounted flashlights and laser-aimers. Five more men suddenly rappelled down out of the trees on black ropes that dropped silently. One of the men reached up and pulled his helmet off. It was Wilcox. He had a tiny bud stuck in one ear and a wrap-around microphone. And he was grinning.

"Nice work, Hacker," he said. "I told you we were good at this."

"It wasn't me," I said. I nodded at Conn, who had lowered his bat while several of the black suits grabbed the prostrate Rico off the ground and frog-marched him off to a black SUV that screeched up.

"Yeah," Wilcox said to Conn. "You'll never know how close you came to getting wasted. Luckily, there was enough light left for me to see your face, and I aborted the open-fire order. Still, I gotta give you credit for guts. Stupid, maybe, but gutsy."

One of the other members of Wilcox' team was shining his light at the base of the headstone where Rico had lost his footing. He bent over and picked something up.

"Yo, Whiskey-One," he called over to Wilcox. "Look at this." He held up his hand. It was a golf ball.

"What the hell?" I went over to look at it, still holding on tight to Mary Jane. It was a brand-new Titleist. I looked down at the ground. There were dozens of balls lying there; new ones, old ones, yellow and pink ones. Plus a few tees, scorecards and even a golf visor.

I brought my eyes up and read the inscription on the headstone. And began to laugh, a slightly hysterical laugh that was right on the edge of madness. The others came over to look.

ROBERT TYRE JONES JR.
March 17, 1902
December 18, 1971

MARY MALONE JONES
July 24, 1902
May 23, 1975

Chapter Twenty-Nine

Wilcox insisted that we take Mary Jane to the hospital and loaded her, Conn and me into another black SUV. The driver stuck a flashing blue light on top of the car and sped off towards downtown. Mary Jane was still sobbing, but she seemed to be in one piece. I held her close, stroking her back and arm.

"How cool was that?" Wilcox said to no one in particular. "Saved by the great Bobby Jones. I'll have to put this in my memoirs."

"I didn't know he was buried in Oaklawn," Conn said. "But I'm sure as hell glad he was."

"Remind me to bring back a dozen Pro V-1s and a bottle of his favorite bourbon," I said.

"Dunno, Hack," Conn said. "You do that and he might lose his amateur status."

"What, exactly, was your plan there?" Wilcox asked Conn.

He shrugged. "I was going to introduce the element surprise," he said. I figured you and your goons needed some kind of incident that would throw Enrico off guard for a split-second. I was hoping you had snipers or something ready to go. I tossed an old brick up into the trees to get his attention and jumped the fence."

"You almost hit one of my guys. What if it hadn't worked?" Wilcox asked, shaking his head.

"Then he would have shot me," Conn said, shrugging. "And that would have given your guys time to pounce."

"Gutsy," he said. "But stupid. You're a lucky man."

"Where did you get the bat?" I wanted to know.

Conn grinned. "As I was walking around to the back of the cemetery, following your car outside the wall, I came across this kid going home from playing some ball. I bought it from him."

"How much?"

He laughed. "I offered him twenty bucks, and he asked for fifty. He settled for forty. Kid has a future in business."

Still wrapped at my side, I felt Mary Jane stir. She put her head up and mumbled something.

"Mary Jane wants to know what happened to Beatrice Samper?" I said. "Geez, I hope she's all right."

Wilcox turned around. "She's OK, darlin'" he said to Mary Jane. "She flew out of here this afternoon on her way to Miami."

"You mean she was part of this?" I was stunned.

"Oh, yeah," Wilcox said, chuckling to himself. "In fact, next time you see Grosvenor, ask him how his sister-in-law is. That poor sumbitch got 'em coming and going in his family."

The SUV pulled up to the emergency entrance at the Crawford Long Hospital. An attendant came out with a wheelchair and whisked Mary Jane inside. We got out of the car and stood on the sidewalk for a minute. The twilight had deepened into evening, with just a faint glow of blue left in the sky.

"Where is Enrico going?" I asked.

Wilcox shrugged. "Secret location," he said. "He'll get treatment for his aching head and then we'll start debriefing him."

"Guantanamo?" I asked.

He smiled. "Nah, that's another division," he said. "We've got our own. It's still secret. For God's sake, don't tell the ***New York Times***. Those bastards like to run our state secrets just for the hell of it."

"What about Grosvenor?" I said. "Are you gonna bust him?"

"We're still looking at that," he said. "Right now, we've got mostly supposition and not that much in hard evidence. But we will certainly be asking him and his wife a few questions before too long."

I left him and Conn outside and went in to stay with Mary Jane. It didn't take long, probably thanks to the influence of Wilcox' alphabet agency. One of the docs came into her emergency-room cubicle and did a quick examination. He shined a pin light in her eyes, listened to her heart, took her blood pressure, quickly felt for any broken bones, palpated her abdomen for internal injuries. She was quiet and teary eyed during the examination, holding my hand tightly the entire time. The doc motioned at me, so I pried her hand away, smiled at her and followed him out into the corridor.

"I think she's OK," he said, making some notes on a chart. "No apparent injuries. I've called our resident OB-GYN to come down and examine her carefully. But I don't think she's been sexually assaulted. I'm going to give you something that will help calm her nerves, probably put her to sleep for a while. I recommend you get her some counseling. These kinds of stressful situations can be traumatic. It's like battle fatigue...the feelings and emotions can come back and probably will. Keep her quiet and resting for a few days. That will help."

He went away for a minute or two, and then came back with a pill bottle. I thanked him and shook his hand. I went back in and sat there with Mary Jane until the OB-GYN came in. She shooed me out of the room. After fifteen minutes, she came back out and gave me a thumbs up. I went back in the room and gave Mary Jane her pill and a cup of water. She took it without any questions. She still had a faraway look in her eyes. I sat there with her, holding her hand. We didn't speak. I wasn't sure what to say, and decided that I'd let her talk about it when she was ready. In a few minutes, I felt her body begin to relax. Her eyes closed and she slept.

I went back outside and found Conn and Wilcox still talking on the sidewalk outside the emergency entrance. My car was parked there.

"She's asleep," I said. "The doctor knocked her out. But she's fine, health wise. Nothing injured. No assault. Said she needs rest for a few days. I guess we should go back to Augusta, if that's OK with you, Conn."

He nodded. "Of course," he said. "But I'm driving. You've had enough stress for one day. Hell, you've had enough for a couple of years."

I was beginning to feel the aftershock setting in. My limbs were suddenly heavy and my face felt flushed. But my heart had returned to a normal rate. I wanted to sleep. I wanted to forget the last couple of hours. I wanted to go back to reporting on golf, telling the world who won and who lost and how.

"Where are you going?" I asked Wilcox.

"I'm heading over to the Varsity," he said. "Get some of their sliders and onion rings. Best greasy food in the world. Perfect after an adventure like this."

"Thanks," I said. "I owe you."

He waved me away. "Nah," he said. "Your friendly government servant, ready at all times to serve and protect. Just doing my job. Besides, your friend here did most of the work."

"I know," I said, my voice breaking down a little. "I owe him, too. Big time."

Conn grabbed my shoulder and gave it a squeeze. "Awww," he said. "Don't let's get all mushy. Saw a chance to help, and luckily no one got hurt. C'mon, let's go home."

We went back inside, put Mary Jane on a stretcher and wheeled her out to the car. We lifted her gently into the back seat, borrowing a pillow and blanket from the hospital. I promised to make a big donation to their next fund-raising program. I got into the front passenger seat and Conn took the wheel. As we pulled away, Wilcox gave us a mock salute.

The ride back to Augusta was quiet. Conn put a classical station on his stereo system, and I soon fell asleep, head lolling back on the headrest. My sleep was deep and dreamless and lasted all the way back to Augusta and Conn's house.

Chapter Thirty

Most of us golf writers don't show up on Sunday much before noon. Most of us, of course, are usually battling monster hangovers from the last night of carousing on Saturday. But few of us are really concerned with whether or not Robert Allenby finishes T-35 or solo 40th. And as any Masters Kool-Aid drinker can tell you, "the Masters really doesn't start until the back nine on Sunday." Except for Allenby, of course, whose Masters really ended Saturday afternoon.

A quick glance at the morning paper told us that O'Shea had finally wilted...a little. He was now three back of Tiger. Ernie Els had carded another fine round to get to two behind and was playing in the last group with Woods. Padraig Harrington, Jim Furyk and Tim "Lumpy" Herron were all within shouting distance. The day promised to deliver another barn-burner of a final round.

Mary Jane slept until about 11 in the morning, brushed her teeth and immediately took another pill. She sat on Conn's leather couch staring at nothing in particular and then fell asleep again. I hoped all the rest was going to help. I knew we'd have to talk about it sooner or later.

Conn said he'd stay with her. He said he preferred to watch the final round on television anyway. "You can see more of the action on TV and you don't have to deal with the crowds," he said. "You go ahead and do your thing. I'll keep an eye on her. She needs rest."

I stayed as long as I could, but around noon I showered and shaved. I checked in on Mary Jane before I left. She was on her side, eyes closed, breathing steady. I could only wonder what dreams she was having. Or nightmares.

It took me 45 minutes to drive the last two miles. Traffic was at a virtual standstill in both directions on Washington Road. The usual assortment of vendors hawking visors and golf shirts and golf towels were crowded in the parking lots on both sides of the busy road. There were even some hopeful, or delusional, property owners still trying to sell a parking space for the fans. But everyone who had a badge was no doubt already inside the gates, packed in five or six deep along the ropes.

I finally made it into the press parking lot, but had to drive up and down the aisles for another fifteen minutes before one of the volunteers, wearing his bright yellow hard-hat, took pity on me and showed me a spot where I could cram my car into a space. I could barely open the car door, but managed to squeeze out. It would have been a good time to have a moon roof.

I could feel the tension in the air that was the unmistakable indication that a major tournament was heading toward its end. It seems the neutrons begin to orbit faster or something, because the atmosphere is completely different on Sunday afternoon than it is even on Thursday morning. It holds the potential for drama, for disaster, and everything in between.

The crowd inside was thick, too. It took me a while to push my way through the milling crowds of people. Dare I say it, the place was mobbed, the word that got Jack Whitaker bounced from the hallowed grounds. When I finally arrived at the media center, Pee Wee was missing from his station at the door. I wondered where he was.

Inside, at the back of the media work area, I saw a group of about fifteen or twenty of the other writers standing around my desk. Quigs Quigley was waving his hands, a phone stuck to his ear. I sidled up, and tapped Johnny Carpenter from the ***L.A. Times*** on the shoulder. "What's up?" I said.

He turned to glance at me, then did a double take, then jumped about three feet and made a strange sound that sounded like "Wraggghhhh!" It made me jump, along with most of the other guys standing there.

"Jesus Christ on wheat toast," Carpenter managed to squeak. "Tell me you're not a ghost!"

I smiled. "Gee, I don't think so," I said.

Everyone else by now was crowding around me, patting me on the back, talking at once, excitedly. I couldn't understand a damn thing any of them were saying and wondered if the entire press corps had suddenly lost every last one of their marbles. Not that it would be easy to tell.

Quigs came up and actually gave me a hug. "Hacker," he said, "My God. We'd heard you were dead!"

"What?" I was dumbfounded. "What the hell are you talking about? And don't hug me again unless you give me a ring first."

Everyone started babbling at once again, the cacophony too much. I held up my hand. "Shut up!" I said. "One at a time. What the hell are you guys talking about?"

Quigs handed me a sheet of paper ripped out from a computer. It was a breaking story that had just come across the AP wires.

AUGUSTA MOTEL FIRE KILLS TWO
Boston golf writer, girlfriend feared dead.

AUGUSTA, GA. –(AP) An early morning fire broke out Sunday before dawn at the Motel 6 in Augusta, Ga. Authorities said that two people were apparently killed in the blaze. Identification has not been confirmed due to the condition of the bodies, but the hotel register indicated that the victims were Peter Hacker, a sportswriter for the ***Boston Journal***, in town to cover the Masters golf tournament at nearby Augusta National Golf Club, and his girlfriend, Mary Jane Cappaletti, also of Boston.

Police have asked for dental records from Boston before making an official identification. Eyewitnesses said the fire broke out in the pre-dawn hours in Room 234, causing a fire of intense heat and smoke. All other motel guests were able to escape the blaze without injuries.

"Holy crap," I said.

Quigs looked at me. "If it wasn't you in that room, who was it?"

I was reading the story again, my mind racing. "Huh?" I finally said, looking up. "Oh. I don't know. Mary Jane and I have spent the week with a friend of ours in town. I told the motel manager to release the room. He said he could rent it fast to someone else." I thought of the poor souls who had been sleeping in my usual Masters room. Two souls who thought they had lucked into a deal. Now, they were reduced to dental records. Which would never match with Mary Jane and me.

I sat down, running a hand over my brow. An early morning fire in my hotel room. That was more coincidental than could be believed. It had to have been set by someone. But who? Certainly, it wasn't Enrico de la Paz, who was tucked safely away in federal custody in one of Wilcox' secret prisons.

"You'd better call the office, Hack," Quigs said. "We already called Frankie Donatello. You'll be glad to know he sounded sad that you were dead."

"Yeah," I said. "Because he's now gotta fill a twenty-inch hole in tomorrow's paper by himself. They'd better notify Mass General. The idea of Frank actually having to do some work is a sure-fire coronary waiting to happen. If I was smart, I'd wait to tell him and get him out of my hair. Permanently."

"Don't make jokes, man," Quigs said, turning back to his laptop. "Especially about death and dying. We were all totally bummed."

"Awww, thanks," I said. "They say if you really want to know what people think of you, go to your own funeral."

My first call, however, was not to the desk back in Beantown, but to Travis Kitchen. He picked up on the second ring.

"This is the ghost of Christmas Past," I said. "I hear people think I'm dead."

There was silence on the other end. "Hacker?" he said, finally.

"Yeah," I said.

"Shit," he said. "Do you know how much paperwork I'm gonna have to do over?"

"Thanks for the sympathy," I said. "Someone thought I was still registered in the Hacker suite at Motel 6. They were wrong. I'm guessing that fire was set. Correct?"

"Yep. Incendiary thrown through the window. Very messy and very deadly."

"Well, I can rule out one suspect," I said.

"Who?"

"Enrico," I said. I quickly filled him in on last night's events.

"Good Christ," he said. "Do you ever just write golf stories for the newspaper, or are you a one-man weapon of mass destruction?"

"Well, I am supposed to be covering this little golf event today," I said. "But I find people everywhere are trying to do me in. I'm beginning to develop a complex."

"With good reason," he said. "Tell you what. Let me pass off most of this grunt work to my crew. I'll come out there and watch your back."

"And maybe watch the back nine?" I said, chuckling.

"Well," he said. "If you're facing the course, I gotta stand there and watch your back. If I happen to see some golfers in the near distance, what am I gonna do? Close my eyes?"

"Fine," I said. "I'll probably be in the media center. Can you get into the place without a ticket?"

"You know," he said, "I've always wanted to face off with those Pinkerton idiots. I'd really make my day to have to shoot one or two of them just for fun."

"OK," I said. "Start with Pee Wee at the door. But bring extra ammo. He's a big fella."

He hung up. Then I called the desk back in Boston and asked for Frankie. His voice was trembling when he came on the line, accompanied by a sniffle or two. Awww.

"Frankie?" I said. "Hacker here."

"Listen," he said heatedly. "I don't know who the fuck you are, but Hacker was my friend. So take your juvenile game and shove it right up your ..."

"Frank," I said. "Really, this is Hacker. It wasn't me that got firebombed this morning. Mary Jane and I decided to bunk in with an old friend here in Augusta who had some extra room. Not that the Motel 6 isn't a fine hotel or anything. Anyway, I just heard about the misidentification, so I thought I'd better call."

"Goddam it," he said, his voice rising. "What do you mean by scaring the hell out of us up here? Do you know what we've been going through? I started in one a page-one feature on you, for Christ sakes. And where the hell have you been? Armand said you split yesterday afternoon for some goddam emergency! What the hell is that? We must have made thirty calls to you last night. We pay you to cover the big golf tournaments, damn it all, not go gallivanting around the South having a high old time. I'm telling you Hacker, this is going in your file. Of all the goddam screwy things you've gotten into, this one takes the cake. I ought a fire your ass right now, you know that? ..."

He went on in that vein for another ten minutes or so. I held the phone out away from my ear and watched the tournament on TV while he ranted. Tiger was still ahead by two shots, but Herron had gone three-under on the front side and was now heading into the back, full of confidence and mojo.

"Frank?" I said when it sounded like he was winding down.

"What?"

"I'm sorry if I worried you," I said. "I'll fill you in completely later. It's a good story. But right now, I've gotta watch the tournament. I'll have all my stuff up there by nine."

"You better have," he started in again, "Because I swear to God ..."

I'd heard enough. I flipped my phone shut. It was time for one of the Masters broadcast's four commercial breaks per hour (I'd once sat there with a stopwatch to see if they really limited commercial interruptions like they say they did. They do.) I sat there thinking.

Who had firebombed that motel room? Obviously I had been the target—no one knew that Mary Jane and I had moved over to Conn's house at the beginning of the week. My first suspicion would have been directed at de la Paz. But I knew it couldn't have been him. So who? Charlie Grosvenor? Someone had told me that he usually didn't use violent means against his enemies, preferring to throw money—not firebombs—at things to solve them. Still, I had learned some interesting things about Charlie and his, and Augusta's past. Could he have snapped? Why? To get rid of a witness who might upend his little apple cart of corruption? Maybe. I remembered the scene in his office with Travis Kitchen, when he had looked worn down and almost fearful. Maybe he had gone over the edge.

Or could it have been Juan Carlos Obrador? The Miami importer with his own wing at the art museum? Who might, or might not, be linked to his family in Colombia, whose business was growing, packaging and exporting cocaine and eliminating all who got in their way. Obrador himself was probably too old to toss a Molotov cocktail through the window at the Motel 6, but how about that bodyguard? He looked strong enough to do it. But why? What did they have against me? I had never once met them.

My phone rang. It was Wilcox.

"Mister Hacker," he said, "Who's winning?"

"Tiger by one," I said. "That's why you called? Don't they have a satellite downlink in the jungle? CBS says that more than 150 million people are watching right now."

"Actually, I wanted to pass on a factoid I just learned," he said. "Been thinking about that Judge boy. You were right. Nobody seemed to give a damn about him with all this other stuff going on. So I dug out the records that we took away from Kitchen. He hadn't had time to look at all of them."

"And?" I was watching Tiger tee off on the 10th. He hit one of his three-wood stingers down the hill with a nice draw.

"And, guess whose tax records young Mr. Judge was doing on the side?"

"Who?" I was paying attention now.

"One Brett Jacoby, employee of Augusta National."

"You are kidding me!"

"I never kid," he said. "But I thought the information might prove useful in tying up any loose ends."

He rang off. I sat there stunned. Then I thought of something else that had been rattling around in the back of my head. I looked over at Quigs, who was typing something in his laptop.

"Quigs?" I said.

He kept typing to the end of the sentence, then cocked an eye at me. "Mmm?"

"Who first announced that I had been barbecued at the motel?" I asked. "Did someone find that AP story on the wires?"

"Naw," he said. "Jacoby came in and told us."

"When?"

He scratched the back of his head. "I dunno," he said, thinking. "Must have been around 11, 11:30. I remember it was right after Lumpy drained a thirty-footer on the fourth."

"What did he say?"

"He went up to the microphone at the front there..." he motioned. "And said something like 'I have some sad news to report...our friend and colleague Hacker has apparently been murdered.' Then someone from the wires found the piece moving and printed it out. We were all trying to figure out when we had last seen you and all that stuff."

"Really?" I asked. "Are you sure that was what he said?"

"Yeah, I think so," he said. "Why?"

"I'll tell you later," I said. I thought some more. Then I re-read the AP newswire.

"God damn!" I said, and jumped up.

"What?" Quigs turned around to face me, his face quizzical.

I didn't answer him. I was heading for the door At a run.

Chapter Thirty-One

Once I got outside, I made a beeline for the main clubhouse. The top of the hill behind the clubhouse was mostly empty. Almost everyone was packing in around the nine holes of the back nine. Tiger and Casey O'Shea had just teed off on the ninth. Tim Herron, making a run, was down on the eleventh, the beginning of Amen Corner.

I came running up to the back entrance to that wide first-floor hallway that led out to the circular drive. I started to push my way in, when someone grabbed my arm.

"I'm sorry sir, but you can't go in this entrance." I looked at the Pinkerton guy standing there in his light grey uniform and hat with its snappy black rim in front. I recognized the friendly kid who had helped me set up the DVD player the other morning when I reviewed the security video. "Oh, hi Mister Hacker," he said. "Sorry, you don't have the right badge to get in here."

"What's your name, kid?" I asked.

"Jackie McCord," he said.

"Well, Jack," I said. "The chairman called me and asked me to come over," I lied. "Don't want to keep him waiting."

He looked uncertain. "I dunno," he said. "My orders are not to let anyone in here unless they have the right bage..."

"Kid," I said. "If you want to piss off the chairman by keeping him waiting, that's OK by me. I got all day."

Now he looked nervous. "Well," he said finally, "I guess he must know you and all, since you was looking at the video an' all. I guess it's OK."

I clapped him on the shoulder. "Thanks, kid," I said.

Inside, I traversed the central hallway and took the stairs two at a time up to the second floor offices. At the end of the hall, Grosvenor's office door was partially open. I strode down and kicked the door open with a crash.

There were three men sitting in Grosvenor's conversation grouping. Two of them had drinks the amber color of whiskey in which floated a couple of ice cubes. Grosvenor, in his green jacket, wasn't drinking. I believe that one of the guests in the room was one of the vice presidents of the U.S. Golf Association, but I had never really bothered to get to know any of those bluebloods, so I couldn't be sure. The other man, who had a ruddy face and receding curly hair that still retained a tint or two of red, I made to be one of the R&A guys over from Scotland.

When the door crashed open, they all jumped and turned around in their seats to look at me with amazement. I pointed at the two gents holding their drinks. "You and you, outta here. Right now," I barked, thumbing at the door.

Grosvenor stood up, his face turning red with fury. "What do you mean by crashing into my office and ordering my guests around?" he demanded hotly. "I'll have you know..."

"You'll have me know nothing, you son-of-a-bitch," I said. I looked at the two men again. "Out. Now." They both put down their drinks on the cocktail table and scurried out. I slammed the door shut behind them and turned to face Charlie Grosvenor.

"You'd better have a good excuse for this behavior, Mister Hacker," he said. "Before I call security and have you arrested."

"Get Jacoby in here ... now," I snarled.

"I can't do that," Grosvenor said. "He's working the press room. I can't ..."

"Now!"

Grosvenor looked at me and shrugged. He picked up the nearest telephone and punched a couple of numbers. He waited. "Brett?" he said. "Can you come to my office right away?" He listened. "Yes, yes, I know. I need to see you. It's important." He hung up.

"He'll be right up," he said. "Now will you please tell me what's wrong?"

"Did he tell you this morning that I had been burned up in a motel fire?" I asked.

"Well, since you obviously haven't been, that would be a ridiculous thing for him to say, wouldn't it?"

"He announced it to the entire press room," I said.

"Why would he do that?"

"I'll tell you when he gets here," I said. And said no more. I took a position somewhat behind the office door, standing against the wall.

It wasn't long before there was a hesitant knock at the door. "Come," said Grosvenor.

Brett Jacoby walked in. He was wearing his own green jacket, over a blue oxford shirt, striped rep tie and khaki trousers, and carried a sheaf of papers under one arm. "Yeah, Charlie," he said, "What's up? I gotta get back to the media center. We've got some early finishers coming in for interviews and ..."

I stepped out from behind the door. Brett turned and looked at me. His eyes widened and his face blanched.

"You!" he said, gasping. "But you're ..."

"Dead, Brett?" I said. "Burned to a crisp in the Motel 6? Gone but not forgotten? Sorry to upset your plan, but that wasn't me in Room 234 last night, bucko. In fact, I haven't been there all week. So that makes four people you've murdered, by my count."

"What?" Grosvenor was stunned. "What are you talking about?"

"I'm talking about John Judge, Christian Geer, and those poor unfortunates who died in the fire early this morning." I said. "Brett here thought I was staying in that motel room. I'll bet Billy Moore rebooked the room for cash and just kept my name on the register. Easy way to make a thou or so under the table. He had my reservation on record and my deposit in the bank. When I told him my girlfriend and I were staying with a friend in town, he took advantage. Then Brett here apparently decided I was too dangerous to his plan to leave town alive, so he came up with the idea of killing me...and Mary Jane...in a hotel fire. Almost worked."

"I don't know what you are talking about," Grosvenor said.

"I'll tell you," I said. "You have been wondering for several weeks now why the Colombian cartels were starting to squeeze you, haven't you? Why did they kill John Judge? Why did they send Juan Obrador personally to talk to you? What the hell was going on? You hadn't done anything. Right?"

Grosvenor nodded, almost against his will. Jacoby stood there, blood drained from his face. His eyes, however, were locked on me. He wasn't moving.

"That's why Brett here was able to convince you to call me in to nose around," I continued. "That was probably the last thing in the world you wanted to do, bring a news reporter inside the gates. But he convinced you that I could ask questions the cops never would, or could. The cops didn't know about RoJo, and the contraband that Grosvenor Group had long been shipping up from South America." The chairman started to protest. I stopped him with a look.

"He figured that I could find out what Enrico and the Obrador cartel wanted. Easier than the cops, anyway. And knowing what a smartass I am, he probably figured that I would end up shot by Enrico de la Paz, or someone else. And if that happened, the police would swoop in and round up the usual suspects. Rico. The Obradors. That would get Brett here off the hook."

"What hook?" Grosvenor asked, casting his eyes at Brett.

"He's been running a shadow operation," I said. "Probably since he got here six years ago. He found out what you've been up to all these years. He wanted a cut, his share, his due. Did he use your name? Or was it your family? By the way, the federal agents I've been hanging around with all week wanted me to tell you that your sister-in-law Beatrice Samper has left town. Probably gonna try and make a run for the border tonight. "

I stopped. A thought occurred to me. "Wait a sec," I said, looking at Brett again. "That's how you did it, isn't it? And why. Once Charlie here became chairman of Augusta National, he had to get out of the smuggling business. Too much to lose if he got caught."

I began pacing back and forth, the ideas coming together in my head.

"But Brett wanted to keep the gravy flowing," I continued. "And I'll bet the Obrador sisters did too. Beatrice and Marta. Your own wife, Charlie." I looked at him. He had sunk down in his chair, shoulders slumped. "They were used to living pretty high off the hog, weren't they? So when you put the official kibosh on the smuggling operation, Marta, Beatrice and Brett here decided to take it over and keep it running. Same operation, new operators. None of the logistics changed, just the ownership group. And Charlie didn't even have to know about it. Perfect!"

I kept pacing. Brett Jacoby was still standing in the middle of the room, his eyes following my every move.

"But he couldn't keep it secret. People talk. Gossip gets around. People have been whispering about Grosvenor since he took over. But they've been whispering about Marta Grosvenor, not Charlie."

I snapped my fingers. "And Christian Geer. Geer was coming to see Grosvenor with information he discovered about the operation. Isn't that right, Brett?" He stared at me. "What did he have? Bank statements showing the millions you three had stashed away in Europe? Questions from international trade sources? Whatever it was, it must have been dangerous enough for you to risk stabbing him with a hypodermic. That took some guts."

"What?" Grosvenor's head snapped up. "Geer was killed?"

"Yup," I said. "Lt. Travis agreed with me that the circumstances were a little too cute and he ordered a fast autopsy. Someone injected Geer with a whole lot of atropine. His heart exploded almost instantly."

I looked at Jacoby. "Too bad, Brett," I said. "Normally, an old foreign guy like him, they would have packed him up in a box and shipped him home for burial. But that was one too many strange deaths in the same place. I convinced Kitchen we had to look."

"But what about the Judge boy?" Grosvenor said. "Why was he killed? And buried here?"

"That's an excellent question," I said. "There's been nothing that connects John Judge to any of this stuff. Until now."

I looked at Brett Jacoby. "I just found out that he was doing your taxes, Brett," I said. "He must have found something in your records that didn't make sense. Asked you about it. He was a straight shooter, wasn't he? He would have been allergic to anything illegal, especially running drugs. Did you try to talk him into going along with the plan? Offer him a bribe to keep quiet? That wouldn't have worked. You'd have to have threatened him with bodily harm. Did you introduce him to Enrico de la Paz? The enforcer. Is that where he heard that name?"

Brett Jacoby stood stock-still, saying nothing.

"Did you have him come over here?" I continued. "Or did you meet him elsewhere? Either way, you were staring right into his face when you pulled the trigger. How does that feel? Shooting some innocent young man to save your own sorry skin? I wondered why he had been shot in the chest. Somebody like Rico would have snuck up and aced him in the back of the head. But sticking him in that bunker was brilliant. That threw all the suspicion onto Enrico and then on to Charlie. His dark past coming back to haunt him. Nice plan."

Grosvenor looked over at Brett Jacoby, who was still standing in the middle of the room, still as a stone, his eyes narrow and never once leaving my face.

"But Brett told me that this la Paz fellow was the killer," Grosvenor said. "How can you be sure he wasn't the one?"

"Ah, we all thought that Rico was the bad guy," I said. "It fit the story. Cold-blooded killer, hired assassin for the cartel. He had to have been the one who killed John Judge. The theory went that he was trying to warn you, Charlie. Put you on notice. But for what? You had no idea what was going on. You thought you were out of that business."

For the first time, Brett Jacoby spoke. "How do you know Rico wasn't the one who set the motel fire last night?"

"Because you announced this morning in the media center that 'Hacker had been murdered.' The story on the wires just said that police were reporting two killed in a motel fire. Nothing was said publically about murder. Just two died in a fire. Could have been an accident. Smoking in bed. Electrical fire. You were the only one who called it a murder. And just now, you said it was a set fire. The only one who could have known that is the one who set the fire. And that'd be you."

"It still could have been Rico," Brett said. "He's a known killer for goodness sakes. You're just jumping on my turn of phrase. That's hardly proof." His lips turned up in a hopeful smile.

"No," I said, shaking my head. "It isn't proof. You're right. But what you may not have known is that Enrico de la Paz was picked up by the feds last night in Atlanta. At about 7:10 p.m., as a matter of fact. I know because I was there. And now Beatrice is on the run. You'd better tell Marta to start hauling ass too, because they're gonna be coming for her pretty soon."

Grosvenor sat there dumbfounded. I was staring at Brett Jacoby so I could watch the emotions playing across his face. The confidence suddenly washed away by fear, the hope by the realization that his goose was pretty much cooked. Grosvenor reached for the phone. "I'm calling security," he said.

Jacoby looked down at his feet. I walked over and stood in front of him.

"So that leaves you, Brett." I said. "You were coordinating the drug operation for the Obrador girls. You killed John Judge when he learned what you had been up to. You killed Christian Geer before he could spill the beans to Charlie here. Then last night, you tried to kill me. You've been a one-man killing machine, huh? It must get easier after the first one. Does it, Brett? "

He nodded, sadly. Then he swept his arms up violently, tossing his armful of papers in my face, and pushing me over backwards. He pivoted and kicked Charlie Grosvenor right in the stomach. I heard the air go out of Grosvenor, and he fell to the floor groaning. When I lwas able to regain my feet, Brett Jacoby was gone. I started to run after him, but, looking down, I could see that Grosvenor was in trouble. He was paper white and gasping for air. I rolled him over onto his knees and tried to help him regain his breath. He was moaning and making horrible raspy sounds that sounded like something inside was broken.

The door crushed open and three Pinkertons burst into the room. Two of them grabbed me roughly and slammed me against the wall. The other one bent over Grosvenor and then pulled out his shoulder radio and began shouting orders for an ambulance. The two guards held me immobile for the nearly two minutes it took before Grosvenor was able to speak. He finally gasped out the words.

"Not...Hacker...Jacoby...He's the killer... Find him."

The two guards let me go. I dashed out into the hall and down the stairs. Halfway down, I leaped over a green jacket lying on the stairs. I stopped and looked inside the right flap. On the label was a small sewn patch that read: B. JACOBY. I left it there, hustled down through the lobby and out the back door. The Pinkerton kid was still guarding the door, but his eyes were big as he listened to the radio reports squawking in his earpiece.

"Jesus," he said when he saw me. "What the hell is going on up there?"

"Did you see Brett Jacoby come out here a minute ago?" I asked.

"Why, yeah, I did," the kid said. "Funny you should ask."

"Why? What?"

"He was wearing a hard hat," he said. "Like one of those" He nodded over by the big old oak, where two of the grounds men were picking up trash with their metal stabbers and putting it into large canvas carriers slung around their shoulders. They were wearing blue coveralls and bright yellow hard hats. "Never seen him in one of those."

He told me in which direction Jacoby had headed. I ran down onto the broad grassy lawn beneath the tree. In the distance, I could hear the bursts of sound that represented cheers after someone dropped a birdie putt, and the low rumble of applause rolling up the hill from the depths of Amen Corner. Everywhere, people were milling, trying to squeeze into a space around the 18th green, or wandering further down the hill to try and find a place along the ropes. Others headed down to 17 and beyond that, the 15th tee. My eye caught sight of several workers wearing yellow hard hats, but they all seemed to also be wearing the blue coveralls of the trash pickers. Jacoby had disappeared into the crowds.

I turned on my heel and ran back to the back entrance. I grabbed Jack the young Pinkerton kid by the arm.

"I need you," I said. "You gotta do what I say. Jacoby is a killer and he's getting away. I need to get up to the Crow's Nest. Now."

He looked into my eyes once, and nodded. He took off to the locker room door and I followed along behind. He pushed several people including, I think, Vijay Singh, roughly out of the way and led me inside and up the stairs. Jack Nicklaus, wearing his own member's green jacket, was coming out of the Champion's Locker Room on the second floor. "Whoa fellas," he said. "Where's the fire?"

I didn't have time to explain, and followed the Pinkerton kid as he took the steep stairway two at a time. Inside, I pointed up at the cupola windows, and he nodded, bent over and hoisted me up onto the beams. I almost fell over backwards, but caught my balance just in time, and yanked myself up where I could stand and look out the windows. I could not believe how many people were scattered across the rolling hills of Augusta National. It seemed every inch of fairway and green on the back nine holes were rimmed with people at least six or seven deep. I began scanning the crowds, trying to pick out a yellow hard had. Again, I saw several, but again, they all seemed to be workers.

Then, down across the 18th fairway, in the woods that protect the right side of the 18th fairway and continue over to the 10th fairway, I saw a yellow hat bobbling. The figure wearing the hat ducked behind one of the scoreboards and came out on the other side. Yes! He was wearing a blue oxford shirt and khakis. I saw him look back over his shoulder and pick up his pace. He was heading down toward Amen Corner.

"There he is!" I yelled. "Looks like he's heading for eleven. "Let's go!"

I jumped down, not caring this time what kind of noise I made, and the Kid and I hightailed it down the stairs and out of the clubhouse. I started running. Behind me, I could hear the kid breathlessly radioing in. I didn't wait for him, but took off running down the hill.

Between the ninth green and the 18th fairway is a wide open field that slopes away from the clubhouse and down the hill. In the old days, it had been used as the practice range, and they even held a long-drive contest for the contestants before the tournament began. But today, it's just a big wide-open grassy hill, where people can walk up from the seventeenth fairway or angle down towards Amen Corner.

Jacoby had already made it around the last fairway, and the people were jammed in all the way down to those fairway bunkers on the left side of the fairway, where many a Masters dream has come to ruin. I could see that almost no one was standing around the bunkers, because with those upswept lips and flashed sand, it's almost impossible to see the green or even another player on the fairway.

So I blasted down that hill at full speed, headed for the bunkers, pushed past some people, ducked under the ropes at the fairway's edge and scampered across the narrow pathway of grass that separates the two huge, yawning bunkers. Behind me,

I heard someone yell "Hey!" as I kept running across the fairway and towards the woods on the far side. One twosome had already played their approach shots and was struggling up the steep hill towards the last green, and I didn't even want to look back down at the tee in the distance to see if I was disrupting play. I gave a quick look over my shoulder and saw the Pinkerton kid following my lead, about twenty paces behind.

Once across the fairway, one of the marshals in his own yellow hard hat tried to corral me, probably thinking I was a streaker who had lost his nerve. I gave him my best Laurence Maroney shoulder fake and juke and left him grasping at air. A second or two later, the Pinkerton kid rumbled past and yelled at the guy not to worry.

Bursting out of the woods, I jumped the ropes again and headed down the last part of the hill on the 10th fairway. That hill is incredibly steep, which is why the hole plays as a par-four even at 500 yards. I got going so fast, I felt my feet begin to spin out, and did an amazing acrobatic roll and slide down the steepest face of the hill. If I were a Titleist, I would have been a good drive. After I stopped rolling, I picked myself up at the bottom and kept going. A couple of beer-soaked patrons, who apparently didn't realize that the tournament had finished with the 10th hole, gave me a nice round of applause. The kid, breathing hard, caught up with me.

Both panting deeply now, we ran up the rise to the 10th green, and down the pinestraw covered ground towards the eleventh fairway, skirting the new monster tee set back to the left deep into the woods. Once on the fairway, we motored down the middle of the empty fairway until we reached the crest of the hill. I slowed and the kid came to a stop beside me. We sounded like a couple of coal-powered locomotives trying to make it up the last bit of grade in the Rockies, geezing, rasping and trying not to throw up.

At our feet was the grandeur of Amen Corner. The fairway we stood on, the eleventh, was tilted from right to left, pushing everything towards the woods that waited on that side. At the base of the hill was that nasty little pond, dark and forboding, and behind that, the green, which also seemed to slope right into the pond. Off to the right at the bottom was the par-three twelfth, the green perched atop a shaved rise that fell down into the blue gash of Rae's Creek where it widened into a deep, still watery fissure. Behind, framed by rows of towering loblolly pines was that narrow sliver of green, the bunker in front and the two behind providing almost nothing in the way of a margin of error. At the same time, the delicate dogwoods and the achingly colorful masses of azaleas made the setting look like it had been borrowed from Heaven.

I scanned the crowd again, looking for Jacoby. Nothing. The kid grabbed my arm. "There he is!" he said, pointing to the left of the eleventh green. Behind that green, Rae's Creek winds around close to the back of the putting surface, backed up and deepened by the dam that creates the hazard in front of 12. Jacoby, still wearing his hard hat, was heading for the wooden dam.

"What's down behind there?" I asked.

"Thick woods, the overspill, some brush and a few snakes," the kid said. "He won't get far." He radioed in our position. I turned around and saw a phalanx of four-wheeled scooters heading down the hill on ten. The cavalry was coming.

We set off down the middle of the fairway again, at a more controlled trot this time. Out of the corner of my eye, I saw Tiger back away from his putt on 12 and hold his hands out as if to say "What the hell is this?" I wondered if CBS would show these two crazies interrupting the first major golf tournament of the year. Maybe I could be a highlight on SportsCenter tonight.

There was no time to stop and explain, apologize to Tiger, make nice to Stevie, or wave to the folks back at home. Jacoby had disappeared over the back of the dam. Jack and I followed him around the left side of the pond in front of the 11th green. We crashed through some hedges, crossed over a hidden maintenance round and threaded our way through the thick stand of young pines before we reached the edge of the creek. While the entire golf course represented the artifice of eternity, as Yeats called it, down behind the dam was the real world. The creek bed below the dam was rocky, almost dry and filled with dead branches and leaves. And it smelled of rotting things, rancid and chemical. Down here, out of sight of the television cameras and the thousands of "patrons," we had come face-to-face with the ugly realities of life, where the world was smelly, untidy, uncontrolled and uncontrollable. It was the antithesis of Augusta National.

And Brett Jacoby was down here, too. He had stopped on a rocky shoal in the middle of that almost dry creek bed. His chest was heaving. He faced away from us, looking at the wall of impenetrable greenery that surrounded the creekbed, filled with thorns and brambles, dark and hidden away from the sun. A burst of sound washed over us from the golf course, a sound that meant Tiger had holed a good putt. Even so, the mass of sound was muted down here, unlike the crystalline beauty of the massed decibels when they rip across the manicured green fairways and played in the branches of the sun-kissed trees.

Jacoby turned to look at us. He bent over and grabbed a baseball-sized rock in each of his hands. His chest was still heaving from the effort of flight, as ours were from the effort of pursuit.

"It's over Brett," I said quietly. "It's finally over."

We all heard the sounds of the others coming behind us, through the woods. Coming from the light into the dark. Brett Jacoby heard it too, and knew. The kid and I watched as he sank to his knees, dropping the rocks, and folded himself over into the shape of an egg. He began to keen, rocking himself slowly back and forth.

Chapter Thirty-Two

They took Jacoby out through the Augusta Country Club, which adjoins the National past Amen Corner on the far side of Rae's Creek. Travis Kitchen had shown up with the other Pinkertons who had followed us down from the clubhouse. The chief Pink decided it would be better to take him out that way, rather than further disrupt play during the tournament. They apparently didn't mind driving their police cars all over the Augusta CC course, however. That's what happens when your neighbor is Augusta National Golf Club. You get trod upon.

Kitchen took Brett downtown. I got one of the other cops to drive me back around to the National and drop me off. I had work to do. Timmy Herron made a hell of a run, playing faultless golf on those last few holes, with birdies on thirteen, fourteen and fifteen. But, a few groups later, Tiger eagled the thirteenth, birdied the fifteenth and nailed the door shut with a spectacular shot on the short sixteenth, that caught the side of the hill on that green and spun back to within six feet. Of course, he made the putt, as all 75,000 souls at the golf course, and the 75 bajillion watching at home knew he would. He strolled home, champion again. We are fortunate to be live in a time when we can watch this remarkable athlete.

When I got back to the press room, Quigs looked at me and said "Where the hell have you been? Swinging through the trees?"

I looked down at myself and noticed, for the first time, that I had a long green grass stain on both knees and one hip from my high-speed spill down the hill at 10, and my shirt wasn't much better after bushwhacking through the forest.

"Hey," he said. "That wasn't you they showed running down the 11th was it? What a couple of idiots. Stevie Williams looked like he was gonna chase after those two and drown them in the pond."

I just smiled enigmatically, and Quigs eventually went back to watching the events unfold.

During the long, long aftermath of the tournament—the ceremony in Butler Cabin, the insipid interview with Jim Nance, the series of press conferences in our comfy little theater, the hour or two writing our stories and notes and sending them to our home desks—I was operating mostly on automatic control. Like the best golfers, I didn't think, I just did. Write down that quote. Check the stats for the back nine. Come up with some narrative theme. Explain what happened and why. All of it done without any conscious thought. Was I thinking about the events of the last several weeks? Of course I was, but not on any recognizable level. All that was just background to doing my job. Writing golf. One step and then the next.

I called Conn to see how Mary Jane was when I had a moment. He told me she was fine. She had risen from bed in late afternoon and watched the end of the tournament with Conn. They hadn't spoken much, he said. At one point during the telecast, he said he looked over at her, and she was weeping, quietly. That didn't sound so good.

Nobody noticed that Brett Jacoby never came back to the media center. Charlie Grosvenor, who had a long list of other things to do, post-tournament, also never reappeared before the media, but then he almost never does. By the time I finished all that I had to do, it was about 10 p.m. I was suddenly bone weary and ravenously hungry.

I grabbed a sandwich, packed up my gear, said goodbye to some of the guys, and drove back to Conn's house. He and Mary Jane were sitting in the living room, reading quietly. Something Mozartian was playing in the background. When I arrived, Conn folded his book closed, nodded at me, and disappeared into his bedroom.

I looked at Mary Jane, but she kept her eyes glued to her book. The silence began to smother me, sucking all the air out of the room, so I went outside onto the deck. The air had chilled after the sun went down and my breath created soft clouds of condensation in the air. The sky was clear and the stars formed interesting patterns.

I shivered once and was about to go back inside, when Mary Jane came out. She went over to the railing, looking out at the darkness where the river was, flowing silently and endlessly down through the land on its way to the sea. I stood there, waiting.

"When he took me, it reminded me of Gerry, my late husband," she said. "Of all the evil that he represented. Of all the bad things he did. In a way, those things became mine, too. I know they really weren't, of course. He was the one who did the shooting and the beating and the stealing. I tried, and I think I succeeded, in keeping that away from Victoria. But as much as I told myself that this was his life and not mine, I knew that wasn't really true. When you are with someone, even if it's not working out all that much, his life is still your life, too. His goodness becomes yours. His evil does too."

I said nothing. She needed to say these things. I needed to listen.

"I thought I had gotten over those feelings," she continued. "But when that man kidnapped me in the mall, it all came back. Those feelings of being wrong, somehow. Not unclean, really, but connected to the wrong things."

"It wasn't you," I said. "It was me."

"But that's just it," she said. "It's neither you nor me. It's us. I am part of what you are. It can't be separated. It's like you don't stop over there, and I don't stop over here. We are."

She stopped and fell silent and looked out at the darkness.

"And?"

She turned to face me, her eyes wet. "And I don't know if I can be us, if it involves living with those feelings again. And I don't know if I can bring Victoria into a life where you might be there one day and gone the next. Where maybe Conn slips instead of Rico. Or you don't get out of the way of the rifle, like Kitchen did. That wouldn't be fair to her. Or to me."

It was my turn to stare out at the night, thinking.

"I called Poppy tonight," she said. "I wanted to talk to Victoria, of course, but when he came on the line, I started telling him all about what had happened down here this week."

"Great," I said, half-seriously. "Your father-in-law the mobster knows that you got kidnapped and almost killed because of me. Tell me, can I ever go back home again?"

"I don't know why I started telling him all this stuff," she said. "But I guess it's because I knew he would understand. That's a life that he's lived his entire life."

"And what did he say?" I asked.

"He said there are two ways you could look at it," she said. "One, that you are irresponsible, you think you have to save the world and that one day you may get us all killed."

"I would never do anything that ..."

She cut me off. "I know you would never do anything to put either me, or worse, Victoria, in any danger. I know that. But I also know that because of the way you are, and the way you go through life, it's unrealistic to think that it would never happen again."

"What's the other way to look at it?" I wasn't sure I really wanted to know.

"He said I could look at it that you are an honorable man, with an over-developed sense of right and wrong," she said. "And he said that perhaps I could look at it that you are a good man and a strong man. And that despite the scrapes you find yourself getting into, you also get yourself out of them, and that I should look at you not as a faulty man, but as a good one. One that I should consider myself lucky to have, because good men are rare."

I let the silence build around us again.

"And what have you decided?" I asked finally.

"I haven't made any decisions," she said. "Except that maybe I don't want to come back here."

"OK," I said.

"It may take me a while to work through this experience," she said.

"OK."

"I may decide that you and your adventures are too much for me and my daughter."

"OK."

"I have decided to put off any further decisions for a while."

"OK."

"I want to go home and hug my daughter."

"OK."

There was more silence.

"I love you, you know," I said.

"And I you," she said, her voice trembling. "And one thing I do know, more than any other," she said. "Is that you are a good man. Poppy is right about that."

"Thank you," I said. "I just wish the recommendation was from someone other than one of New England's greatest mobsters."

She stared at me for a moment, her eyes wide. Then she chortled. I stepped forward and took her in my arms, and we stood like that for a long time, while the stars overhead blinked down at us unconcernedly.

ABOUT THE AUTHOR

James Y. Bartlett is one of the most-published golf writers of his generation. His work has appeared in golf and lifestyle publications around the world for nearly twenty years. He was an editor with Golfweek *and* Luxury Golf *and even was the editor of* Caribbean Travel & Life *magazine during what he calls his "golf hiatus" period.*

Yet even while reclining on various tropical beaches swilling down countless pina coladas, he was still writing about the world of golf. He was the golf columnist for Forbes FYI *magazine for more than twelve years, and continues to churn out witty and informative golf pieces for* Hemispheres, *the inflight magazine of United Airlines under the pseudonym "A.G. Pollard, Jr." The best of Bartlett's nonfiction golf writing has been published in the Yeoman House book* Back Swings: A Golf Omnibus.

His first Hacker golf mystery novel, Death is a Two-Stroke Penalty *was published by St. Martin's Press/Thomas Dunne Books in 1991, followed soon thereafter by* Death from the Ladies Tee. *The third Hacker novel,* Death at the Member-Guest, *was published by Yeoman House in 2005.Today, Bartlett's Hacker novels are published in trade softcover editions by Yeoman House.*

A native of Massachusetts, former resident of Atlanta, Orlando and Manhattan, Bartlett currently lives in Rhode Island.

Printed in the United States
207556BV00005B/6/A

9 780975 467664